## PRAISE FOR LIS



"Lisa Gray explodes onto the literary stage with this taut, edge-of-the-seat thriller, and her headstrong protagonist Jessica Shaw, reminiscent of Lee Child's Jack Reacher, delivers a serious punch."

—Robert Dugoni, *New York Times* bestselling author

"Atmospheric and beautifully written. Lisa Gray is becoming a firm favorite in this house."

—Ian Rankin, bestselling author of the Inspector Rebus series

"Slick, smart, and sassy as hell, *To Die For* has more twists than the Pacific Coast Highway. Lisa knows how to grab your attention from the get-go with this memorable ensemble and it never lets up. Her best book yet."

—John Marrs, author of *The Stranger in Her House*

"A glossy, glamorous surface gives way to a dark undercurrent in this oh-so-clever mystery."

—Marion Todd, author of the Detective Clare Mackay series

"*Thin Air* is an exciting whodunit that kept me guessing until the end. PI Jessica Shaw is so capable and strong, I couldn't get enough of her!"

—T.R. Ragan, bestselling author of the Lizzy Gardner series

"One of this year's best new thrillers . . ."

—*Evening Standard*

"You'll find this one hard to put down."

—*Daily Record*

"Sets off at a fantastic pace, with plenty of twists and turns."

—Claire McGowan, author of *Truth Truth Lie*

"A fast-paced, perfectly plotted killer of a thriller with a fantastic female lead and a cracking premise."

—Susi Holliday, author of *The Hike*

"A terrifically entertaining and intriguing story."

—Liz Nugent, author of *Strange Sally Diamond*

"*Thin Air* is an assured and fast-paced debut with a compelling central character and plenty of twists to keep you guessing until the very end."

—Victoria Selman, author of *All the Little Liars*

"An assured and explosive debut with a premise that grabs you by the throat and refuses to let go. The pace never drops as it hurtles to a stunning conclusion."

—C.S. Robertson, author of *The Undiscovered Deaths of Grace McGill*

"Smart, sassy, and adrenaline-fueled, this kick-ass debut is a must-read for thriller fans."

—Steph Broadribb, author of *Death in the Sunshine*

"Lisa Gray's thriller is so assured it's hard to believe it's a debut. It's so fast-paced it should be pulled over for speeding!"

—Douglas Skelton, author of *A Thief's Justice*

# THE FINAL ACT

# ALSO BY LISA GRAY

## The Jessica Shaw thriller series

*Thin Air*

*Bad Memory*

*Dark Highway*

*Lonely Hearts*

## Standalone books

*The Dark Room*

*To Die For*

# THE FINAL ACT

LISA GRAY

This is a work of fiction. Names, characters, organizations, places, events, and incidents are either products of the author's imagination or are used fictitiously. Any resemblance to actual persons, living or dead, or actual events is purely coincidental.



Published by Thomas & Mercer, Seattle

www.apub.com

Amazon, the Amazon logo, and Thomas & Mercer are trademarks of Amazon.com, Inc., or its affiliates.

ISBN-13: 9781662519154
eISBN: 9781662519147

Cover design by Will Speed
Cover image: © Pierre Dal Corso / Gallery Stock

Printed in the United States of America

*This one's for the readers—each and every one of you.*

# PROLOGUE

## FALL, 2001

*The night thrummed with malice.*

*Murder was in the air.*

*She ran into the cabin and slammed the door hard behind her. Her dress was torn, her arms were scratched, and the soles of her bare feet were bleeding.*

*Her breathing came in sharp, ragged bursts. She rammed the deadbolt into place with the heel of her hand and reached for the big metal key in the lock. Her trembling fingers knocked it to the floor and it landed with a dull thud on the rotting wood.*

*"Shit, shit, shit."*

*That was NOT supposed to happen.*

*Her heart thudded as she bent down and scooped up the key. She inserted it into the lock and managed to steady her hand just enough to twist it all the way this time, until she heard the click.*

*There was a telephone on the nightstand next to the queen bed. The sheets were still mussed up from when she'd been fooling around with Jake just a couple of hours earlier.*

*Now she was fighting for her life.*

*She ran for the phone and grabbed up the receiver and held it to her ear while stabbing 911 on the number pad.*

*But there was nothing.*

*Only silence.*

*She pressed down frantically on the switch hook but there was no dial tone, no voice on the other end of the line, no one to assure her that help was on the way. She pulled at the cord and saw that the end had been crudely cut, exposing the wires.*

*She slid to the floor in despair.*

*"No. Please, God. No. Please, somebody help me." Her voice was nothing more than a hoarse whisper.*

*Somewhere in the woods outside, a scream shattered the silent night.*

*"It's just an animal," she whispered. "Just an animal."*

*But she knew it wasn't. The scream had sounded human. Female. Ashley or Brooke. A sob escaped from her lips. Her cheeks were wet with sooty mascara tears. Her chest heaved as she tried to swallow down the panic that threatened to engulf her.*

*She crawled toward the door. Barely felt the splinters from the wooden floor pierce the skin on her knees and the palms of her hands. She pressed an ear to the door and listened. The screaming had stopped. All she heard now was the electric hum of the porch light outside the cabin and the drumming of her own heartbeat.*

*A minute passed.*

*Then she heard it.*

*A noise outside.*

*Footsteps on the porch stairs. Slow and deliberate. Getting louder, getting closer, coming this way. The footsteps stopped right outside the door. A whimper escaped from her lips, and she clamped both hands over her mouth to stifle the sobs.*

*The doorknob rattled.*

*She closed her eyes and sent up a silent prayer.*

*A fist banged hard on the door, sending a jolt down her spine. There was more pounding. Each blow vibrated through her body. Fear pumped through her veins.*

*Then . . . nothing.*

*Silence.*

*For a brief moment, she dared to hope that he might leave and that she would live.*

*Then the doorframe splintered with a crack as a boot connected solidly with the flimsy ancient timber.*

*"NO!"*

*She scrabbled backward until she hit the wall. Could only watch in horror as the frame gave way completely and the door crashed open.*

*A dark, menacing figure stood on the threshold. His bulk seemed to fill the entire space. He wore a black sweater, black pants, and—most terrifyingly of all—a black ski mask. The masked man was holding a knife. He walked slowly toward her and raised the blade, and she screamed even though she knew there was no one who could save her now.*

*She would die on the floor of this filthy cabin in the woods . . .*

"CUT!"

The director's voice boomed out from the darkness of video village, where he'd been watching the action on a monitor alongside the assistant director and cinematographer.

Dan Cassidy—aka "The Slasher"—pulled off the ski mask and tossed the prop knife onto the bed. He held out a hand to help Madison James up from the floor. She was still trembling from the adrenaline buzz. The actor's handsome face broke into a big smile and his hazel eyes sparkled under the set lighting. He was way less scary without the horrible mask.

"Nailed it," he whispered. "That final scream? Man, I almost believed it myself."

"Thanks. You were great too."

Madison was grateful for the positive feedback, but there was only one person's approval that really mattered. She turned as Kent LaMarr strode across the soundstage and stood in front of them. The director nodded enthusiastically, and she breathed a sigh of relief.

"That was fucking fantastic. We got the shot on the first take." LaMarr gave her shoulder a squeeze. "Great job, Madison. Loved the ad-lib with the key. Nice touch."

She smiled and accepted the praise and didn't tell him the key drop had been a total accident because her hands really had been shaking so much.

*Survive the Night* was her first real acting job and her first movie role. She'd lucked out big-time landing the part. Madison had barely gotten off the Greyhound bus from Indiana when she'd signed with a talent management agency thanks to Mr. Pepper, her high-school drama teacher, and his contacts in the industry. Her new manager, Annie Kline, had lined up auditions for some commercials and Madison had been beyond excited.

Then the actress Gabby McCarthy had broken her leg right before she was due to start filming a new horror movie. The director needed a replacement fast—and the stand-in had to be a redhead. Kent LaMarr had already cast a blonde and a brunette in the other key roles, and he wanted the full set. Annie had thrown Madison's name into the mix, she'd auditioned for LaMarr, and she'd gotten the part.

An actual movie! That would be shown in theaters!

Madison's folks hadn't exactly been thrilled about her plans to move to Hollywood to be an actress, but they'd agreed to release a chunk of the college fund they'd saved for her so she could buy an old station wagon and pay her rent and bills in shared accommodation in Los Angeles for a year. If it didn't work out in that time, she'd come home to Dutton and go to community college or get a real job.

But Madison didn't need a year. After just a few short months, she'd already made it.

She was going to be a movie star.

She might be playing a dead girl, but Madison had never felt more alive.

As she drove down Sunset Strip after leaving the studio, she popped a cassette into the deck and blasted "Bootylicious" by Destiny's Child at full volume. She sang along and tapped her fingers on the steering wheel and breathed in the cool October air through the open window.

A billboard for the new movie *Donnie Darko* flashed past. Then another for *Mulholland Drive*, Naomi Watts' beautiful face twenty feet tall and lighting up the Strip.

Madison smiled to herself. One day soon, she would be on those billboards.

One day, the whole world would know the name Madison James.

# SILVER SCREAM MAGAZINE

REVIEW: *SURVIVE THE NIGHT*

By Seth Midnight, October 2002

Director Kent LaMarr is clearly a big fan of the classic slasher movies of the '70s and '80s (aren't we all?) and with *Survive the Night* he has aimed for a nostalgic pastiche of a bygone era.

Unfortunately, what he's actually delivered is a wander down a well-trodden path littered with tired old tropes.

Sure, there's plenty of gore, some nice snappy dialogue, and the occasional jump-scare to make you spill your popcorn. The problem with LaMarr's third directorial outing is it just doesn't offer anything new in the genre.

Here's the premise: A trio of friends, Brooke (Ally Hagen), Kate (Madison James), and Ashley (Rachel Rayner) decide to celebrate their high-school graduation by spending a weekend partying at a remote cabin in the woods.

Yeah, because nothing bad ever happened to a group of teens getting lit in the middle of no-where, right? Did none of these kids ever watch old horror flicks after their folks had gone to bed? Apparently not.

Studious, single girl Ashley is pissed when Brooke and Kate's boyfriends come along for the ride but, pretty soon, she has a lot more to worry about than being a fifth wheel when a knife-wielding maniac hunts them down one by one.

Sexy brunette Rayner—daughter of Hollywood royalty and Oscar-winner Rodger Rayner—fails to convince as the meek and virginal Ashley in the early scenes. She does come into her own in the final act, as the last girl standing who must bravely battle Dan Cassidy's "The Slasher" if she's to survive the night (see what I did there!). But let's just say Rayner is unlikely to follow in Daddy's footsteps by taking home a golden statuette any time soon.

Instead, it was James, making her film acting debut, who had this reviewer's pad filled with notes—and got his blood pumping.

Gabby McCarthy was initially cast in the role of kooky Kate, but had to pull out shortly before filming was due to start following a skiing accident that sounds far more horrific than some of the scenes in the movie.

James was cast last minute. This proved to be a stroke of luck for the ingenue and a masterstroke by LaMarr.

With her red hair (think Hayworth rather than Lohan) and alabaster skin and mesmerizing blue eyes, James steals every shot she's in. And boy can she act too.

In conclusion: *Survive the Night* won't live long in the memory—but Madison James certainly will. You heard it here first.

Move aside, Neve Campbell, because a new "Scream Queen" is in town and she's coming for your crown.

RATING: ** ½

# 1

# SARAH

## SEPTEMBER 2022

The discovery of the purse changed everything.

Until then, no one—at least, no one with a gun and a badge—was too concerned about the missing woman. There was nothing initially to set alarm bells ringing about the actress. No reason to suspect foul play or that she had come to harm or had harmed herself. She'd simply failed to show up for work for a couple of days and had stopped answering her cell phone. No reason to worry. Not really.

Then her purse had turned up in a place where it shouldn't have been, and that was when things switched up a gear.

Detective Sarah Delaney pulled into the parking lot at the entrance to the Brush Canyon Trail in Griffith Park. It was a popular spot with local hikers and tourists, because it snaked through picturesque terrain all the way to the iconic Hollywood sign high in the hills. The lot would usually be packed this time of day but, right now, there were just three vehicles: a cherry-red Dodge Charger, an ocean-blue Kia Soul, and a black and white LAPD patrol car. Sarah parked next to the cruiser, stuffed a lukewarm bottle of water into her shoulder bag, and got out.

A uniformed cop was standing guard in front of a chain-link fence gate at the trailhead. He straightened up, widened his stance, and folded his arms across his chest like a nightclub doorman. When she was about six feet away, he held up a hand in a halting gesture and Sarah could see the irritation on her face reflected in the lenses of his wraparound shades.

"Can't let you through," he said. "The trail is closed until further notice. There's been an incident."

The sun had burned his bald head the color of rare steak. The metal nameplate above his right breast identified him as Meadows.

"Please lower your hand, Officer Meadows. You're not directing traffic and I *will* be requiring access to the trail." Sarah indicated the LAPD detective's badge clipped to the waistband of her jeans that Meadows had clearly failed to notice. "Detective Delaney from the . . ."—she paused—"Missing Persons Unit."

It was the first time she'd said the words out loud and they felt strange in her mouth, like trying out a new food that she wasn't sure she liked.

"Apologies, Detective." Meadows didn't sound sorry but at least he lowered the hand. "I've had to turn away a bunch of hikers while my partner, that's Officer Powell, searches the area. I've also had some 'citizen detectives' trying to get up there for a look-see." He made air quotations with his fingers when he said the words "citizen detectives." "There's been five here already asking about the missing actress. I guess she did kind of used to be famous back in the day. Well, almost famous. These TikTokers seem to think they're gonna solve the case, that they can do a better job than us professionals."

"Is that so?" Sarah said. "Well, I guess we can all take the rest of the day off then."

It actually was her day off. She was supposed to be having some downtime before officially transferring over from Robbery-Homicide Division to her new role with the MPU. She'd only stopped by the Police Administration Building downtown to move her stuff from one desk to another on a different floor.

After seeking out her new partner to introduce herself, Sarah had discovered he was out working a case he'd just caught, and she'd figured there was no time like the present. That was why she was casually dressed in jeans and a tee and sneakers, and had apparently been mistaken for a citizen detective.

"How'd these amateur sleuths even know to come here?" she asked Meadows.

He shrugged. "Beats me."

She narrowed her eyes. "You didn't post anything on TikTok about the purse, did you?"

Meadows looked insulted. "Absolutely not. I don't even have a TikTok account. Those dumb twerking and lip-syncing videos are for kids. In any case, I've been trying to keep those assholes and their camera phones out, not encourage them."

"How about your partner up there on the trail?"

"I doubt it. He's still trying to figure out how Facebook works." Meadows jabbed a thumb at the trailhead behind him. "You'll find the welcome party after a couple miles. Might want to be quick about it though. The park rangers have been busting my ass about the trail being shut off and they want it opened up again ASAP."

Sarah nodded and set off along the wide, dusty track, enjoying the rugged natural beauty of the scrubland and trees and wildflowers. She'd hiked it several times before, but always early morning when the temperature was cooler and always with plenty of other folk around. It felt kind of special, if a little eerie, having it all to herself.

After more than a mile of traipsing uphill, it was no longer feeling quite so special.

The sun was beating down hard, and her leg muscles ached. She was starting to wish she'd waited until Monday to relocate the cardboard boxes of files, mugs, potted plants, stationery, and other knickknacks she'd accumulated over the years (the single framed photo she'd once kept on her desk had been trashed months ago). Perspiration dampened her brow and she gulped down half the bottle of water before pulling her long dark hair into a low ponytail. Sweat pooled in the small of her back.

At a fork in the track, Sarah hooked a left and carried on along the Mulholland Trail until she came across a small group of people. The Hollywood sign and radio tower were both visible above them, and she sent up a silent thank you that her destination wasn't all the way to the Mount Lee summit, where the trail ended right behind the famous sign.

Another uniformed officer—red-faced and sweating and presumably Meadows' partner, Powell—was poking around in the chaparral. A dark-haired man dressed in a summer-weight gray suit watched him as he worked. A young blonde woman in denim cutoffs and a tight tank top and gleaming white sneakers stood off to the side, swiping furiously at a cell phone. Sarah figured at least one mystery had been solved already.

The guy in the suit came over to greet her. He was holding some evidence bags in one hand and stuck out the other for an awkward handshake. His grip was firm and cool, and Sarah was aware of her own sweaty palms.

"Detective Rob Moreno," he said by way of introduction. "You must be Detective Delaney. The boss said you'd be coming out here." He grinned, showing off impressive dental work. "Talk about keen, huh? You weren't scheduled to start until next week, right?"

Sarah guessed her new partner's age to be around thirty, maybe even younger.

"Right." She gestured to the evidence bags. "What do we have?"

"Blue leather purse found in some scrubland," Moreno said. "Belongs to a woman by the name of Madison James, according to the driver's license inside. She was reported missing yesterday by her boss at the restaurant where she works."

Sarah nodded. She'd read the MP report before leaving the office. Madison James—who was an actress as well as a waitress—had swapped her Monday morning shift so she could attend an important audition. She'd been a no-show for the rearranged shift that evening, and then again for her regular morning slot the following day. Her boss had thus far been unable to reach her at home or on her cell phone. Apparently, Madison was very reliable, and it was out of character for her to go off-grid like this. She was last seen Monday morning, setting off for the audition, wearing a blue floral dress, blue leather purse, and gold strappy sandals. Today was Wednesday.

Moreno went on, "The paperwork was logged with the National Crime Information Center but, hey, we both know how many MP reports are filed in a month and most missing persons reappear after a day or two. She wasn't deemed to be a vulnerable adult and there was no indication of foul play. Then her purse somehow wound up in Griffith Park and here we are."

"The blonde found it?"

"That's right," Moreno said. "Chloe Reid. Twenty-one years old. Lives with her folks in the Valley. Works at a Jack in the Box in Van Nuys. No known connection to the missing woman."

"Have you found anything else?"

Moreno shook his head. "Officer Powell has been over the immediate terrain and, so far, nada. No body, no clothing, no blood. Nothing—other than the purse—to suggest anything bad went down here. That being said, the park covers more than four thousand acres of natural terrain. There's no way we can search it all. No cameras up here either. It's all canyons and chaparral and mountains and dirt."

"Might be worth checking social media for any selfies taken here in the last few days. With the Hollywood sign above us, it's a good spot. A long shot, I know—and it does mean some grunt work—but one of those photos might turn up something useful."

Moreno nodded. "It's worth a try. I'll get on it."

They walked over to Chloe Reid, who reluctantly slipped her cell phone into the back pocket of her shorts. Moreno tucked the evidence bags under an arm and withdrew a notepad and pen from his inside pocket. Sarah introduced herself and asked the woman to talk them through finding the purse.

Chloe said, "I was hiking the trail and stopped for a drink of water. That's when I saw something glinting in the scrubland. I was curious, so I went over to have a look and noticed a purse behind some bushes. The glinting I'd seen was the sun shining off the metal chain strap."

"Was there anyone else around, nearby the purse?" Sarah asked.

"Not really. No one who it could have belonged to, just a group of guys with backpacks. So, I picked it up and looked inside. Figured if there was ID, I might be able to find the owner on socials and DM them, try to return it. I know if it were me, I'd be freaking out. It's a real pain in the ass trying to cancel credit cards and arrange for new ones. I did a search for the name on the driver's license and saw a Facebook post saying she was an actress and that she was missing—so I called the cops."

Sarah sighed. "So, you handled the bag and its contents?"

"Hey, I didn't steal anything," Chloe said defensively. "Check the wallet. Fifty dollars cash still in there. All her cards too."

"Okay. But we'll need you to provide elimination prints, seeing as you've touched everything."

The younger woman shrugged, annoyed. "Sure, whatever."

"Did you also post about the purse—and who it belongs to—on social media?"

Chloe brightened, her brown eyes shining. "Yeah, I did a TikTok video, and it's been super-popular. Last I checked, it had almost four thousand views and over two hundred reposts. Only my pranked-neighbor video has done better. Who knew so many people were interested in an actress from forever-ago who wasn't even that famous back then?"

Sarah gave her a hard stare. "There have been people showing up at the trailhead trying to come up here to film their own videos and take photos because they saw your post. Not helpful, Chloe."

The blonde got defensive again. "My video might help to find this woman. Four thousand views so far—that's a lot more effective than a missing person poster stapled to a tree." She pulled her phone from her pocket, tapped it a few times, and thrust it in Sarah's face. "See? Even more people have watched it now. Almost five thousand."

Sure enough, the numbers on the screen continued to tick up. The post wasn't viral, far from it, but Sarah had to grudgingly admit that Chloe Reid might have a point. Someone who viewed the video might have information that could help locate Madison James.

"Do you know the missing woman?" she asked. "Any idea where she might be or why her purse was in the park?"

Sarah knew Moreno had already asked these questions, but it didn't hurt to go over them again.

Chloe shook her head. "Nope. Don't know her. Never met her. Never even heard of her until today. But I'm totally going to check out her IMDb page later, see if I can stream any of her movies. Probably only available on DVD though. Maybe even videotape. I mean, she's pretty old now according to the DOB on her driver's license."

Sarah raised an eyebrow. Pretty old? Madison James was thirty-nine (although her Wikipedia page claimed she was thirty-one) and two years younger than Sarah.

Chloe consulted her smartwatch. "Can I go now? I need to get home and get changed before my shift starts in an hour. And my shoulders are starting to burn."

Sarah said, "We'll be in touch about those prints."

Chloe bounded off down the dirt track, her ponytail bouncing, the phone's screen held out in front of her face.

"What do you think?" Sarah asked Moreno. "Dumb luck finding the purse like that?"

He shrugged. "I guess so."

"Show me where it was."

Moreno pointed to a cluster of bushes that were far enough away from the main trail to suggest the purse hadn't been dropped there by accident. Not unless Madison James had been up here after dark, fooling around with someone in the bushes. Which wasn't impossible but seemed unlikely, seeing as she was a grown woman and not a horny high schooler.

A bad feeling began to settle in the pit of Sarah's belly. She hoped the purse had been dumped by a thief or a junkie after finding something inside worth stealing and selling, but that didn't explain why they would have left behind the cash and the cards.

Or where Madison James had been since Monday.

Sarah and Moreno left Powell to finish up his search and made their way back to the trailhead, where Meadows was still turning away disgruntled tourists. Chloe Reid's Kia Soul was gone. Moreno laid out his collection of evidence bags on the hood of the Dodge Charger at the far end of the lot for Sarah to inspect. It was a relief to get out of the blazing sun and into the cool shade offered by a canopy of trees.

The clear bags contained a wallet, a ten-dollar bill and two twenties, a Chase bank card, an Amex card, a tube of lipstick, a set of house keys, a car key for a Ford Mustang, and a driver's license. There was no cell phone.

Sarah picked up the bag with the driver's license and studied it. Most folk looked like convicts in their DL photo. Madison James was a rare exception. With her auburn waves, ice-blue eyes, and pale skin, she was still strikingly beautiful at almost forty.

Sarah had a vague recollection of watching one of her movies at the theater years ago. It'd been a slasher flick, with lots of blood and gore and a high body count, but she couldn't recall the title or anything else about the plot.

She gloved up with a pair of latexes she'd picked up at the PAB and gestured for Moreno to hand over the brown paper evidence bag with the purse inside. After checking the interior compartments were empty, she flipped it over and saw a small slip pocket on the back. She poked a gloved finger into the tight space and felt something wedged inside. It was a crisply folded square of yellow paper. Sarah teased it out and unfolded it to reveal small, neat handwriting in blue biro. The note read:

*FM HTL 12 CASH??*

As well as the two question marks, the word "CASH" had been underlined twice and emphatically enough for the pen to go right through the paper.

Sarah held up the note for Moreno to see.

He read it and frowned. "What does it mean?"

"That, partner, is what we need to find out."

# 2

# SARAH

## SEPTEMBER 2022

Madison James' address led to a bubblegum-pink apartment complex in Studio City, close to the Hollywood Freeway. It was sandwiched between similarly modest lemon-yellow and pistachio-green buildings on a pleasant tree-lined street.

The detectives made the twenty-minute journey separately in their respective cars, the Charger on Sarah's rear bumper the whole way like the world's worst tail. She was glad to avoid the awkward small talk that came from being enclosed in a confined space with a stranger—or, worse, the questions that she knew Moreno would be itching to ask:

*Why give up a plumb gig with the elite RHD to work missing persons?*

*Was it your choice to leave or were you pushed?*

*Did you mess up a case or get on the wrong side of the top brass?*

*Do you really want a rookie detective who looks about twelve to be your new partner?*

Okay, so maybe he wouldn't ask that last one.

But Sarah wasn't ready for that conversation yet. She'd hopefully build a rapport with Moreno in time—maybe even a friendship—but it was way too soon for all that cozy getting-to-know-each-other stuff.

They met at the front of Madison's building, which was protected by a secure entry system. Moreno pressed the buzzer long enough to seriously piss off anyone who might be inside the apartment. Sarah held her breath, hoping to hear a hiss of static and the tinny voice of an angry woman, but there was only silence. She breathed out again, disappointed but not surprised.

Moreno produced the evidence bag with the set of house keys and Sarah squeezed her hands into another pair of gloves and found the key that opened the front door.

The entrance hall was big and bright, with whitewashed walls and terracotta floor tiles and a large wooden ceiling fan that was just about winning the battle against the mid-afternoon heat.

Two doors to the left led to a laundry room and on-site parking according to their signs. To the right was a mail room with a bank of mailboxes and some bubble envelopes and packages dumped on top. Straight ahead, a patio door offered a glimpse of an interior courtyard and a small residents' pool. A brunette with big hair and a full-length house dress—who presumably resided at the apartment complex—was sitting on a lawn chair by the pool, smoking a cigarette, her face turned up to the sun.

"I'll try the garage," Moreno said. "See if Madison's Mustang is there."

Sarah nodded. There had been no Ford Mustangs—black or otherwise—parked on the street outside. She located the mailbox for unit 305 and a handwritten sticker on front confirmed it belonged to "M. James." Sarah tried the smallest key on the ring and the mailbox sprung open. It wasn't stuffed full because Madison hadn't been gone long, but there was a small pile of unopened mail and some menus for local takeout places stacked inside. One of the envelopes was stamped "PAST DUE" in big red capital letters and bore the insignia of a property rental company.

Moreno returned from the garage, the heels of his dress shoes clicking loudly on the tiled floor. Sarah wondered how he'd managed to hike the Griffith Park trail in such inappropriate footwear.

"No sign of her car," he reported.

She held up the envelope from the property rental company.

"Interesting," Moreno said.

"Not good," Sarah said.

In her experience, people with money worries often resorted to desperate measures that often led to a whole world of trouble.

They climbed the staircase to the third floor, where Madison's apartment was located at the end of a walkway overlooking the interior courtyard. The big-haired brunette was done smoking and appeared to have fallen asleep. Moreno rapped his knuckles on the door. They waited. There was no answer. He knocked again, harder this time. Still nothing.

"Ms. James?" he called. "This is the LAPD. If you're in there, please open up." He pressed an ear to the door and listened, then met Sarah's eye with a shake of the head. "Neighbors?"

"Yep."

A friendly neighbor might know about any plans Madison had to take off for a few days, and a nosy one would likely have spotted any unusual comings and goings and unfamiliar visitors.

Sarah pressed the nearest apartment's doorbell, expecting a standard ding-dong, and heard a familiar tune echoing inside instead. It was from a TV show, but it took a moment for her to place it.

"*Cheers,*" she said.

"Huh?" Moreno said.

"The doorbell's tune. It's the theme song from *Cheers.*"

He gave her a blank look.

"You're kidding me, right? Everybody knows *Cheers*. Hugely popular TV show from the '80s? Set in a friendly bar, starring Kirstie Alley and Ted Danson? Any of this ringing any bells?"

Moreno grinned. "I wasn't born until '95."

Sarah rolled her eyes. "Whatever. Anyway, no one's home."

The next door along was a bust too. They returned to Madison's unit and Sarah tried the doorknob. It was locked.

Madison's mother had granted permission to search her daughter's apartment and vehicle—assuming they were able to locate it—when the MPU had contacted her earlier to inform her about the purse being found. The woman still lived in Madison's hometown in Indiana and hadn't seen her daughter in months, and hadn't spoken to her in days.

The first thing Sarah noticed when she opened the door was the smell inside the apartment. Thankfully it wasn't the copper tang of blood or the pungent odor of death. Murder had been her business for more than a decade and she was all too familiar with its scent, but her nose wasn't picking that up here. Only the smell of dry heat and undisturbed air, the result of hot weather and no open windows.

They stepped inside, straight into a living room with a tiny kitchen off it. The decor was modern and minimal, with polished parquet flooring and cream walls. A leather corner sofa and a glass coffee table and a white glossy sideboard that Sarah recognized as one she'd almost purchased from IKEA took up most of the small space. A flat-screen TV hung on one wall, a trio of cheap landscape canvases on another.

The place was tidy. Really tidy. The cushions on the couch had been fluffed up and expertly karate-chopped to create sharp dents. The remote controls were lined up perfectly on the table. There were no dirty dishes in the kitchen sink or half-empty coffee mugs on the counter or overflowing trash cans stinking the place out.

Sarah thought of the mess she'd left behind in her own home this morning and felt a twinge of shame. Admittedly, she'd let things slide now that there was no one around to judge if she didn't load the dishwasher or scrub out the toilet bowl or make the bed.

"A neat freak," said Moreno. "I wish my roommate was this tidy."

On closer inspection, Sarah noticed that a fine layer of dust covered all the surfaces. Yellow carnations in a glass vase on the sideboard were starting to wilt, and the water had turned cloudy. A "word a day" calendar next to the vase still showed Monday's word. The word was "flummoxed," meaning "confused and bewildered," and Sarah found it apt.

Three strides took her into the kitchen, where another calendar, this one featuring funny photos of cats, was stuck to the side of the refrigerator. The current month was displayed, and Monday's date had been ringed in black marker pen but there were no additional notes or details to explain its significance. None of the other dates in September had been circled. Sarah flipped through the eight previous months. A half-peeled "70 percent off" label was stuck on the back of the calendar, indicating it had been purchased well into the current year at a reduced price.

"This is weird," she said.

Moreno joined her in the cramped space, close enough to identify his brand of deodorant. "A cat wearing roller skates and sunglasses? Yeah, you're right. That is weird."

"Not the picture, which is Photoshopped by the way. The calendar itself. Only one date is circled."

"Maybe it's her acting calendar? Maybe she only marks the dates when she has an audition, or a callback, and it's been a quiet month so far?"

"Look at the other months."

Moreno looked at the other months. "Okay. A quiet year so far."

Next, they searched the bedroom. The queen bed was neatly made up and unoccupied. No bleary-eyed woman under the sheets, with smudged makeup and crumpled days-old clothes, demanding to know why the LAPD were snooping around her apartment.

But no dead woman either. Sometimes you had to take the small wins.

Two dresses were laid out on the bed, like Madison had been trying to decide what to wear the last time she'd been here. Assuming that was Monday morning, she'd opted for a blue floral dress and blue leather purse and gold strappy sandals to wear to her audition.

On the nightstand was a paperback novel and a reading lamp. Sarah fanned the pages of the book but there were no notes or tickets or receipts tucked inside.

Moreno snapped on some gloves and slid open the closet door. Sarah's heartbeat kicked up a notch. It wouldn't be the first time she'd found a stiff stuffed inside a closet, but there was nothing more sinister than sneakers and shoes and a set of lightweight dumbbells on the floor this time. Two orange shirts bearing Madison's name and the name of the diner where she worked hung among the dresses and pants and blouses on the rail.

Moreno moved over to the bed and got down on his hands and knees to check underneath. Sarah went over to a dressing table by the window, where she found a yellow notepad and ballpoint pen that had likely been used to write the note found in the purse.

A photograph in an ornate silver frame showed a younger Madison with an older man and woman. She resembled both in different ways—same auburn hair as the woman, same ice-blue eyes as the man. Sarah knew from reading the MP report that the father was now deceased, and the mother was in a care home and was no doubt worried sick about her daughter but too frail to travel to Los Angeles. Madison had no siblings.

The only other item on the dressing table was an old jewelry box decorated with pink and blue butterflies. The lid was open, revealing mostly cheap costume jewelry. Sitting on top of the bangles and earrings and chunky necklaces was a clear plastic bag, like the kind used to store batch-cooked food in the freezer.

Sarah held it up to the light streaming in through the window, and saw that it contained a little rose-shaped gold pendant with a tiny diamond at the center. The clasp was still fastened but the delicate chain had been snapped.

"This is weird too," she said.

Moreno got up from the floor, dusted off the knees of his suit pants, and joined her at the dressing table. She showed him the bag with the necklace. "Looks like it's broken," he said. "Why weird though?"

"Nice piece of jewelry like this and it's in a plastic bag?"

"Looks like a real diamond. Maybe it's to protect it from getting damaged?"

"Most people keep diamonds and other expensive jewelry in velvet boxes or pouches, not plastic freezer bags. This makes no sense."

Moreno shrugged, and Sarah returned the necklace to the jewelry box.

"Anything under the bed?" she asked.

"Negative," Moreno said. "And still no sign of her cell phone."

The last place to be searched was a compact bathroom. Like the rest of the apartment, it was clean and uncluttered. The shower curtain was pulled all the way back to reveal an empty bathtub. The tub was bone dry and so was the washbasin. Sarah looked inside the vanity unit beneath the sink and saw an open box of tampons, but no birth control pills or condoms. She lifted the toilet seat. No telltale urine stains either. If Madison James had a boyfriend on the scene, they must have been doing the dirty someplace else.

Moreno bagged Madison's toothbrush and hairbrush in case a DNA sample would be required further down the line. Sarah hoped that it wouldn't.

When they returned to the living room, a woman was standing in the open doorway of the apartment and she was holding a gun.

# 3

# MADISON

## SPRING, 2002

Madison pushed through the old-fashioned polished brass and wood revolving door and her eyes widened.

"Oh, wow," she whispered in awe. "This place is gorgeous."

The hotel lobby was like something out of a movie. Old paintings that were probably worth a fortune hung on walls covered in fancy wallpaper. Her heels sunk into a deep-pile carpet. A dozen crystal chandeliers glittered. A floral display that was taller than she was dominated the center of the room and she could smell its heady perfume from where she stood.

Madison could just imagine herself filming a big-budget production in a hotel like this, maybe playing the role of Daisy Buchanan in *The Great Gatsby*. She would be adorned in strings of beads and sequins, and holding a champagne coupe, and enjoying an illicit rendezvous with Gatsby.

"Yeah, I suppose it's okay if you like old shit," said her friend Ally Hagen, and the daydream evaporated.

"It's not old shit, it's classy."

"Whatever you say, Mads. Just don't get too excited, huh? We ain't here for a spa treatment or a slap-up meal in the restaurant. We're about to be herded like cattle into that glorified barn over there."

Ally pointed to a conference room with big wood-paneled doors that had been opened wide to reveal dozens of young women, just like Madison and Ally, milling around inside.

A woman wearing a pink velvet baker-boy cap and ripped jeans approached them, holding a clipboard. "Are you ladies here to audition?"

"We sure are." Ally snapped her gum, and the woman pooched her lips in disapproval. "I'm Ally Hagan. She's Madison James. Stick a star next to our names because that's exactly what we are."

"Is that so?" The woman licked a finger and turned a sheet of paper filled with names, then another, and then a third. She wrote their names on the fourth page.

Madison's heart sank. They were all here for the same part. It was bad enough that she had to go up against Ally, but so many other girls too? What chance did she have? Then she told herself to be optimistic. She was just as talented as every other actress here. And everything would change once *Survive the Night* was released in the fall, just in time for Halloween. Then she'd be inundated with scripts, and casting directors would be chasing her for parts instead of her having to attend these cattle-call auditions. That was what her manager Annie Kline said anyway.

Her spirits lifted and then plummeted right back into her shoes again when she entered the conference room. She glanced around in dismay. Most of the girls were dressed like Ally. Sexy. Trendy. Youthful. Ally, with her Doc Martens and satin slip dress and slim diamanté choker around her throat, fitted right in.

Madison stood out like a plain gray pebble in a pile of sparkling diamonds.

Annie had told her to dress demurely because the part she was trying out for was demure, so she'd picked a sensible blouse and a skirt that fell below the knee and kitten-heeled slingbacks. She felt like a frump among all the minidresses and low-rise jeans and cropped halter tops.

Ally lifted the hem of her dress to reveal a small silver hip flask strapped to her skinny thigh. "You want a little Dutch courage?" She smiled wryly. "Actually, it's Scotch, not Dutch. Scotch courage."

Madison laughed but shook her head. Ally slipped the flask from the elastic, took a long slug, and winced, before returning it to its hiding place under the dress. "That's better. Now let's get this fucking show on the road."

The woman with the clipboard started calling out names, and girls were led into another room where the auditions were taking place. An hour passed. Ally drank from the flask two more times. Boredom set in. Madison's toes felt pinched by the kitten heels. Another half hour crawled by.

Then Madison had the strangest sensation of eyes being on her, could feel the weight of a heavy stare. Goosebumps prickled her bare arms. She turned and saw a man standing in the doorway, half in shadow. He cradled what looked like a tumbler of whisky. He was looking straight at her.

"Who's the guy over by the door?" she asked.

Ally turned just before the man stepped back into the lobby. She squinted. "My eyesight is so shit. I swear, I'm gonna need to get glasses soon. I think it was Cash."

"Cash? Who's Cash?"

Ally snorted. "You don't know?"

"No, should I?"

"Oh, kid. You've got a lot to learn. You'll know soon enough who he is. Trust me. Everyone does. They call him Cash because he likes to flash the cash." Ally leaned in closer and Madison could smell the booze on her breath. "But all the girls call him Dirty Cash behind his back."

Madison's eyes widened. "Why do they call him Dirty Cash?" she whispered. "Is he a gangster?"

Ally laughed. "No, they call him Dirty Cash because he's a dirty bastard. You know, a creep. Like I said, you'll learn."

Ally was twenty-two, just three years older than Madison, but she'd been in Hollywood since she was sixteen so she knew a lot more about the industry—who the key players were, who to impress, who to avoid, how things worked, how to play the game.

They'd met on the set of *Survive the Night.* On the first day of filming, Ally had strolled up to Madison and taken a strand of Madison's auburn hair in her hand and twirled it around her index finger. She'd said, "I guess you think you're going to be the next Julia Roberts?"

Madison had replied, "I'd rather be the first Madison James."

Ally had dropped the hair and stared at her, and Madison had silently berated herself for making such a stupid, conceited remark. Then the bottle blonde had broken into a big grin and said, "I like you, Mads. You're funny. Green, but funny. Stick with me and you'll be just fine, kid. Ally Hagen. Your new best friend."

Madison hated being called anything other than Madison, but Ally Hagen didn't seem like the kind of person you corrected.

A woman of around forty entered the conference room from the lobby now. She wore a silk blouse and smart pants and designer heels and had an air of confidence about her that suggested she was more important than her coworker with the clipboard. She went over to where a young blonde was standing on her own and whispered in her ear.

Madison's breath caught. The girl was beautiful. Her long hair was naturally sun-kissed, her eyes were the color of a frozen lake, and her lips were pink and full. She was around five-five and slender and, like Madison, had dressed modestly in a knee-length summer dress. But she didn't look dowdy, or even cutesy in a Doris Day kind of way; she was classy and elegant like Grace Kelly. Madison knew she herself was pretty, maybe even regarded as beautiful back in her hometown of Dutton, but this girl was in a different league altogether. Hers was the kind of beauty that should come with its own slow-motion sequence and soundtrack every time she walked into a room or down the street.

The blonde followed the older woman out of the conference room.

"No fucking way," said Ally. She darted after them and disappeared into the lobby. A minute later she returned. She looked pissed. "They went into an elevator. It went up to the penthouse suites."

"So?" said Madison.

"So, we're wasting our time, Mads. We've no chance of getting the part. Not now."

"Why?"

"What do I always tell you, kid? You've got a lot to learn."

"Ally Hagen!" the woman with the clipboard yelled. "No star next to the name. And lose the gum!"

"I'm up." Ally spat the gum into a potted plant. "Catch you after? We can go drown our sorrows in some dive bar with loud music and cheap hooch."

Madison grabbed Ally's arm. "Where did the blonde go? Why did she leave the audition?"

Ally looked sad. "I hope you never have to find out, Mads."

She was right. They both missed out on the part. The blonde was announced as the lead actress in the movie a few weeks later.

Her name was Taylor Rose.

# 4

# SARAH

## SEPTEMBER 2022

Up close, the smoker from the pool was much older than she'd initially appeared from earlier glimpses.

The woman was at least seventy, with sun-worn skin the texture and color of buckskin. The big hair was courtesy of a Raquel Welch–style wig that was slightly askew. The house dress hung loosely on her skinny frame and was accessorized with fluffy slippers peeking out below the hem and a nickel and pearl revolver held down by her side.

The gun looked as old as its owner, and Sarah thought it was an odd choice for home protection. But at least it wasn't being pointed at her and Moreno. Not yet anyway.

"What the hell do you think you're doing?" the old woman demanded in a voice that sounded like she'd been sucking on gravel. The hand holding the revolver trembled. Age or illness rather than fear or nerves, because her stare was pure steel. Sarah figured the only thing worse than a steady hand holding a gun was an unsteady one.

"Ma'am, I'm going to need you to slowly put the weapon on the floor," Sarah said calmly.

From the corner of her eye, she saw Moreno's hand go to his hip holster and unclip it, but he didn't pull his sidearm. Not yet anyway.

The old lady ignored Sarah. "If this is a robbery then bad luck," she rasped. "I called the cops already and they're on their way."

"Ma'am, we *are* the cops. Put the weapon on the floor. Now."

"Cops, huh? You don't look like cops. You look like a soccer mom, and he looks like a trainee realtor. Show me some ID."

For the second time today, Sarah indicated the detective's badge on the waistband of her jeans.

"You expect me to see that thing from all the way over here? Fire it over. If it's a fake, I'll know it's a fake. I've seen a million of them."

Sarah sighed. First a four-mile hike in hundred-degree heat and now a gun-toting senior. And to think she could be at home right now, scrubbing out the toilet bowl instead. She took her ID from her jeans pocket and slid it across the shiny floor. Moreno's fingers gripped the butt of his Beretta 92FS.

The old lady leaned over and squinted at the ID at her feet. "Uh-huh. Okay, seems legit." She kicked it back to Sarah. "So, what're the cops doing here? Where's Madison?"

"Gun," Sarah said. "Then we can talk."

"Relax, relax." The old-timer waved the revolver in the air. "It's a prop."

"Lay it on the floor right now. I mean it."

"You seriously think that's going to happen with my arthritis?"

The woman's shriveled hand creaked open like an arcade claw machine and the gun hit the parquet with a loud clatter.

"Shit," said Sarah.

"Jesus!" gasped Moreno. "You could've taken one of us out if that had gone off, including yourself."

The woman glared at him. "What part of 'prop' don't you understand, son? That thing's about as much use in a gunfight as a water pistol." She toed what appeared to be a Colt Peacemaker toward them, same as she'd done with Sarah's ID. Moreno snatched it up and quickly inspected it.

"Prop," he confirmed, showing it to Sarah, who nodded her agreement.

"That's what I said," the woman wheezed. "From the spaghetti western *Bullet for a Blind Man* starring Ed Baynes. Mostly shot in Andalusia back in '76. Now give it back. It's worth at least a C-note."

Moreno returned the gun, and it was quickly dispatched into a deep pocket on the front of the house dress.

"Wait," Sarah said. "Did you really call the cops?"

"Of course I didn't. Don't trust them, no offense. Not since that time I was arrested for indecent exposure for peeing outside. When you gotta go, you gotta go—that's what I tried to tell them. But would they listen? No. Why are you nosing around Madison's apartment? And where the hell is she?"

"That's what we're trying to find out," Sarah said. "Madison James is missing."

"Missing, huh? Well, shit. That doesn't sound good. Now that you mention it, I haven't seen her around for a day or two."

"And you are?" Sarah asked.

"Kitty Duvall. Concerned neighbor. Apartment 304, right next door. And no relation to Shelley or Robert before you ask."

"Who?" asked Moreno.

"Here we go again," muttered Sarah.

"Are you shitting me?" Kitty gaped. "Robert Duvall, who only spoke one of the most famous lines in cinematic history in

*Apocalypse Now*? Then won the Academy Award for Best Actor in '84 for *Tender Mercies*?"

Moreno gave her a blank look.

"Surely you know who the hell Shelley Duvall is? *The Shining*? Jack Nicholson smashing in a door with an axe? Shelley giving the performance of her career?"

"Trust me, you're wasting your breath," Sarah said. "He wasn't born until '95. Can we talk about Madison James, please?"

Kitty's eyes went to the wall clock in the kitchen. "Sure, but let's go next door to my place. It's almost three o'clock."

"What happens at three o'clock?" Moreno asked.

"A cigarette and a vodka martini with a crisp olive on a toothpick, that's what. Follow me."

Sarah locked up behind them, and they followed slowly behind Kitty Duvall as she shuffled along the walkway. Inside apartment 304, the layout was identical to the one they'd just been in but that was where any similarities ended. While Madison's was like touring a show home, Kitty's was like wandering into an old curiosity shop.

Every corner of the living room was jammed full of weird and wonderful things, including a banjo, a frilly parasol, and a unicycle. Framed black and white photos hung on the walls showing a much younger Kitty Duvall posing alongside Clint Eastwood and Charlton Heston and Joan Collins and the real Raquel Welch. There were some not so wonderful things too, Sarah thought with a shudder, noticing a ventriloquist dummy dressed in a tweed suit and sitting on a director's chair.

Kitty slipped Ed Baynes' revolver into the drawer of a writing bureau, then ambled over to a well-stocked bar cart.

"You want to join me in a vodka martini?" She unscrewed the lid from a bottle of Tito's. "Or I can do you a gimlet or an old-fashioned or a manhattan?"

"We're on duty, remember?" Sarah pointed out.

"Never stopped the cops I knew back in the day." Kitty lifted her bony shoulders in a shrug. "But suit yourself. All I got otherwise is water."

"Water would be good," Moreno said.

Kitty flicked a hand toward the kitchen. "The faucet is right over there, son. Tumblers are in the cabinet above it."

Sarah bit back a smile and Moreno rolled his eyes but headed for the kitchen. Kitty finished mixing the martini and took the drink and a Betty Boop ashtray to a mustard velvet wing chair. She balanced the cocktail on a side table and positioned the ashtray in her lap. Then she pulled a crumpled pack of Camels from her pocket and lit a cigarette.

Moreno returned with two glasses of water and Sarah drank hers gratefully. It was hotter in here than it was outside, and the smoke was making her throat scratchy.

Kitty gestured to a two-seater velvet couch. "Sit or I'll get a crick in my neck looking up at the pair of you."

They sank onto the small purple sofa and Sarah gestured around the room. "What is all this stuff?"

Kitty took a deep drag on the cigarette. "Some of it was picked up in thrift stores and garage sales. Mostly it's from old movie sets. I worked props for over fifty years for all the major studios. A few of the crappy ones too."

"They just allowed you to take it all?" Moreno asked.

Kitty chuckled and it sounded like car gears grinding. "I'm not sure 'allowed' is the right word. I guess you could say I 'liberated' it."

Moreno raised his eyebrows. "You mean you stole it?"

Kitty shrugged and smiled, and tapped ash into the Betty Boop ashtray. "I like to think of it as saving it from cold storage or—even worse—gawking tourists on those dreadful studio tours." She eyeballed

Moreno. "What? You gonna arrest me? Are you gonna slap your handcuffs on an old lady? Hey, speaking of cuffs, you didn't find any in Madison's apartment, did you? Or a blonde Julia Roberts wig?"

Sarah frowned. "A blonde Julia Roberts wig?"

"You know, like the one she wears in *Pretty Woman* when she's wearing her hooker outfit and picks up Richard Gere on Hollywood Boulevard in his fancy car that he can't drive? Mine isn't the real deal sadly—I never worked on that set—but you get the idea. Anyway, Madison borrowed the wig and the handcuffs a few weeks ago for some community play she was appearing in, and I never got them back." Kitty winked at Moreno. "You never know when that stuff might come in handy, huh?"

Moreno reddened and coughed and took out his notepad. "Um, so, Madison James. When was the last time you saw her?"

"Monday morning." Kitty crushed the cigarette butt and took a sip of the cocktail. "I was by the pool smoking. She was dressed up all fancy. I said to her, 'Those tips are gonna be rolling in today, sweetheart. You should make an effort more often.' She told me she had the morning off work and was on her way to an audition. Seemed to think it was a big deal. She said, 'Kitty, this is the breakthrough role I've been waiting for—it's going to make me a star.' I said, 'Well, good luck with that.' She mentioned something about wearing her lucky blue dress and I figured it hadn't been too lucky for her so far. That girl has lived next door for near on seven years and I've never once known her to land a part on a TV show or a movie in all that time. A couple of community plays and a few advertisements that you hope no one ever sees—that's it." Kitty gulped down another mouthful of martini. "Madison was never going to give up on the dream though. You could smell it on her like cheap drugstore perfume."

"Smell what?" asked Sarah.

"Desperation. She was desperate for stardom, desperate to be somebody. When you've worked in the movies for as long as I did, you see it all the time. Young girls willing to do just about anything to see their name on a billboard on Sunset Strip." Kitty's leathery forehead creased like an accordion. "You don't think something's happened to her, do you? You don't think she got herself into a bad situation?"

"It's too soon to jump to any conclusions." Sarah decided not to mention the purse. "All we know for sure is that Madison hasn't been at work the last few days and isn't answering her cell phone. Do you know if she had a boyfriend or was dating anyone?"

"A few deadbeats in the past. Never anything serious. A good-looking woman like her, I always wondered why she was single. Figured she'd had her heart broken once or was just really smart. No deadbeats recently though. If there were any sleepovers happening next door, I'd know about it."

"Any visitors?"

"Just the other waitress from the restaurant. Loretta or Larissa. I'm guessing she's the one who called the cops."

"Anything suspicious or out of the ordinary? Any strangers hanging around the building?"

"Not that I've noticed, and I notice plenty that goes on around here."

Sarah didn't doubt it. She thought of the "past due" letter in Madison's mailbox. "Was there anything worrying Madison? Any unusual behavior recently?"

Kitty drained the glass and slid the olive from the toothpick and popped it in her mouth. Crunched it and nodded grimly. "Yeah, maybe. There was this one night not so long ago. Book club night. There are five of us who meet once a month and we take it in turns to host. On this occasion, it was my turn. One of the girls had overstayed her welcome as usual. It's always the same with Irene. Makes like she wants to discuss the book some more when what she really wants to do is drink my good liquor and save on her own electricity. Anyway, it was late by the time I convinced her to order an Uber. I was seeing Irene out when I noticed Madison at her front door, like she'd just arrived home. She seemed upset. Even paler than usual. I remember she dropped her keys but before I could say anything, she'd gotten the door unlocked and shut it behind her."

"When was this?" Sarah said.

Kitty thought about it. "Well, we've had book club at Irene's place since then. She wasn't happy about that, let me tell you. So, maybe six weeks ago? It's hard to keep track, what with book club, bridge club, wine club, and movie club. Let me check my day planner."

Kitty put the ashtray on the side table and gripped the arms of the chair, and hauled herself up to a symphony of groans, cracking bones, and rustling polyester. She pulled a leather-bound diary from the drawer where she'd stored the fake Colt Peacemaker and thumbed through the pages until she found the right date. She read it out and Moreno made a note of it.

"The next day, I knocked on Madison's door to make sure she was okay," Kitty said. "She'd been all dressed up that night too—in fact, it might've been the lucky blue dress—and I'd assumed she'd been on a date with a guy who'd turned out to be a jerk. Believe me, I've been in that movie a million times. She told me she was fine—then she said the strangest thing."

Sarah and Moreno exchanged a look. "What did she say?"

"She said, 'Kitty, if anyone shows up asking about me, tell them I don't live here anymore. It doesn't matter who they are or what they want. Tell them I've left town and I'm never coming back.'"

"Why would she say that?" Sarah asked.

Kitty hugged the diary to her scrawny chest and shook her head. "I have no idea. I guess I thought she was just being melodramatic, what with her being an actress and all. But now you're telling me she's missing and I'm thinking that maybe she wasn't just upset that night. Maybe she was scared too."

# 5

# SARAH

## SEPTEMBER 2022

One of Sarah's pet peeves was overpriced restaurants that served tiny portions in the name of haute cuisine and left her craving a huge slice of pizza on the way home.

The Joneses wasn't one of those places. A squat building in the Fairfax district with buzzy neon even in the daytime and early-to-late opening hours, it was the kind of old-school diner where breakfast was served all day, "diet" was a dirty word, and five-thousand-calorie chocolate malts were encouraged as an accompaniment to the jumbo burger and fries.

Sarah was flying solo for the interview with Larissa Jones because Moreno had returned downtown to get the ball rolling on the paperwork for Madison's cell phone and bank records, as well as issuing a BOLO on the Mustang. He was also going to contact the major studios about auditions that had taken place on Monday, and trawl through Brush Canyon Trail photos and videos posted on social media in the last few days.

It was well after lunch and still early for dinner but most of the parking spaces were occupied. Sarah eased her Chevy Equinox into a vacant spot right next to the front entrance, where a woman stood out front smoking a cigarette. In a world where everyone vaped now, it seemed like Sarah was destined to inhale more secondhand smoke in one day than she had in the last decade.

The woman was early forties, with blonde streaks burned into long afro curls. She wore a fitted orange shirt, like the ones hanging in Madison's closet, that complemented her dark skin. Bootcut blue jeans and Converse hi-tops completed the uniform.

"Larissa Jones?" Sarah asked, getting out of the car, even though "Larissa" was stitched in a curlicue font on the shirt, along with "The Joneses."

"That's me," the woman said. "Are you here about Madison? Is she okay?"

Sarah introduced herself. "I'm afraid we haven't located Madison yet. I just wanted to follow up on the report you filed yesterday, if that's okay?"

"Sure thing." Larissa held up the cigarette. "You know, I've been off the cancer sticks for two years—cold turkey, not even so much as a vape in all that time—and this is my third pack since Madison vanished." She stubbed it out on top of a trash can. "Let's go inside."

White Formica and orange leatherette booths lined one side of the busy restaurant, and a chrome counter with orange swing stools occupied the other. Funky vintage artwork adorned the walls and a retro jukebox played "Twilight Time" by The Platters loud enough to hear but low enough to be heard over.

Sarah's heart clenched. When she was a kid, her mom used to listen to The Platters and Neil Sedaka and Paul Anka on a cassette player in the kitchen, while weeping quietly, after Sarah's father had passed out drunk on his chair for the night.

They sat in a booth by the window with a view of an outside patio, where a handful of patrons were enjoying tuna melts and

Cobb salads and the late afternoon sun. Larissa signaled to a waitress behind the counter to bring over a pot of coffee. Sarah's stomach growled in response to the aroma of fried onions and grilled meat drifting from the kitchen, and she realized she hadn't eaten since breakfast. Even so, it didn't seem an appropriate time to be ordering a side of fries.

They waited for the coffee to arrive and for the waitress to return to the counter, then Larissa said, "I saw something on social media about Madison's purse being found. What was she doing in Griffith Park?"

"I was hoping you might be able to tell me?"

"I have no idea. I couldn't even tell you the last time she visited the park. Madison is not what you would call the outdoorsy type." Larissa sighed and pinched the bridge of her nose. Dark circles stood out like bruises beneath her eyes, under the harsh ceiling lights. "This is all just so unlike her, disappearing like this. It's completely out of character. That's what I told the police officer when I filed the report."

"She's never done anything like this before?"

"No. Never."

"Often in missing persons cases, the individual just needs a break from their own life for a while," Sarah said. "Sometimes stress and worry can reach a breaking point and they remove themselves from the situation without informing anyone of their plans. Is there a chance that's what's happening with Madison?"

"I really don't think so," Larissa said. "I'm not just Madison's boss, I'm her friend too. We've been tight ever since we started waitressing together around fifteen years ago. When my husband and I took over this place, Madison was the first person we hired. The only time she ever cried off sick was when she got Covid. So, no, I don't think she would just take off and not tell me. She'd know how much I'd worry."

"When you filed the missing person report, you provided a description of what she was wearing on Monday—so you saw her before the audition?"

"Yeah, she stopped by the restaurant."

"Why did she stop by the restaurant if she'd scheduled the morning off?"

Larissa thought about it. "It'd been a while since she'd had any auditions—and a long time since she'd been this excited about an acting job—so I guess she just wanted a pep talk. For me to tell her she looked great, which she did, and assure her that she was going to smash it, which I was sure she would."

Sarah sipped her coffee. Larissa hadn't touched her own drink.

"Did Madison tell you anything about the audition? Where it was being held? Who she was trying out for? The names of any casting directors or studios or production companies?"

Larissa said, "All I know is she was up for the lead role, and it was a movie that would be shown in theaters, so not a TV show or one of the streamers. I didn't ask for any other details, and she didn't offer any. I'm not part of that world so, unless we're talking Steven Spielberg or James Cameron—and I don't think we are because she would have been shouting it from the rooftops—the names of directors and producers wouldn't mean anything to me."

"Does Madison have a manager or an agent?"

"Her manager is Annie Kline. That's K-L-I-N-E. They've worked together forever, pretty much since Madison first arrived in Hollywood."

"This Annie Kline would know all about the audition then? She'd have been the one who set it up?"

"You'd think so," Larissa said. "I haven't been able to reach her. I've tried her office a bunch of times and left messages with her assistant, but she hasn't returned my calls. I don't know her. We've never met. Like I said, different worlds."

Sarah made a mental note to speak to Annie Kline as a priority.

"Madison's neighbor seemed to think she'd been worried or upset about something recently. Any idea what that might be?"

Larissa considered the question and nodded in agreement. "I guess she has been acting a little different lately," she said. "Quieter. Maybe a little distracted. Sometimes, I'd catch her staring out the window, like she was a million miles away. I put it down to her turning forty soon. I know it bothered her, her life not looking how she thought it would by now. When I saw her on Monday, it was the happiest she'd been in a while. Like a weight had been lifted."

"Any boyfriends or casual dates?"

"Not for a while."

"Other friends?"

"Madison is friendly with a couple of the girls who work here. I already spoke to them, and they don't know where she is. Then there's the old crow who lives next door to her. I think Madison enjoys her stories even though I'm convinced most of them are fiction. She has the occasional coffee with one or two ladies from her SoulCycle class. That's it, really."

"No friends from the acting world?" Sarah asked.

"Years ago, yes. But they're either dead or quit Tinseltown a long time ago. I guess it's a tough industry. Madison also meets Annie Kline socially occasionally."

Sarah showed Larissa a photo of the note they'd found in Madison's purse. "Any idea what this note means?"

She shook her head. "It's Madison's writing but I have no idea. Looks like some kind of shorthand."

Sarah's next question was a difficult one. She said carefully, "Larissa, can you think of anyone who may have had a grudge against Madison or would have had reason to harm her?"

"No!" Larissa was shocked. "Madison is just the nicest, sweetest person." She gestured with her hand around the restaurant. "Ask anyone in here. The customers all love her. Why would anyone want to hurt her? You really think that's what happened?"

"That's not what I'm saying. We're just trying to cover all the bases here." Sarah decided to change tack. "There was a key for a Ford Mustang in Madison's purse, but so far, we've been unable to locate the vehicle. It's not in the garage at her—"

"It's in the staff lot out back," Larissa interrupted. She slid out of the booth. "I can show you. Follow me."

They made their way through a steamy kitchen that could have doubled as a sauna. A tall chef flipped burgers with one hand and stirred a pot with the other. A shorter chef rapid-chopped cucumber and tomatoes. The sizzling and clanging and chopping thankfully camouflaged the rumble that erupted from Sarah's belly. Larissa pushed down on the lever on a fire exit door, and they stepped outside to a back alleyway.

A row of dumpsters piled high with trash bags lined the back wall. Steam pumped out of an air vent. Three cars occupied four spaces marked "Reserved." One of them was a black '98 Ford Mustang.

Sarah took out her cell phone and sent a message to Moreno: *Cancel the BOLO on Madison's car. It's at the restaurant.*

"It's been here since Monday," Larissa confirmed.

"Why didn't Madison drive it to the audition?"

"I guess she didn't think a beat-up old banger was the right kind of image. She set off on foot down the street toward the strip mall. Said she was getting a lift."

"As in a ride with someone, or Lyft the cab company?"

"That's a good question," Larissa said. "I'd assumed she meant the cab company, but I guess she could have meant a ride. A driver from the studio or something?"

Sarah circled Madison's car and peered inside. All the worn, red leather seats were empty. She got down on her haunches at the rear of the vehicle to check if the suspension was lower than it should be. It wasn't. She sniffed the air but didn't detect any suspicious odors either. In this heat, a corpse would be ripe by now.

Larissa noticed what she was doing. "You don't think she's in the trunk, do you?" There was a trace of panic in her voice.

"I think it's unlikely."

"You need to open it and make sure."

"I don't have the key."

Moreno had taken the Mustang's fob to log as evidence, along with the purse and the rest of its contents.

"You don't need one." Larissa went to the driver's side door and yanked it open. "Madison never locks it. I'm always on at her for leaving it unlocked and she just laughs and says a thief would be doing her a favor stealing this heap of junk."

"Okay, don't touch anything else, Larissa."

Sarah pulled another pair of gloves from her bag. She swore some days she wore more latex than a '70s gigolo. She got into the driver's seat and, after a few moments of searching, found a button in the glove compartment to pop the trunk.

Larissa stood by the back door, wringing her hands.

Sarah returned to the trunk and heaved it all the way open. Gym gear was strewn everywhere: running shoes, leggings, crumpled t-shirt, sports bra, empty water bottle, towel. The mess was in stark contrast to the show-home apartment in Studio City.

"Anything in there?" Larissa called nervously.

"Just some workout stuff."

Larissa appeared next to Sarah and peered inside. "We do yoga together and Madison also goes to that SoulCycle class in Hollywood. She likes to stay in shape, but I think she mostly goes there for the networking opportunities."

"She doesn't keep this stuff in a gym bag?"

"Yeah, usually. A neon pink and yellow duffel."

Sarah slammed the trunk shut and went around to the driver's side, and slid back in behind the wheel. The center console contained sunglasses, mints, and some loose change. The side pockets on both doors were empty. She opened the glove compartment again and withdrew a pile of receipts. They were for groceries at Ralphs, filling up the tank at a local gas station, toiletries and household stuff from Target, and another gas station fill-up, this one in Palm Springs. The date on that receipt gave her pause. Sarah quickly tapped out a text to Moreno.

She got out of the car and leaned on the open door. "Why was Madison in Palm Springs?"

"I didn't know that she was," Larissa said.

"What's in Palm Springs? Does she have any friends out there?"

"Not that I know of."

Sarah's cell phone pinged with a text.

She'd asked Moreno to check his notes for the date of Kitty Duvall's book club meeting on the night Madison James had returned home from a date or a party or some other event visibly shaken and upset.

Sarah read her partner's response:

*August 8th.*

It was same date as the Palm Springs gas station receipt.

# 6
# MADISON
## FALL, 2002

The *Survive the Night* premiere was crazy.

Madison and Ally weren't famous enough for any of the big fashion houses to offer them the loan of dresses for the event. Not yet anyway. But Ally had managed to convince a small designer boutique in West Hollywood to give her and Madison 50 percent off if they plugged the store on the red carpet.

Ally had picked out tight black leather pants, a corset top with skinny straps, and a velvet choker, while Madison had chosen a green paisley-print boho dress because the sales assistant had said it complemented her red hair and pale skin.

Even with the discount, it was still a lot of cash to splurge on a single outfit, but Madison figured if you couldn't splash out for the premiere of your movie, when could you?

They'd gotten dressed and done their own hair and makeup at Ally's studio apartment, while listening to Linkin Park turned up loud and drinking a bottle of wine to steady their nerves. Okay, to steady Madison's nerves. Ally never got nervous about anything.

Then it was off to the Village Theater in Westwood in a sleek car with tinted windows that the studio had sent for them. A whole block had been closed off when they got there. Fans were crammed behind metal barriers, and shouted their names and thrust glossy photos and notebooks at them and demanded autographs.

Madison suddenly felt overwhelmed by all the chaos and noise. A wave of dizziness washed over her and, for a horrible moment, she thought she might pass out. Ally noticed and grabbed her hand and whispered, "You got this, kid. Just breathe." Madison did as she was told and took a breath and her head cleared and the roaring in her ears subsided and the panic passed.

This was what she wanted, she told herself. This was what she'd dreamed of since she was a little girl.

They walked the red carpet for an hour, and were photographed and interviewed in front of a step-and-repeat backdrop. Madison smiled the smile she'd practiced for years in front of the bathroom mirror until her face muscles ached. Flashbulbs popped and photographers yelled for them to turn this way and that way and "that's great Madison" and "just one more shot Madison, looking straight down the lens."

The star of the movie, Rachel Rayner, then appeared wearing a silver one-shouldered sheath that turned sheer when the cameras flashed and showed off her breasts, because her stylist had screwed up and forgotten the nipple covers. Ally was convinced the screw-up was deliberate to secure extra column inches, same as she was convinced Rachel only got the good parts because her dad had been a big movie star in the '70s and '80s.

After the screening, Ally suggested they ditch the catered reception with its canapés and formal small talk and warm fizz and go somewhere livelier, and Madison was relieved to escape the mayhem.

Their car dropped them at The Volcano Club on Sunset Strip where the line snaked all the way around the block. Ally hooked an arm through Madison's and led her right up to the entrance, where a doorman who could have been Vin Diesel's twin stood behind a red velvet rope.

"We're on the VIP list," Ally said confidently. "Ally Hagen and Madison James."

Madison stared at her in surprise and Ally winked.

The Vin Diesel lookalike touched a Bluetooth earpiece and spoke to someone, and Madison's heart pounded as she waited for the inevitable, humiliating knock-back. Then he lifted the rope and said "Enjoy your night, ladies," and the people at the front of the line glared at them as they were ushered inside the club.

"We're on the list at The Volcano?" Madison asked, wide-eyed and impressed. "How the hell did you swing that, Hagen?"

Ally grinned. "I'd love to take all the credit, but the studio sorted it. A VIP table too. Now let's party!"

The club was dark, with dry ice rising from the floor and sweaty bodies packed together as they gyrated to "Hot in Herre" by Nelly, blasting so loudly through the speaker system that Madison's teeth vibrated.

They were shown to a private booth, and before they'd even placed a drinks order, a server in a short skirt and low-cut top deposited an ice bucket containing a bottle of Dom Pérignon and two flutes onto the table.

"The studio?" Madison's words were swallowed up by the music.

Ally, lipreading, shrugged.

The server leaned down to be heard, her huge breasts almost spilling out of the top. "For Madison," she yelled. "A gift from the gentleman in the next booth. Enjoy." Then she left.

The booths were curved, the occupant of the one next to theirs obscured from view.

"I bet it's Jimmy Grand!" Ally shrieked. "Your new co-star. It must be him, right? He's always throwing his cash around in clubs on the Strip."

Madison had just been cast in a supporting role in a romantic comedy alongside Grand, who was the male lead. The director, Buck Bendich, had seen the teaser trailers for *Survive the Night* and had reached out to Annie and Madison's agent, Solly Jenkins, to personally request that she audition for his next project.

She'd tried out for Bendich at the studios and was offered the part the next day.

Ally stuck her head around the side of the booth, then turned back to Madison with a sour expression. "Urgh. Not Jimmy Grand. It's that creepy fucker Cantwell."

Madison leaned over Ally to see for herself who her mystery benefactor was, and saw a man she vaguely recognized sitting on his own. He raised a glass of whisky in a "cheers" gesture and her skin crawled. She forced a smile and sat back in the booth.

"What do we do? Send back the champagne and say we don't want it?"

Ally pulled the Dom Pérignon from the ice, condensation dripping from the bottle. "Like hell we do. We drink it is what we do. And we definitely don't invite him to join us. That's what he wants. Seriously, who comes to a club on their own?"

Ally filled the flutes and they clinked.

"To *Survive the Night*!" Madison shouted over the pounding beat.

"And *The One Year Hitch* too," Ally yelled back. "My girl Mads is the toast of freakin' Tinseltown!"

They drank the fizz and another bottle appeared and Madison again smiled her thanks at the stranger in the next booth, and this time the smile came more easily because she was a little drunk.

It was after 3 a.m. by the time they spilled out of a back door to avoid the paparazzi, clutching each other, and stumbling in their heels, and laughing so hard Madison thought she might pee herself.

It had been the best night of her life.

The studio car had only been available until midnight, so they called a cab and Ally was dropped off first at her place and then Madison carried on to the apartment she shared with her roommates.

She didn't notice the dark-green SUV that tailed the taxi the whole way.

# 7
# SARAH
## SEPTEMBER 2022

Sarah snapped a photo of each of the receipts with her phone before returning them to the glove compartment. The Palm Springs trip might be nothing, but it might be something.

The back door opened and the tall chef who'd been flipping burgers in the kitchen stuck his head out, a dishcloth slung over his shoulder and sweat dappling his brow.

"Sorry, babe," he said to Larissa. "But we need you back here. The place is really filling up."

"I'll be right there," she said.

He nodded and retreated inside.

"My husband, Tre," Larissa explained. "The staff don't usually call me 'babe.'" She gave a little laugh and Sarah realized it was the first time she'd seen the woman smile. Just as quickly it was gone again.

Sarah pointed to a discreet camera mounted above the back door. "Is that the only security camera you have?"

"We have three: front door, back door, and above the counter."

"Could you shoot me over all your footage from Monday?"

"Sure thing."

She gave Larissa her card and they went back inside, and Sarah saw that Tre hadn't been exaggerating. The number of customers had almost doubled in the time they'd been outside. Larissa walked Sarah through the busy restaurant to the front door and promised to email the camera footage as soon as she had five minutes to spare.

Then she gripped Sarah's arm tightly, her eyes wet and worried. "Promise me you'll find her."

Sarah knew better than to make promises she wasn't sure she could keep. "I'll be in touch as soon as I have any news," was all she said.

Instead of climbing into her car, Sarah wove past the other vehicles in the lot until she reached the street. Then she turned in the direction of the strip mall, same as Madison had three days earlier.

She passed a coin laundry with a rusted padlock on the door and grime coating the windows, and a shuttered auto shop with a "Closed for Vacation" sign, and a liquor store that was open. Sarah went inside. Behind the counter was a burly man with a drinker's nose and a smoker's teeth. She showed him the photo of Madison that Larissa had included on her Facebook post.

"Have you seen this woman around here the last few days?"

The cashier eyed the photo appreciatively. "Nah. She's a honey. I'd remember."

"Any cameras inside or outside the store?"

"No cameras but I got plenty of beer."

"It's a little early in the day for me."

Sarah left. A narrow alleyway separated the liquor store from the auto shop. She stepped from bright daylight into the gloom and shadows. Trash bags and cardboard boxes bearing the names of popular booze brands were piled alongside each other. Beyond a stack of balding tires was a small pool of dried vomit. The alley stank of urine and gasoline. Sarah followed its path, which led to another main thoroughfare. She quickly retraced her steps back through the darkness and piss and puke and emerged onto the first street again. Shielded her eyes from the glare of the sun and looked around. There didn't appear to be any cameras nearby. A blind spot.

She continued toward the strip mall, which was only a hundred yards or so from The Joneses. It housed a dentist, a budget menswear outlet, a shipping and postal service point, a vacant unit, and a convenience store. It was covered by a security camera at the entrance to the parking lot. Whether it was operational or not was a different matter.

Sarah wondered why Madison had set off on foot instead of using the restaurant as her pickup point.

Her stomach growled loudly, providing another reminder that it had been hours since she'd last eaten. Sarah entered the convenience store and picked out a tuna salad sandwich and a bottle of Coke from the fridge. A bored-looking young guy sat behind the counter scrolling on his phone. He wore an old Green Day tour t-shirt and his hair in curtains and Sarah wondered if the '90s were making yet another comeback. She could see herself on a small screen behind him as she approached. She placed her ID on the counter along with her purchases and pointed at the screen.

"Is that live feed only or does it record too?" she asked.

"Yeah, it records." He spoke slowly and she wondered if he was stoned.

"How long do you keep the footage?"

Sarah didn't think Madison had been seeking a dental checkup or to purchase a men's suit or to send a parcel before her audition, but maybe she'd come in here for a bottle of water or some breath mints. Maybe she'd had company. Maybe she'd been with the mystery driver.

The kid shrugged like it was a huge effort and didn't look any less bored. "No idea." He swiped the sandwich and soda across the scanner.

She tapped her ID again. "Do you think you could check? I'd like to see any footage you have from Monday."

He peered at her through the curtains. "I get paid twelve dollars an hour."

"Okay. And?"

"And it's a shitty wage but it's all I've got, and I don't plan on losing it because I took some cop out back and let them go through the boss's computer without a warrant. You want to see the tapes, ask Bobby. His shift starts at ten." He shook the hair out of his face. "That'll be five dollars."

She paid and left and went back to The Joneses, pausing briefly for another glance down the alleyway. Back in the car, the sandwich was a disappointment. Sarah could smell Larissa's burgers from where she sat, and she cursed her own professionalism.

An online search for "Annie Kline Talent Management" provided an address in North Hollywood and a landline number. It rang and rang before the message service kicked in. Sarah left her details, same as Larissa Jones had apparently done. It was just gone five thirty. Annie Kline clearly didn't hang around beyond regular office hours. Lucky her.

Next, Sarah opened the TikTok app and found Chloe Reid's account. The Griffith Park video had more than eight thousand views now. The video auto-played and showed Chloe—wide-eyed and mock-serious—holding up the blue purse while recounting her "seriously crazy" day.

"Okay, listen up guys," she was telling her followers. "The weirdest thing just happened. I'm out hiking the Brush Canyon Trail right now and I've just found this purse hidden in some bushes. Weird, right? I guess I'm nosy, so I've had a look inside and found some ID. I can't believe who it belongs to." Chloe paused for dramatic effect. "An actress called Madison James. I know, I know, I hadn't heard of her either until I googled her just now. But, get this, she's *missing*. No one's seen her in *days*. And now I've just found her purse in Griffith Park. That can't be good, huh? Anyway, the cops are on their way. I guess I'm, like, a witness or something. If they make a TV show about it, I'll probably be in it. Seriously crazy, right? Anyway, I'll keep you guys posted!"

Chloe signed off by blowing a kiss to the camera, which seemed kind of inappropriate in the circumstances.

More videos loaded in Sarah's "For You" feed showing other TikTokers at the same spot under the Hollywood sign—claiming to be "assisting in the search for Madison James" and "hunting down clues"—having apparently been able to access the trail after it was reopened by Meadows.

"Jeez," Sarah muttered.

She started the car and headed downtown, quickly getting tangled up in the start-stop crawl of the 101 in rush hour. When she finally reached the PAB, Sarah moved the cardboard boxes from her desk to the floor and fired up her computer.

Moreno stuck his head over the privacy divider and provided an update. He'd requested—and already viewed—the footage from the LAPD's own cameras, mounted on top of traffic signals and light poles, in Madison's neighborhood. Nothing useful. The major studios were a bust too. None of them had been holding auditions on Monday. He was still waiting for Madison's cell phone and bank records and had started to go through the social media images from Brush Canyon Trail.

Moreno returned to his work and Sarah found a website for the company who operated security at the strip mall. A recorded message informed her the office was now closed. She emailed a request to view Monday's footage of the strip mall entrance.

Larissa Jones had emailed Sarah the restaurant's own footage, as promised. Three files were attached, named "Front," "Rear," and "Counter." Sarah decided to view them in the order that Madison would appear on each one.

She clicked on the "Rear" file and hit fast-forward until she saw the Mustang pull into the back lot. The time stamp read 11:02. Madison got out and slammed the door shut. She didn't lock it, just dropped the key into a blue purse. It looked like the same purse Chloe Reid had found in Griffith Park. As far as Sarah could tell, there were no other passengers in the car. Madison didn't make a call or take anything from the car or open the trunk or do anything else, other than head for the back door.

Sarah clicked on the file marked "Counter" next. Again, she whizzed past all the earlier, irrelevant activity, the actions of Larissa and the diner's patrons moving comically fast at triple speed. When the time stamp showed 11 a.m., Sarah slowed the video to its regular speed and waited for Madison to enter the frame. She approached from the direction of the kitchen and climbed onto a stool at the counter and waited for Larissa to finish serving a customer. The two women chatted for a little over five minutes, and Sarah thought that Larissa was right—Madison *did* seem happy. Then they hugged over the counter and Madison slid off the stool and headed for the front door.

Sarah closed the attachment and opened the last of the files, this one named "Front." Madison emerged from the restaurant into the customer parking lot. She paused briefly and took something from her purse, glanced at it, then dropped it back inside. Sarah was almost certain it was the missing cell phone. Then Madison turned in the direction of the strip mall and was gone.

Sarah watched all the footage again and screen-grabbed one of the frames from inside the diner that provided a clear view of Madison's face and the outfit she'd been wearing when she was last seen. The image would be useful for the media conference and press release that would both happen in the coming days if the woman wasn't found by then. The LAPD had yet to post about the disappearance of Madison James on their own social media channels, but plenty of other folk had. The hashtags #FindMadison and #MadisonIsMissing were now trending in the Los Angeles area.

Next, Sarah turned her attention to the Palm Springs gas station, a small Valero off State Route 111 and around six miles from the desert city's downtown area. She picked up the desk phone and punched in the telephone number onscreen. Two minutes later she had confirmation of what she'd suspected would be the case—the gas station didn't keep security footage as far back as six weeks ago. Leaning back in her chair, Sarah tapped a pen against her teeth and stared at the screen-grab.

*Where are you, Madison?*

The office was almost empty. It was late. The streets outside were dark, the room inside illuminated by the dim glow of a few desk lights and computer screens. It was quiet too. Only the occasional tap of a keyboard and the rhythmic ticking of a wall clock and the faint drone of a vacuum from down the hall to break the silence in a space that was usually humming with activity.

"How're you getting on, partner?" Sarah asked.

Moreno's head popped up over the privacy divider like a jack-in-the-box. His hair was mussed up, the knot of his tie was loosened, and his eyes were bleary, like he was a toddler fighting sleep.

"No dice with the social media posts," he said wearily. "Dozens of variations of the same photo over and over again, folks posing with the

Hollywood sign above them, but no sign of Madison or anyone else with a blue purse. I'm still waiting on her cell phone and bank records."

Sarah suggested they both call it a night and pay a visit to Annie Kline's office early the next morning.

On the way home, Sarah picked up a takeout meal of minestrone soup and homemade *tagliatelle con piselli e prosciutto* from her favorite Italian in Laurel Canyon—a treat to compensate for the bad strip-mall sandwich. The streets were quiet and the drive was smooth, and her head was filled with thoughts of Madison James as she navigated the steep curves of Laurel Canyon Boulevard.

It was only once she'd passed the Houdini Estate that Sarah realized the same headlights had been in her rearview mirror since leaving the restaurant. She stole another glance and caught a flash of dark metallic green as the car—a big boxy SUV—passed under a streetlight, but the interior was too dark to get a visual on the driver. As she continued toward home, the SUV stayed with her. When she turned onto her street, it turned too. Sarah's heart slammed against her chest.

She pulled into the empty driveway of a house that wasn't her own and kept her eyes on the rearview, her hands white-knuckled as she gripped the steering wheel. The SUV cruised past without slowing down, the driver still obscured from view, and continued down the street. When it reached the corner, its blinker flashed, and then it was gone.

Sarah let out a breath, backed out of the driveway, and carried on to her own house.

Once inside, she double-locked the front door and slid the two-barrel bolt latches into place, which she'd had installed when the locks were changed not so long ago. As a cop she had always been vigilant about home security, but even more so now that she was on her own. It was the first time she'd lived alone—having previously shared a home with her parents then roommates then romantic partners—and it was taking some getting used to.

She switched on lamps and dumped the takeout bag on the kitchen counter and made sure the back door was secured. Upstairs, she drew the curtains and changed into pajamas. The street outside was empty. No green SUV. No one lurking in the shadows. Back in the kitchen, Sarah settled into a chair at the dining table which also doubled as her workspace. She opened the laptop and turned to a fresh page of a yellow legal pad and did what Chloe Reid had planned on doing, and checked out Madison James' IMDb page.

Sarah ate the soup while she read. It didn't take long to complete either task because she was ravenous and Madison had only appeared in three movies. Two of them were horror flicks either side of a romantic comedy:

*Survive the Night* (2002)

*The One Year Hitch* (2003)

*Do Not Disturb* (2004)

Having made fast work of the soup, Sarah moved onto the pasta container while making a note of the key cast and crew from each of the productions. The three directors Madison had worked with were Kent LaMarr, Buck Bendich, and Ted Clayton. None of their names were familiar to Sarah. The movies had all performed okay at the box office—not roaring successes but not flops either—so she guessed the trio of filmmakers had been a few steps below A-listers like Spielberg, Scorsese, and Stone at the time.

The names of some of Madison's fellow cast members rang distant bells, but the only one who stood out was Jimmy Grand, the male lead in *The One Year Hitch*.

Jimmy Grand.

*Jeez.*

Talk about a blast from the past.

With his square jaw, sexy grin, and dark hair falling into his flame-blue eyes, Jimmy Grand had been quite the heartthrob two decades ago. His image had graced the covers of magazines and the bedroom walls of teenage girls, but Sarah hadn't heard his name in years. Back then, he'd had a reputation for partying hard—drugs, booze, and a lot of beautiful women—and she had no idea if he was even still alive. A quick Google search confirmed that he was, but he'd dropped out of the limelight a long time ago after a couple of spells in rehab.

Sarah then found on-demand access to all three movies—Chloe Reid was wrong about them only being available on DVD or videotape—but the only one she watched all the way through was the romantic comedy.

In the movie, Madison played the younger sister of the unlucky-in-love female lead who set herself a year to get married, humorously assisted by her platonic best friend and next-door neighbor played by Jimmy Grand. Of course, the female lead realized she was in love with Grand's character and married him in the end, unaware that her sister had been carrying a torch for him for years. Larissa Jones was right—Madison was a very good actress. Sarah was particularly impressed by the final scenes when she bravely performed her bridesmaid duties, despite nursing a broken heart.

There was no need to watch the two horror films all the way to the final credits because Madison's characters met a gruesome end early on in both. She was the second girl to die in *Survive the Night* and the first victim in *Do Not Disturb*, which proved to be her last movie role to date. That was the one Sarah had seen at the theater.

She closed the laptop and wearily climbed the stairs to the bedroom. Somewhere in the hills, the cry of a coyote shattered the quiet night. She thought of Madison's blood-curdling screams as she was attacked by an axe-wielding madman in *Do Not Disturb*. As Sarah got into bed and turned off the lamp, it occurred to her that none of the roles Madison James had played had gotten a happy ending.

Sarah hoped life wasn't about to imitate art.

# 8

# SARAH

## SEPTEMBER 2022

The two detectives met at the PAB and rode together to North Hollywood, Sarah driving and Moreno riding shotgun.

"I see you ditched the soccer mom look," he said with a grin.

Today, Sarah was dressed in navy suit pants and a cream satin blouse, and ankle boots with a modest heel. Moreno had swapped the gray suit for a beige one. "I see you're still digging the trainee realtor look," she shot back.

Sarah had barely cleared West 1st Street when Moreno started with the questions.

"So . . ." he said. "Missing Persons, huh? You get tired of clearing homicides or what?"

"I'm not in the mood for a game of 'Twenty Questions' about my career, so let's change the subject, okay?"

"Okay."

Neither of them spoke as they drove along North Broadway. Sarah was about to turn on the radio to drown out the silence when Moreno finally said, "I watched her movies last night."

She glanced at him as she joined the freeway. "You did? What did you think?"

"If I was feeling generous, I'd give them all a three-star rating. Madison four stars. She was pretty good, and she looked great onscreen."

"I agree," Sarah said.

"You watched them too?"

"I did."

"Don't you think it's weird though? The trajectory of her career?"

"How do you mean?"

"Let's forget the rom-com and focus on the slasher flicks," Moreno said. "The 'final girl' is the star of the movie, right? The one who survives, the last woman standing. In *Survive the Night*, Madison was second to die. She performed well—and so did the movie. So, she should've been able to build on that for *Do Not Disturb,* surely? The last girl to die, maybe even the final girl role. Instead, she was killed off first. More nudity, less screen time."

Moreno was right. In *Survive the Night*, Madison's character had lasted more than half the movie and had died while wearing a ripped dress with just a flash of underwear showing. In *Do Not Disturb*, she was in bed with her boyfriend and her breasts were briefly on show when the axe fell just twenty minutes in.

"And then her career crashed and burned," Sarah said, thinking out loud.

"Right," Moreno said. "Weird."

They turned into a business park off Lankershim Boulevard. The offices of Annie Kline Talent Management were located in a faded red-brick single-story building alongside a catering company, a dry cleaner, and an insurance broker.

"Doesn't exactly look like a dream factory where stars are made," Moreno observed.

They entered a reception area that was furnished with a cream leather couch and a glass desk and several cheese plants. Attempts had clearly been made to offer a more aesthetically pleasing interior than the building's drab exterior.

On the walls were framed movie prints, some of which Sarah recognized but most of which she didn't. She spotted posters for *Survive the Night* and *The One Year Hitch.* In the latter, Jimmy Grand sported a lopsided grin and blue jeans and a crisp white t-shirt, and posed alongside the lead actress who was resplendent in a huge taffeta puffball wedding dress. Madison's name was in small print on both posters but there was no photo of her on either.

Sarah didn't see a framed print for *Do Not Disturb*, but she did spot another glossy poster featuring Jimmy Grand. Both the title of the movie—*The Murder Book*—and his co-star's name—Rachel Rayner—seemed familiar, but she couldn't put her finger on why. Maybe the actress was related to the old movie star Rodger Rayner. Or maybe it was another movie Sarah had watched at the theater a long time ago that had failed to make enough of an impression to prevent it from being consigned to hazy memory.

Behind the glass desk sat a straight-backed young blonde who was a carbon copy of Chloe Reid. Same perky ponytail and baby-pink glossy lips and summer tan, which was accented by a sleeveless white dress. She was frowning at a ringing phone, a manicured nail hovering above the buttons.

"One moment, please," she said without looking up.

The phone eventually stopped ringing and an iMac pinged once, then twice, and the receptionist directed her frown at the computer screen and pursed her lips and finally turned her attention to Sarah and Moreno, the lips now rearranged into a welcoming smile.

"Hi, how can I . . ."

The words trailed off and the smile faltered as her eyes went straight to the detective's badge on Sarah's waistband. The blonde might be stressed, but at least she was observant.

"We're here to see Annie Kline," Sarah said. "Detective Delaney—that's me—and Detective Moreno—that's him—from the LAPD."

"Oh. Okay." The receptionist turned back to the computer screen, her French-tipped nails tapping hesitantly at the keys. "Let me just pull up Ms. Kline's schedule for today. I think she's on a call just now though."

"We don't have an appointment."

"Oh. Well, I'm not sure I can disturb her . . ."

"It's a police matter."

"Oh."

The blonde appeared undecided, then pained when the phone began ringing again.

A door opened behind the desk to reveal a woman in her fifties with a sleek platinum bob, an even sleeker dress suit, and tortoise-shell glasses. Sarah recognized Annie Kline from the professional head shot on her company's website.

To the blonde, Annie Kline said, "Kayla, the button with the little green receiver." To Sarah and Moreno, she said, "You'd better come on through."

They followed her into a modern office that was not unlike Madison's apartment in both decor and tidiness. A bowl of potpourri filled the room with an artificially floral scent. The attempts to style the office were tempered by the view of a brick wall outside the window. Annie Kline settled into a high-backed leather chair behind an identical glass desk to the one in reception and gestured for the two detectives to take a seat facing her.

"Kayla is new," she explained. "I doubt she'll last the month, which will still be an improvement on my last assistant. It's always the same story; they apply for the job and come armed with résumés boasting office experience that they clearly don't have because it very quickly becomes apparent that they don't know the first thing about spreadsheets or virtual calendars or how to transfer a telephone call."

"Why would they lie to get the job?" asked Moreno.

Annie sighed. "They're all aspiring actresses who think working for a talent agency will help them be 'discovered', or that they'll meet an A-list actor here who'll fall in love with them, and they'll become rich and famous that way. Once they realize neither scenario is going to happen, they leave. If they're not sacked first, that is."

Annie called through to reception and told Kayla to hold all her calls, and Sarah wondered if Kayla had passed on any of the messages left by Larissa or herself, and if Annie Kline was even aware that her client was missing.

"So, what do two detectives from the LAPD want with me?" Annie laughed nervously. "Should I be worried? Did I forget to pay a speeding ticket or parking fine?"

So, she didn't know that Madison James had vanished then.

"We're from the LAPD's Missing Persons Unit," Sarah said. "I left a voice message yesterday evening."

"Kayla is still trying to master how to access voicemails. Who's missing?"

A light knock was followed by Kayla sticking her head around the door and looking uncertain again. "Can I offer anyone a drink? Iced tea, coffee, water?"

Annie said, "Thank you, Kayla, but I already had a cortado at Amp this morning so I won't be ready for any more caffeine until noon. Detectives?"

"We're fine," Sarah said.

Kayla seemed relieved, and Sarah guessed she'd also yet to master some overly complicated coffee machine in the back kitchen. She waited until the receptionist had returned to the outer office, then said, "Your client Madison James is missing."

A little upside-down V appeared on Annie's forehead. Then it disappeared again as realization dawned.

"Ah, right," she said. "Is this about Larissa Jones? Kayla did mention she'd called and left some messages. Something about Madison not turning up for her shifts at the restaurant. To be perfectly frank, my job is to secure acting work for Madison. The waitressing isn't really my concern."

"When was the last time you spoke to Madison?"

Moreno once again took the notes, while Sarah took the lead with the questions. She was glad that her new partner wasn't pulling any macho bullshit stuff and that he was willing to acknowledge her seniority even if she was the most recent addition to the MPU team.

"I'm not sure," Annie said. "I could ask Kayla to check my planner but that could take a while."

"Ballpark."

"A couple of weeks. Maybe longer. Why? How long has she been gone?"

"Since Monday."

"Monday?" Annie gave an incredulous laugh. "And the police are involved? She's probably gone away for a few days, and it'll be crossed wires with Larissa at the restaurant. Or she met a guy. Madison is an attractive, single woman. Maybe she hooked up with someone and they wanted to spend some time together with no distractions or interruptions. I'm sure she'll show up in a day or two full of apologies and very embarrassed that the LAPD were called."

Sarah told Annie about Madison's purse and her belongings being found in Griffith Park.

The upside-down V returned. "Okay, that is concerning. Could it have been stolen?"

"Maybe," Sarah said. "Madison had booked some time off work Monday to attend an audition. Did you arrange the audition?"

The V deepened. "I don't know anything about an audition."

"Madison didn't mention it?"

Annie held Sarah's gaze. "No. Not a word."

"You're her manager. Isn't that unusual?"

"Yes, I suppose."

Sarah went on, "According to what she told friends, Madison seemed to think the audition was a big deal. It was for the lead role in a movie, and she said it was going to make her a star. Yet she didn't mention it to you?"

"Perhaps she wanted to surprise me with the good news if it happened," Annie said. "There hasn't been a whole lot of good news where Madison's concerned for a long time."

"How would Madison even know about the audition? Does she have an agent?"

"She's between agents."

"When was her last one?"

"Almost two decades ago."

"Why did they part company?"

"Madison wasn't making him any money, so he fired her."

"Seems kind of brutal."

"It's a brutal industry."

"Could Madison have reunited with this agent for the audition?"

"I doubt it," Annie said. "I believe Solly Jenkins returned to London some years ago. And, like I said, they didn't part on the best of terms."

"You've worked with Madison for how long?"

Annie considered. "Around twenty years. Madison was recommended to an industry contact of mine by her high-school drama teacher. The contact set up a meeting. I was impressed and signed her."

"And you've never fired her? Despite there not having been a whole lot of good news where Madison is concerned for a long time?"

"I'm a manager." Annie's lips became a thin scarlet slash. "I manage careers and I look at the long term. Madison is a great actress and I've always believed she'll have the success she deserves one day. Many actors have breakthrough performances at an older age. Look at Glenn Close in *Fatal Attraction* and Connie Britton in *Friday Night Lights* and Octavia Spencer in *The Help*. It can happen at any time. All it takes is one role. In any case, I treat all my clients as people, not cash cows. I also regard Madison as a friend."

"But you don't know where she is."

A statement, not a question.

"I don't," Annie answered anyway. "And now I *am* worried. All these questions . . . you're clearly concerned about her well-being. What I'd like to know is what exactly you're going to do about it?"

"What do you mean?"

"I haven't seen anything on the news about Madison being missing."

"It's trending on Twitter and TikTok," said Moreno.

"I don't do social media. I'm a talent manager, not an actress." Annie turned her attention back to Sarah. "Why isn't it being reported on TV or the radio? Why isn't there a press conference? The public should be made aware. People should be out looking for her."

Sarah said, "We'll decide in due course whether to release a statement to the press. Right now, we're just trying to establish where exactly Madison's audition was taking place and with whom, and where she's been since Monday."

Annie spread her hands in a helpless gesture. "I wish I could be of more help."

"Perhaps you could ask around your industry contacts, see if they're aware of any auditions that Madison could have attended?"

Annie nodded solemnly. "Of course."

"This role that Madison was trying out for," Sarah said. "Could it have been a cash job?"

Annie looked confused. "A cash job? I don't follow."

"You know, if Madison was offered the part, would she be paid in cash for the work?"

The woman seemed even more bewildered now. "No, that's not how it works. When a client is offered a role, we agree a contract and payment is then made via wire transfer. It would be me who would handle all the paperwork."

"But you didn't know about the audition," Sarah pointed out. "So, it's possible Madison could have lined up a gig herself that would pay cash? Something both you and the IRS wouldn't need to know about—where she'd get to keep all of her earnings?"

Annie said, "Maybe if the work was with a less than reputable production company, but I don't deal with people like that, and Madison doesn't either. Plus, you said it was a major film role that could make her a star, so that makes no sense. Why are you asking?"

Sarah withdrew her cell phone from her pants pocket and opened the photos app. She said, "As well as her personal belongings, there was a note in Madison's purse when it was discovered in Griffith Park."

Annie's eyebrows disappeared beneath her platinum bangs. "A note?" she asked sharply. "What kind of note?"

Sarah and Moreno exchanged a look.

*Why was Annie Kline so rattled by the mention of a note?*

Sarah slid the cell phone across the desk. On the screen was a photograph of the yellow sheet of paper from the purse. "Do you know what it means?"

Annie stared at the screen. "No. I have no idea."

"Are you sure?" Sarah pushed. "Could it be the details of the audition? Think, Ms. Kline. This could be important."

"I'm sorry, but I don't know what those letters and numbers mean or who Cash is."

Sarah and Moreno shared another look. They hadn't considered that "Cash" might be a person.

But Annie Kline clearly thought so.

"Okay, I think we're done here," Sarah said.

She gave Annie her card and ushered Moreno out of the office. Sarah closed the door quietly behind her. Kayla was at the front desk, focused on a spreadsheet on the computer screen. Moreno opened his mouth to speak, but Sarah hushed him with a raised finger.

She pressed an ear to the office door. Waited. Listened. A long moment of silence passed. Then she heard Annie Kline speaking softly from the other side of the door. She was on the phone.

Bingo.

Sarah strained to hear the words.

". . . Annie Kline . . . yes, good . . . yes, it has . . . Can I speak to him?" A pause. "It's important . . . won't take long . . ."

"Was there anything else, Detective Delaney?"

Kayla had swung around in her chair and was watching Sarah with narrowed eyes.

*Dammit.*

Sarah held up her cell phone. "Just replying to an email." To Moreno, she said, "Let's go."

Once outside, she asked, "What do you think?"

"I think the note spooked her," Moreno said.

Sarah nodded slowly. "Exactly. And it spooked her enough for her to make a call as soon as we were out of the door."

# 9

# SARAH

## SEPTEMBER 2022

"Who do you think she was calling?" Moreno asked.

"Cash?" Sarah turned onto Lankershim and then headed west along Oxnard Street.

"You picked up on that too? That Annie Kline immediately assumed that Cash was a person."

"Maybe it wasn't an assumption. Maybe she knew."

They dropped south onto the Hollywood Freeway in the direction of Fairfax.

"So, who is Cash?" Moreno asked. "I'm guessing we're not talking Johnny Cash or Pat Cash?"

Sarah glanced at him, surprised. "I thought the world didn't exist for you prior to 1995?"

Moreno grinned. "My dad is a big country music fan and I'm a total sports nerd. I'm just not so great with ancient movies and TV shows."

*Ancient.*

"Tell me, did a favorite aunt or a kindly neighbor or a friendly cashier in a grocery store once tell you that you have a great smile?"

"Maybe. I don't know. Why?"

"You grin a lot."

He grinned again. "I guess I'm just a happy guy."

"It's annoying."

"My happiness annoys you?"

"Not the happiness. The grinning."

Moreno shrugged good-naturedly and turned to stare out of the window. Traffic was free-moving for once and Sarah navigated the lanes of the freeway while thinking about the case.

"Back to Cash," she said. "Can you pull up Madison's IMDb page and check the lists of cast and crew from her three movies? See if there's a Cash in there. First or last name. I had a look last night, but I was mainly focused on the key players. It could be someone more minor like a grip or a sound mixer."

Moreno opened the internet search browser on his cell phone and found the IMDb page. He was silent as he read through the long lists of names.

"There's no one named Cash," he said at length.

"Dammit." Sarah slammed her hands against the wheel. "I guess that would have been too easy."

"Maybe Annie Kline didn't call Cash. Maybe the call was to someone else who knows who Cash is or where Madison's at or what happened to her."

"Kline knows more than she's telling us, that's for sure."

"How do we find out who she made the call to?"

Sarah frowned. "We don't. It's not possible."

"It is if we get a warrant for her call records."

"On what grounds?" Sarah asked. "Eavesdropping for a few seconds on a one-sided private conversation that didn't yield any concrete information? Even if I offered sexual favors and VIP tickets for the Dodgers as a bribe, we still wouldn't find a judge in the whole of Los Angeles willing to sign off on a warrant."

"I think you're underestimating how much the city's judges love their baseball."

The corners of Sarah's mouth tugged up. "Funny."

"Are you grinning?" Moreno asked.

"Cringing more like."

The customer lot at The Joneses was rammed again, but with people rather than cars. There was no vehicular access this morning, the entrance blocked by a couple of traffic cones. Sarah drove to the end of the street, turned, and headed for the strip mall. Everyone else apparently had the same idea because that lot was full too, a couple of satellite vans from local TV stations among the cars. She parked on the street outside the liquor store. The bad-teeth cashier spotted her through the window grille as she got out of the Chevy, waved, and pointed hopefully to the selection of beers in the fridge behind him. She shook her head.

"Friend of yours?" Moreno asked.

"One almost-funny quip doesn't make you a comedian, you know."

Several folding tables were set up in the restaurant's lot, holding platters of breakfast food and dozens of bottles of water jammed into metal ice buckets and stacks of flyers with Madison's photo on the front. Larissa had posted on Facebook last night about getting a search party together and had requested volunteers meet at The Joneses this morning.

She'd had a good response. There were about a hundred people milling around. Tre, dressed casually in jeans and an orange polo shirt with the diner's insignia, was stationed behind one table, making notes on a clipboard and handing out flyers and little round colored stickers that volunteers were attaching to their lapels.

Larissa was being interviewed by a sharp-suited radio reporter with a foam-topped mike and a sympathetic expression who was of similar age and style as Moreno. Two TV cameras were set up on tripods nearby, glossy female presenters hovering with their respective cameramen, awaiting their turn for interviews.

A slender, balding man of about fifty stood back from the crowd, his cell phone raised as though filming the hive of activity. His lips were moving under his pencil mustache. If Sarah made the law, Errol Flynn mustaches would be a criminal offense. He was expensively dressed in a Ralph Lauren shirt and tan chinos and leather boat shoes but still managed to look untidy. There was something familiar about him but Sarah couldn't place him.

Chloe Reid was also there filming. Unlike the older skinny guy, she was right in the middle of the action and had her cell phone on selfie mode, so that she was front and center of her own video. She finished recording and spotted Sarah, who glared at her. Chloe lifted her chin and looked away.

"I guess you saw her latest video?" Moreno said.

"I watched it this morning."

Chloe had filmed the video while making her way back to the trailhead the previous afternoon. In it, she'd recounted breathlessly how she'd been "grilled" by LAPD detectives who'd subjected her to a "good cop, bad cop" routine. The female detective, according to Chloe, had been "old and mean," whereas the young male detective had been "kind of hot." The "lady cop" had insisted on Chloe having her prints taken like she was "some kind of suspect."

"You'd better not be grinning," Sarah warned.

"I wouldn't dream of it," Moreno said.

The shorter chef emerged from the restaurant. Unlike Tre, he was dressed in a uniform of double-breasted white jacket and monochrome houndstooth pants. He was carrying two more platters piled high with pancakes and waffles and bacon, and Sarah watched him like a hawk eyeing roadkill.

"Let's eat while we wait for Larissa," she said.

She wasn't going to make the same mistake as yesterday.

As soon as the chef had deposited the platters onto the table and gone, Sarah picked up a set of tongs and filled a paper plate and grabbed a chilled bottle of water. Moreno stood staring at the food but not moving. Eventually, he pulled a water from the bucket.

"Not hungry?" Sarah asked.

"I could eat. But my PT won't be happy."

"Your PT doesn't need to know. Do some extra star jumps next time you're in the gym if it makes you feel better."

Moreno shrugged and picked up a plate and added a small pancake and a single slice of bacon.

They moved away from the food table and ate, and Sarah tuned in to the conversation taking place between two men, also eating, who were standing nearby. They were both bearded with ponytails and were dressed almost identically, in jeans, hiking boots, and slasher movie t-shirts. The white-haired one's tee displayed a faded image from *The Texas Chainsaw Massacre*; his ginger friend had opted for the original *Scream* movie from the mid-'90s. Their t-shirts were both accessorized with little green stickers.

"I couldn't believe it when I saw on social media that Madison James was missing," the *Massacre* fan was saying. "I absolutely loved her in *Survive the Night*. Back then, I would have put money on her being one of the great scream queens of her generation."

"I know what you mean," agreed the ginger. "You ask me, she had the beauty of Heather Langenkamp, the acting chops of Neve Campbell, and the screen presence of Marilyn Burns. That's a helluva combination."

"I met her once at HorrorCon and she was a real sweetheart too. It's a shame she never quite made it."

"Who knows? Maybe once we find her safe and well, Madison will make a comeback. Look at Jamie Lee Curtis. Still killing it more than forty years after *Halloween*."

The slick radio reporter lowered his microphone and shook Larissa's hand.

"Larissa is free," Sarah said, trashing her paper plate and water bottle. She made a beeline for the woman, Moreno trailing in her wake, and reached her just before the two TV reporters.

"Hey," said the hard-faced blonde one. "No cutting in, okay? I need to get this interview in the can in time for the top-of-the-hour news."

"And I need to find a missing woman," Sarah snapped.

"Wait, are you investigating the disappearance? Can I get a comment on camera?"

"I know you," said the other reporter, a heavily made-up brunette whose hairstyle was not dissimilar to Kitty Duvall's Raquel Welch wig. "You work homicide. Did you find Madison James' body? Is that why you're here?"

Larissa looked stricken.

Sarah said, "I work for the Missing Persons Unit. Now back up and let me do my job."

"That comment?" asked the blonde again.

"No comment on camera or otherwise. If you want a statement, contact the LAPD's media relations office. You know the drill."

Sarah steered Larissa away from the TV crews and turned her back to them, aware that both cameramen had removed their cameras from the tripods, and now had them hoisted on shoulders and rolling.

"Did Madison know anyone by the name of Cash?" Sarah asked in a low voice.

Larissa's brow furrowed. "Cash? I don't think so."

"Could be a first name or a last name?"

"I'm pretty sure she's never mentioned that name. Why?"

Sarah said, "We think the reference to 'Cash' on the note we found may be a person. Someone she'd arranged to meet."

"Let me ask Tre. Maybe he knows who this guy is."

Larissa called her husband's name and motioned him over. He excused himself from the line of volunteers and joined them. He didn't know who Cash was either.

"Would you mind looking at the note?" Sarah said. "See if its contents make any sense to you?"

"Sure thing," Tre said.

"Tre is great at puzzles," Larissa said hopefully. "If it's some kind of code, maybe he'll be able to crack it."

Sarah opened the photos app on her cell phone and handed it to him. He studied the screen for a long moment.

Finally, he said, "The 'HTL'—could that be an abbreviation for the word 'hotel'?"

Sarah looked at Moreno, who gave a small nod. A hotel. It was possible.

To Larissa, she said, "Did Madison ever mention any auditions taking place in hotels?"

Larissa nodded slowly. "She did, but this was years ago, when she was just starting out. She'd tell me stories about waiting for hours in line to try out for a part. It was how she got to know some of the other actresses back then."

Sarah felt adrenaline start to fizz. "Do you remember which hotels?"

Larissa scrunched up her face like she was thinking hard. Tre watched her intently. Sarah willed her to come up with a name.

"I don't know," Larissa said helplessly. "I wish I'd paid more attention to those conversations. Maybe the Beverly Hills Hotel?"

"Think Larissa," Sarah urged. "'FM HTL.' A hotel with the initials FM?"

All four of them were silent, racking their brains.

Tre broke the silence. "How about the Fulton Majestic? You know, that fancy old place downtown? We supplied the buffet for a conference there once. This was back when we did occasional outside catering to help pay the bills."

Larissa's eyes lit up with recognition. "The Fulton Majestic. Yes! That's the place."

"The place where you supplied the buffet?" said Moreno.

"No. I mean, yes. Yes, we did do a job there. What I meant was that's the place where Madison tried out for some of her movie roles."

Larissa frowned suddenly.

"What is it?" Sarah asked.

"Yesterday, when I told you that the only time Madison ever cried off sick was that time that she had Covid?"

"Uh-huh."

"I was wrong," Larissa said. "I just remembered. The day we supplied the buffet for the Fulton Majestic, Madison was supposed to help. But it turned out to be a crazy busy day with just me and Tre because she called last-minute to say she was sick. She didn't show up at the hotel that day."

# 10
# MADISON
## SUMMER, 2003

Madison was back at the Fulton Majestic for another cattle call audition.

She thought she'd be done with those by now. But *The One Year Hitch*, while not a box office bomb, hadn't been the hit that everyone expected it to be. The movie had been universally panned by the critics for the "predicable plot" and "lack of laughs" and "zero chemistry" between its two stars.

Madison's own performance had been one of the few positives, one reviewer wrote, but not enough to save a "forgettable rom-com that's short on both the rom and the com."

Her performance hadn't been enough to catapult her into the big time either. Not even close. The scripts and offers didn't start rolling in. The major studios weren't interested. The only parts she did get offered were for low-budget, limited-release indies that were hardly going to be the launchpad her career badly needed. She'd turned them all down, against the advice of Annie and Solly.

Her manager had summoned Madison to her office a few days ago, and she'd expected to be fired. Annie hadn't fired her. She'd asked, "How much do you want it, Madison? The big movie roles, the money, the stardom?"

"More than anything," Madison had said passionately.

She'd meant it.

Annie had been grim-faced. "Hollywood is the toughest—and most competitive—industry in the world. You need to be tough to survive it. To succeed? To rise to the top? You must be prepared to do whatever it takes. And I mean anything."

Madison had nodded in agreement.

Then Annie had told her to be at the Fulton Majestic at noon on Wednesday.

So here she was. This time, the flowers and chandeliers barely registered. The first person she saw when she entered the lobby was the guy from The Volcano Club who'd bought her the expensive champagne after the *Survive the Night* premiere. That night seemed like a million years ago.

He was carrying an expensive-looking camera, like the ones the paparazzi used but with a smaller lens.

"Hi, Madison. Could I trouble you for a photo?"

"Sure."

"I love the dress. Is it new?"

The guy was a creep, but at least he thought she was still relevant instead of a failing actress whose career was stalling worse than an old station wagon. Madison tried not to flinch when he put his arm around her and asked a member of staff to take shot after shot after shot.

The conference room was busy. Madison gave her name to the same woman with the same clipboard and prepared for a long wait. She didn't even have Ally for company this time. She hadn't seen her friend in months. Ally had been filming on location in

Canada and had spent a lot of time partying since getting back to Los Angeles. There had been a series of unflattering photos in one of the trashy magazines showing Ally staggering from The Volcano Club with her makeup smeared and her hair a mess and flashing her underwear as she got into a limo. She'd looked totally wasted.

The stylish woman who'd once plucked the now-in-demand Taylor Rose from the conference room—and, apparently, obscurity—was back. A different silk blouse and pants and heels but the same confident air. She made a beeline for Madison.

"Madison James?"

Madison swallowed hard. "That's me." She could feel every eye in the room on her.

The woman spoke in a low voice. "The director, Mr. Clayton, is a big fan of your work. He would like to see you in his suite. Would you mind coming with me?"

"Um, sure."

They crossed the lobby to the ornate gold elevators and, once inside, the woman stabbed the button marked "P" for the penthouse suites on the top floor.

She didn't say a word to Madison. Didn't look at her either. Just kept her eyes straight ahead. Jazzy muzak played softly. Madison watched each number light up as the elevator climbed higher. The doors finally slid open after what felt like forever.

There were only three doors on the entire floor. The woman knocked on one, ignoring the "Do Not Disturb" sign hooked onto the handle, which Madison found amusing because that was the title of the movie she was auditioning for. The woman swiped a key card and pushed open the door. She called out, "I have Madison James." Then she gestured for Madison to enter and closed the door behind her, leaving Madison alone in the huge suite.

It was decorated in luxuriously rich, warm tones. The living space had a fireplace, dining table, and even a piano! There was also a personal kitchen, which baffled Madison, because if she was rich enough to be a guest here, she'd order every item on the room service menu. Wouldn't even think about cooking.

An open door led to a separate bedroom with a king-size canopy bed draped in chintzy material. The closed door was presumably the bathroom. The views of downtown were breathtaking and took in the fountains, monuments, and lush greenery of Pershing Square way down below.

While she waited, Madison considered what to read for Ted Clayton. She knew the script wasn't finished yet, but he might have some early scenes that he wanted her to run through.

The closed door opened and Clayton stepped out of a marble-tiled bathroom. Behind him was a Jacuzzi big enough for five people. He was dressed in a white terry cloth robe with "FM" stitched on in big gold letters. On his feet were hotel slippers. He went over to a crystal decanter filled with whisky at a bar area and poured himself a double.

"Would you like one?" he asked.

"No, thank you."

He nodded and gulped down the drink in one go and then took a seat on a red velvet camelback sofa.

Clayton motioned for her to stand in front of him.

"Pretty dress. I like it."

The guy downstairs, Cantwell, had been right. The dress was new. A blue floral pattern. She hoped it would be lucky for her.

"I'm a big fan of your work, Madison," Clayton said. "Particularly *Survive the Night*. I think you'd be perfect for *Do Not Disturb*."

Her legs turned to rubber. The palms of her hands were damp. One of the biggest names in the horror genre was about to offer her a role in a movie that was being tipped to be the next *Scream*. She could feel it.

Then he said, "I need to ask you something first. I need to be sure that you're the right girl to star in my movie."

*Star? Oh wow!*

*Play it cool.*

"Okay."

"How do you feel about nudity?"

*Huh?*

It wasn't what she'd been expecting him to ask but it made sense, seeing as Ted Clayton always had nudity in his movies. She weighed it up quickly and decided she was comfortable with showing her butt and her breasts but nothing else. She didn't think full frontal would be required but she'd be able to thrash out the details in the contract talks.

"I'm okay with nudity."

Ted Clayton smiled. "Right answer."

He stood and undid the belt on the robe and let it fall open.

"Oh."

Madison had assumed that when he'd brought up nudity he'd meant her, not him.

Clayton was mid-forties and not in great shape. His chest was carpeted in thick black hair that was turning gray. So was his pubic area. He was aroused.

Her heart pounded so hard she thought it might explode from her chest. Her already weak legs threatened to buckle beneath her. She felt sick.

This couldn't be happening.

"I could do a lot for a woman like you, Madison," he said conversationally, like he wasn't standing there, completely exposed. "Young, talented, beautiful. I could make you rich. I could make you famous. I could make you a star. The question is—how much do you want it?"

Her eyes filled with tears.

"More than anything in the world."

"Right answer. Now get down on your knees and show me how much."

Madison was not particularly sexually experienced, not like Ally.

She'd lost her virginity at sixteen in the backseat of Jesse Fischer's Toyota Camry, and it had been awkward and painful and mercifully quick and they'd both been too embarrassed to see each other again. Then, a year later, she'd stupidly put out on a first date with Chad Bowman from the football team after three beers, and he'd told the entire school and never called her again.

All Madison had gotten from those experiences was embarrassment, shame, and regret.

This would be different. This would be a transaction. Clayton would get what he wanted but so would she. It would be horrible and disgusting and she would hate herself. But she'd hate herself more if she had to return to Dutton a failure. The girl who wasn't good enough for Hollywood.

Tears streaked her cheeks, but her voice was strong and resolute.

"I want to be the final girl."

Clayton nodded. "You got it."

His meaty hands pressed down roughly on her shoulders, and she sank to her knees and the plush carpet felt like razor blades on her skin.

Afterwards, when it was over, she left without saying a word. There was no sign of the confident woman in the corridor outside. Madison rode the elevator alone and found a restroom off the lobby. She washed her mouth out with luxurious handwash and avoided looking at her reflection in the mirror.

Then she locked herself in a stall and dropped to her knees once more and leaned over the toilet bowl and threw up.

# 11

# SARAH

## SEPTEMBER 2022

The Fulton Majestic was designed in the Beaux Arts style, with an imposing frontage boasting lavish sculptures and tall arched windows framed with heavy drapes and elaborate cornicing. Almost one hundred years old, it occupied an entire city block, and stood out among the glass and steel of downtown's modern structures like a classic Rolls-Royce in a showroom full of Teslas.

Passing through the hotel's polished brass and wood revolving door was like stepping into a time machine. On the other side, guests were greeted with an expansive carpeted lobby with high ceilings and mahogany paneling and William Morris–print wallpaper and oil paintings in ornate gold frames. A huge marble table with a ten-foot fresh flower display occupied the center of the room.

It was the kind of establishment where rich men with fat wallets had once smoked cigars and drunk neat whisky in dark corners of the bar, and pretty girls had tried to get themselves noticed, and the extravagant suites had played witness to the secret affairs and exuberant parties of long-ago starlets.

Today, a retractable banner welcomed delegates to a business convention that was being held in a conference room on the other side of the lobby, where the double doors were thrown open to reveal men and women in stuffy work attire and matching lanyards milling around clutching champagne flutes even though it wasn't yet noon.

Sarah wondered if that same room had hosted Madison James and all the other Hollywood hopefuls two decades ago. She wondered if it had hosted Madison just a few days ago.

As she crossed the lobby to the reception desk, Sarah was struck by a memory that was sudden and vivid and hit like a gut punch. She had spent a night in this hotel once years ago. It had been a surprise treat for a birthday, although she couldn't remember which one. There had been a four-poster bed and a claw-foot tub in the room and, even though she'd found the place too stuffy and old-fashioned for her taste, she remembered now how she'd made good use of both.

Sarah shut down the memory like it was an internet browser tab and asked to speak to the manager. The receptionist made a call, and after a short wait the elevator doors opened with a ping and jazzy muzak leached into the lobby. A silver-haired man stepped out and the doors whooshed shut behind him. He wore a suit that wasn't off the rack and a pale pink satin tie that was a perfect match for his pocket square, and he made Moreno look like he'd spent the night sleeping on a bench in comparison. The man walked toward them and didn't look happy. If it had been yesterday and Sarah had fronted up in her jeans and sneakers, he would probably have been even more pissed.

He introduced himself as Mr. Michaels, the general manager, and ushered them away from the desk where rich folk with designer luggage were beginning to stare. Sarah explained that they were investigating the disappearance of a woman by the name of

Madison James, who they believed had been planning on attending an audition at the hotel on Monday.

"There was no audition," said Michaels.

"Are you sure? Perhaps you could check with your events manager?"

"I don't need to check with my staff. There was no audition this week or last week or last month or last year. We no longer host those kinds of events and haven't done for a long time."

"Why not?"

Michaels wrinkled his nose. "All those young women hanging around, dressed like they were attending a Beyoncé concert, it wasn't the right image. When the new owners took over several years ago, they decided to stop the auditions and focus on corporate events instead."

"Did Madison James have a reservation at the hotel earlier in the week?"

Michaels pursed his lips and sighed but made his way to the desk and spoke to the receptionist, who clicked on a computer keyboard and then shook her head.

"No reservation," he confirmed when he returned. "She didn't have a room and she didn't book a table in the restaurant. Will that be all?"

"No, it won't," Sarah said. "We're still trying to establish if she was here on Monday and who she was meeting. Was there a reservation under the name of Cash? Room or restaurant?"

"I can't give out any information about our guests. Not without a warrant."

"A woman is missing," Sarah reminded him. "It will take two seconds for the receptionist to hit some keys and tell us."

"I wish I could help but I can't. I have the privacy of my guests to consider."

"Look, Mr. Michaels, we couldn't care less if you have a Grammy-award winner shacked up with a bunch of groupies or a high-profile politician enjoying an afternoon delight with his mistress. All we're interested in is finding Madison James."

He puffed out some more air, glanced around him. "If I check, then will you leave?"

"Of course."

Michaels went over to the reception desk again.

"Are we going to leave?" Moreno asked.

"Not a chance," Sarah said.

They watched the receptionist. More clacking. Another shake of the head. Michaels looked relieved. He walked back to them. "No guest named Cash. Let me show you out."

He started walking toward the revolving door.

Sarah and Moreno didn't move.

She said, "A classy joint like this, I'm assuming you have cameras covering the lobby? For the security of your staff and guests."

Michaels' face flushed. "You said you would leave."

"We will. Just as soon as we see the feed from Monday."

"No warrant, no footage."

"Okay, fair enough." Sarah turned to Moreno. "But it'll take, what, a couple of hours to get a warrant signed?"

"I'd say closer to three. It's almost lunch. The judges don't like to be disturbed during lunch."

"Good point. So, I guess I'll stay here while you sort the paperwork. Maybe have a soft drink in the bar while I pass the time."

Moreno said, "You could ask the other patrons in the bar about Madison James while you wait for the warrant to be signed off. Show them her photo too."

"Excellent suggestion, Detective Moreno."

"The bar is for residents only," Michaels snapped. His face was even redder now.

Sarah took out her cell phone. "No problem. I'll go online and book a room now. That way, I can enjoy a drink in the bar and chat to the other guests. Maybe have some lunch in the restaurant too. Show her photo to the other diners."

"The hotel is fully booked."

She tapped at the phone and showed the manager the website for a popular hotel booking site. "Oh, look. Rooms available on this site. Special offer too. Must be my lucky day."

Moreno said, "I think what Mr. Michaels is trying to say is that he doesn't want a cop hanging around his bar. Or his restaurant or the lobby for that matter. Not the right image, Mr. Michaels—isn't that correct?"

Moreno inclined his head toward the reception desk, where a businessman with a laptop case and a garment carrier was watching them with a frown. Behind him in the check-in line was an older woman wearing a Chanel purse and a Hermès silk scarf and a concerned expression.

Michaels loosened the knot on his pink tie. He lowered his voice. "That missing woman is all over the internet. I don't want the Fulton Majestic being dragged into this circus."

"You don't have a choice," Sarah said. "Either Madison James was here, or she wasn't. We are going to find out which one it is. How long that takes is up to you."

The manager looked furious, then defeated. "Okay, okay. Just be quick about it—and then get the hell out of my hotel."

He stalked over to reception and opened the door to an office behind the desk and motioned them inside. The office led to a smaller, windowless room where a security guard in a starched uniform sat in front of a bank of computers showing different camera views of locations around the hotel.

To the uniformed man, Michaels said, "Mr. Silva, these detectives need to view the lobby feed from Monday. Can you assist them, please?"

To Sarah, he said, "Mr. Silva is our head of security. He'll take it from here. I need to get back to my duties."

"Before you go, Mr. Michaels, did you work here in the early 2000s?"

"No, I joined the Fulton Group in 2011. Why?"

"Do you know which studios or production companies hired the conference room for auditions back then?"

"I'd need to go through our old records to find that information."

"Could you?"

"Don't push your luck, Detective."

Michaels left and Silva queued up the feed from Monday. Madison had left The Joneses at around 11:15 a.m. and it would have taken at least twenty minutes to make the drive downtown. Sarah asked Silva to start playing the recording from 11:30 a.m. She assumed the "12" on the note meant noon, so they watched all the way through to 1 p.m.

No Madison James.

No one else hanging around the lobby like they might be waiting for her either.

"Are there any other ways in and out of the hotel besides the revolving door?" Sarah asked.

"There's a staff entrance around the back, but you need a key card to enter," Silva said. "Fire exits too, but those are all alarmed and can't be accessed from outside."

"Can we see the footage from the camera that covers the staff entrance?"

Silva tapped some keys, and a different view filled the screen. They watched. Staff clocked on and off. Still no Madison James.

They checked the feeds from the bar and the restaurant too, and they didn't see Madison James or anyone else drinking or dining alone who appeared to have been stood up.

They went back to the lobby feed and this time they fast-watched all the way from 11 a.m. to midnight. They watched until their eyes stung and their heads began to pound and they were absolutely sure that Madison James had never made it to her rendezvous at the Fulton Majestic hotel.

# 12

# MADISON

## LATE SUMMER/FALL, 2003

Madison didn't leave the apartment for four days after the encounter with Ted Clayton. She didn't shower or wash her hair. She barely ate.

Her roommates constantly asked what was wrong, but she didn't confide in them. They thought her low mood was down to a guy and they were right, but they were also wrong. They weren't a part of the industry. They wouldn't understand what had happened in that grand hotel suite and why she'd agreed to it.

Madison gargled with mouthwash all the time. It didn't help. She tried Chardonnay and it didn't get rid of the memory of the taste, but it made her loose and fuzzy and not care so much.

On the fifth day she got a call on her cell phone. The ID displayed Annie Kline's office number. Madison flipped open her Motorola and answered.

"Please hold for Ms. Kline and Mr. Jenkins," said Annie's assistant, who sounded like a different assistant to the one who'd been behind the reception desk a week ago.

Madison waited for the calls to be conferenced together. After a few moments, Annie's voice came on the line.

"Madison, we have wonderful news. You've been offered the role of Jodi Todd in *Do Not Disturb*."

"Huge congratulations, Madison!" Solly boomed in his posh English accent that sounded like it belonged in a period drama.

Madison should have been elated. She felt only a deep emptiness. She would have to call her parents later to tell them the news and they would be so proud of her.

If only they knew.

"Jodi Todd, that's the final girl part, right?" she said dully.

There was a long silence.

"We don't have the script yet," Annie said eventually.

Solly changed the subject to talk money. He always wanted to talk money. He told her how much she'd be getting paid. It was more than double her fee for *The One Year Hitch*. It sounded about right for prostituting herself so she could finally be a leading lady.

"Okay. That sounds fine."

"Super!" Solly roared. "Annie and I will go over the contract with a fine-tooth comb. Make sure there are no issues, but I don't expect there will be. Then we'll get you to sign. And then it's off to North Carolina in a few weeks' time for filming. Don't forget your toothbrush!"

◆ ◆ ◆

The shoot was scheduled to last for twenty days.

On the first day on set, Madison still hadn't had sight of the script.

She knew the general premise of the movie: Six college students are heading off on spring break when their truck breaks down and they're forced to check in to an isolated motel. Over the course of one terrible night, the motel's creepy owner murders them one by one with an axe before the ultimate showdown between the killer and the final girl.

The Jodi Todd character.

But still no script.

Whenever she'd raised the subject with Annie, she'd dismissed Madison's concerns, assuring her that Clayton had requested the writers make a few changes and that he was a perfectionist and just wanted everything to be right, and there really was nothing to worry about.

Madison was shown to her trailer, and it was a huge double banger. Her name was on the door. "Madison James/Jodi Todd." For the first time in weeks, she smiled. She'd been assigned honey wagons—the smallest-sized trailers that didn't even have their own bathroom—for the on-location shoots for both *Survive the Night* and *The One Year Hitch*.

She opened the door. There was a vanity mirror with bulb lights around it and a TV and a refrigerator and a microwave and a private bathroom and a couch.

Cantwell was sitting on the couch.

Madison's brain couldn't make sense of why a fan who'd bought her drinks in a nightclub and asked for a photo together in a hotel in Los Angeles was sitting in her trailer in North Carolina.

"What the hell are you doing here?" she stuttered.

He smiled and it creeped her out.

"I brought you flowers to brighten the place and some champagne for later." Cantwell gestured to a huge vase filled with lilies and a bottle of Dom Pérignon. "I also filled the fridge with food and snacks and bottled water. I thought it would be nice to have lunch together?"

Madison stared at him. Was this guy completely insane? Fear shot through her. Then fury. "Get the fuck out of my trailer."

He laughed. Didn't budge from the couch. "Such a little diva now, aren't you, Madison James?"

Madison threw open the trailer door and went in search of the location manager.

"There's a fucking stalker in my trailer!" she yelled.

She knew she was causing a scene, but she didn't care.

A half hour later Madison was assured that it was all a big misunderstanding. Jeff Cantwell had recently started working for the studio as a production assistant and thought it was part of his duties to make the actors' trailers more welcoming. He hadn't realized he had overstepped and certainly hadn't meant to scare her. Jeff had been advised to keep his distance from Madison for the duration of filming.

A misunderstanding. Right.

If Madison's morning had gotten off to a bad start, the afternoon was going to get a whole lot worse.

When she was finally handed the script, she retired to the trailer to read through her lines. Thankfully there was no Cantwell lurking around this time. Madison started reading. She stopped when she came to the scene where Jodi Todd was attacked by the axe-wielding motel owner while straddling her boyfriend naked in bed.

Jodi Todd was the first character to die in *Do Not Disturb*. (The boyfriend was a close second.)

Madison frantically flicked through the pages, her fingers trembling, panic starting to rise. There had to have been a mistake. This couldn't be right. She reached the climactic scene where the final girl—bloodied, bruised, but still alive—turned the killer's own axe on him.

That character's name was Maya Swanson. She was being played by Taylor Rose.

Taylor Rose was the final girl.

Madison found Clayton on the motel set with a couple of the producers and an assistant director and—of course—Taylor Rose.

Madison lost it. She accused Clayton of using her and lying to her. She accused Taylor Rose of screwing the director to steal the lead role that had been promised to Madison. She almost got fired. She almost quit. In the end, she stayed for the three days it took to get her scenes in the can. Those scenes were overseen by the assistant director. She didn't see Clayton or Cantwell for the remainder of her time in North Carolina.

When she returned to Los Angeles, Madison called Annie Kline and told her she never wanted to work with Ted Clayton on another movie.

Annie said, "You won't have to. His choice, not yours. You'll be lucky to work in this town again."

# 13
# SARAH
## SEPTEMBER 2022

The office was a short drive from the Fulton Majestic, but they'd barely traveled a block when Sarah realized there was a problem.

The green SUV was back.

"Asshole," she muttered through gritted teeth.

"What did I do now?" Moreno asked.

Sarah ignored him. She maintained a steady speed and flipped her blinker on as she approached the next turn.

"I thought we were heading back to base?" Moreno said.

"We were. Change of plan."

She made the turn and then eyeballed the rearview. The SUV also made the turn and stayed with her. Did this jerk never watch any cop shows that taught you how to tail someone without being spotted?

Sarah repeated the steps at the next intersection. Blinker. Turn. Mirror. The tail was still there. Last night she'd been scared. Now she was just pissed.

Moreno turned all the way in his seat so he could see out of the back window. "Green SUV?"

"Uh-huh."

He withdrew his notepad and pen from his inside pocket.

Sarah made the next turn and waited for the tail to reappear in her rearview.

It didn't.

Maybe the driver had watched those old cop shows after all. She pulled into a parking lane and shut off the engine. "Dammit. He made us make him."

"Who is he? Do you think it could be the elusive Cash?"

"I don't think so. Kline only made the tip-off call this morning."

"So?"

"So, this jerk followed me home last night too."

"Seriously?"

"I think so," Sarah said. "It was a dark-green metallic SUV, like just now. Too much of a coincidence. Did you get the plate number?"

"I did."

"Good work, partner. Call it in."

Moreno made the call and tucked his phone between his ear and shoulder so he could take notes. When he ended the call he said, "The car, a brand-new Mercedes-Benz GLS 450, is registered to a Jefferson David Burton Cantwell III."

"Quite a mouthful. Must be a nightmare ordering in Starbucks."

"Address in Bel-Air. Fancy."

Sarah restarted the car. "Let's find out how fancy."

Jefferson Cantwell's home was a grand structure located in a private enclave just off Mulholland Drive. A light-colored two-story traditional construction with a wraparound balcony, it had probably been built in the '50s or '60s. The green SUV was in the driveway.

"Super-fancy," Moreno said.

They climbed the stairs to an imposing front door and knocked, and a man Sarah instantly recognized answered. It was the balding social media influencer from The Joneses this morning. He was still wearing the Ralph Lauren shirt and tan chinos and boat shoes, and still looked untidy. Wary too. As he should be. Instead of getting a colored sticker and joining in the search with the rest of the volunteers he'd apparently decided to follow Sarah all over town.

"Jefferson Cantwell?"

"Yes, that's me. Although I prefer Jeff."

They badged him and introduced themselves and explained that they were investigating the disappearance of Madison James, like he didn't already know.

"Okay. What does that have to do with me?"

"We have a few questions. May we come in?"

"Do I need to call my lawyer?"

Sarah raised an eyebrow. "Not unless you've done something wrong, Mr. Cantwell."

He ran a finger along the pencil mustache. Sarah's teeth itched.

"Okay." He opened the door wider. "Follow me."

Cantwell led them down a hallway into an open-plan kitchen and living area with maple hardwood flooring and lots of mahogany. The styling was traditional inside and out, like he'd inherited the place from an elderly aunt. Sliding doors led to a deck with a kidney-shaped pool and panoramic views of the canyons, city, and ocean. He didn't offer them a drink. Just crossed his arms over his chest. Defensive.

"So, how can I help you, Detectives?"

Sarah said, "I saw you at The Joneses this morning, didn't I? At the search event? You were filming on your cell phone."

"That's right. I recorded some video for social media."

"You didn't want to participate in the search?"

He smiled. It would have been a creepy smile even without the mustache. "I did, but I had some other errands to run."

"Errands. Uh-huh."

"I figure I'm helping in a different way, by spreading the word about Madison online to my followers. They're very engaged."

"Do you know Madison James?"

Cantwell stroked the mustache again. "We met once or twice. Many years ago."

"How did you meet?"

"I briefly worked in the film industry. Madison was an aspiring actress. Our paths crossed a couple of times."

"But you haven't spoken to her recently?"

"Not for a long time."

"Do you know where she is right now, Mr. Cantwell?"

"Of course not. Why would I?"

"Why did you follow me to my home last night?"

Cantwell blinked rapidly at the sudden change of subject. "I have no idea what you're talking about, Detective Delaney."

"The green Mercedes in your driveway. It was in Laurel Canyon last night. I saw it. Same make and model. Same license plate."

That last part was a bluff, but Cantwell didn't know that.

"Yes, it was." The creepy smile was back and so was his composure. "I picked up some takeout food at one of my favorite restaurants. An Italian at the foot of Laurel Canyon Boulevard. I'm sure if you call them, they'll confirm my order. I paid by card. Then I drove home."

Sarah knew that if she did contact the restaurant, they'd confirm his food order. Cantwell was smart enough to cover his tracks.

"Kind of out of your way, is it not?"

"Not really. Twenty minutes each way. And the food is worth it. Especially the *tagliatelle con piselli e prosciutto*. It's divine."

Sarah's blood turned cold. She narrowed her eyes. "How about the hotel just now? You were at the Fulton Majestic too, right? Was following us there one of the errands you had to run?"

Cantwell stared at her and then grinned and spread his hands. "Okay, you got me, Detective Delaney. I did follow you to the hotel, but only to get ahead of the competition. I'm surprised the rest of the media didn't have the same idea."

"You're a journalist?" Moreno asked.

"Podcast host. *Hollywood's Broken Dolls*. It's very popular. You may have heard of it?"

"Can't say that I have. Interesting title."

Cantwell shrugged with his mouth. "Well, that's what they are, aren't they? Hollywood actresses? Dolls to be painted and posed and played with, until they're of no use anymore and then they're discarded. Broken dolls. Even the very famous ones."

"What does your podcast have to do with Madison James?"

"The podcast focuses on the dark side of the Hollywood dream." Cantwell's beady eyes glittered darkly. He grew animated, clearly excited by the subject. "The untimely deaths. The murders. The mysteries. Think Marilyn Monroe, Natalie Wood, the Black Dahlia. Now that Madison has vanished, she's a story too. People are interested. She's like a modern-day Jean Spangler."

"Who?" Sarah beat Moreno to the punch this time.

Cantwell's eyes took on a faraway gaze. "Jean Spangler was a dancer, a model, and an actress." His voice had changed tone and he'd adopted a "conversational journalism" style as though he were narrating an episode of his show. "With her long legs, and killer curves, and million-dollar smile, she could have been a star. She'd had some bit parts in movies such as *When My Baby Smiles at Me* and *Chicken Every Sunday* and she was intent on becoming one of Tinseltown's leading ladies. Then, on the evening of October 7, 1949, Jean Spangler disappeared after telling her family she was going to work as an extra on a film set. More than seventy years later, what happened to Jean Spangler that night remains a mystery." Cantwell's eyes refocused and he looked at Sarah. "Her purse was also found in Griffith Park with a handwritten note inside. Just like Madison James. Isn't that odd?"

"How do you know about the note?" Sarah asked, surprised.

"The trailhead yesterday. I saw you pluck it from the blue purse."

Sarah remembered now why Cantwell had been familiar when she'd seen him at the restaurant earlier. One of the disgruntled hikers who was turned away at the trail's entrance while Sarah and Moreno went through the evidence on the trunk of the Dodge Charger. Except it hadn't been a hiker. Cantwell had been at Griffith Park too.

He said, "I've posted some videos on TikTok and photos on Instagram to tease the episode I'm putting together on Madison James. I would love to interview you, Detective Delaney. I could set up my equipment right now?"

"We're done here," Sarah said. "And if you follow me again, you will need to call that lawyer."

Back in the car, Sarah took off angrily down Mulholland and had to force herself to slow down on the twisty two-lane. She shook her head. "Can you believe that creep? He even knew my order at the Italian restaurant."

"I tell you what else he knew," Moreno said. "That Madison used to audition at the Fulton Majestic." He held up his cell phone. "It's right here in Cantwell's latest TikTok. The one he filmed after following us to the hotel."

Sarah glanced at the phone. She couldn't hear the audio but could see big, splashy subtitles rolling on the screen.

A call came through the speaker system. "Ellen-Media" flashed up as the caller ID. Sarah accepted the call.

"How long have you been in the new job for, Delaney? A day? Two? And already you're pissing off our friends in the media again."

Ellen Downey was head of media relations at the LAPD, and one of Sarah's best buddies outside of work too when she needed wine or sympathy or advice. But mostly wine.

"They're sharks, the whole damn lot of them," Sarah said.

"Sharks that we need to feed occasionally," Ellen pointed out. "We're about to post an appeal for information about Madison James on MPU's Facebook and Twitter feeds. There's lots of interest in the case now. We've even had *Dateline* and *People* magazine on the phone."

"Am I supposed to be impressed?"

Sarah was kind of impressed.

"There's also a press conference scheduled for ten tomorrow morning. Look sharp, Delaney."

Ellen hung up.

Moreno looked up from his cell phone. "This Cantwell guy is seriously obsessed with dead and missing Hollywood stars," he said. "His *Hollywood's Broken Dolls* podcast is split into four categories. 'Dead by Forty' is about actresses who died young—Marilyn Monroe, Jean Harlow, Barbara Payton, and so on. 'Twist of Fate' focuses on tragic accidents involving the likes of Grace Kelly and Natalie Wood. 'Hollywood Homicides' recounts famous murders such as the Black Dahlia and Dominique Dunne. And then there's 'Vanishing Acts', which features the disappearances of Jean Spangler and Tammy Lynn Leppert. That section has a 'coming soon' teaser trailer for an episode about Madison James."

Sarah said, "I want to know everything there is to know about Jefferson David Burton Cantwell III. There's something off about him, and it's not just his facial hair."

Back at her desk, Sarah called Larissa Jones and asked if she would be willing to take part in tomorrow's press conference and make an appeal for information. Larissa said that she would. Sarah picked up the phone again and this time punched in the number for the care facility where Madison's mom lived in Indiana. She wanted to introduce herself personally to Norah James as the lead on the case, and bring her up to speed on the LAPD's efforts to find her daughter.

A woman answered identifying herself as Senior Nurse Ramirez. Sarah explained why she was calling.

"Norah is resting just now," Ramirez said. "She's been very upset about Madison. It's made the news out here in Indiana what with Madison being a local girl."

"The LAPD are holding a press conference tomorrow morning," Sarah said. "I know Norah isn't well enough to travel to Los Angeles, but if we could read out a statement from Madison's mother it would be very useful."

"Of course. I'll see what I can do."

Sarah provided her direct email address. Then asked, "When did Madison last speak to her mother?"

"They Facetimed a few weeks ago," Ramirez said. "I was there. I help Norah operate the iPad. Madison seemed fine. It was just the usual conversation about her work and what books they had read and movies they'd watched. Nothing out of the ordinary. No one in Dutton can believe what's happened."

"And that was the last time Norah had any contact with Madison?"

"Yes. Other than the flowers."

"Flowers?"

"Yellow carnations. Very pretty. They arrived last week."

"Did Madison usually send her mother flowers?"

"On her birthday, yes."

"Was it Norah's birthday?"

"No. I guess she just wanted to tell her mom that she loved her. That's what the card said: *I love you, Mom. Madison x.* Norah still has it on her dresser."

Sarah thanked the nurse and ended the call. She thought about the flowers Madison had sent her mom. Not a birthday or a special occasion. Just to tell Norah James that she loved her.

The week before she vanished.

# 14

# SARAH

## SEPTEMBER 2022

Friday morning.

Fifth day gone.

Sarah leaned over the washbasin and peered at her reflection in the smeared, cracked mirror. She slicked mascara on her eyelashes and applied her usual deep-rose lipstick. She took a step back and appraised herself. Frowned.

"Too much."

She pulled a paper towel from the wall dispenser and wiped off the deep-rose stain. Fished in her purse for another, older lipstick tube. Pale pink. She applied that one. Nodded at her reflection.

"Better."

Sarah pulled her hair back into a ponytail.

"Nope. Too severe."

She let the hair fall back loose around her shoulders.

She'd opted for black heels and slim black pants and a crisp white shirt. She wanted to demonstrate authority and look like she was in charge. Plus, the white wouldn't show the sweat patches underneath her armpits so much. After a final appraisal in the mirror, Sarah decided that she'd do. She wasn't Madison James, the camera didn't love her, but she at least wanted it to like her. A glance at her watch told her it was ten to ten. She took a deep breath and opened the restroom door.

Moreno was skulking in the corridor outside.

"How do I look?" she asked.

"Sharp," he said.

"Wish me luck."

"Are you nervous? You must have done a ton of these things."

"Yep, and I've hated every single one of them."

"I had a peek inside the room where the press is assembled just now. The place is rammed."

"You're not helping."

Moreno was right, the presser was busy. All the seats were filled, and an overspill of reporters huddled at the back of the room where a dozen cameras lined the rear wall. A bouquet of mikes was set up on a table that was littered with Dictaphones. The screen-grab Sarah had taken of Madison from the camera footage at The Joneses had been blown up to poster size and was on a stand behind the table.

She took a seat alongside Larissa Jones and Ellen Downey. Photographers kneeled in front of them and snapped off shot after shot, their flashes blinding, before Ellen signaled that the photoshoot was over.

Sarah kicked off the press conference by describing the circumstances surrounding the disappearance of Madison James—how she'd last been seen at the restaurant where she worked before setting off for an audition; how her purse had been discovered in Griffith Park; how a handwritten note inside suggested a meeting at the Fulton Majestic hotel. If Michaels was watching, he'd probably be bursting a blood vessel right now. Sarah pointed out that she didn't know if the meeting was planned for Monday, when

Madison vanished, or had been arranged for a different date. That was true, but Sarah felt it in her gut that the note was significant somehow.

Larissa then knocked it out of the park with an appeal that was emotional and heartfelt, but also clear and concise. Then it was back to Sarah to read out a short statement from Norah James that Senior Nurse Ramirez had emailed.

> *Madison is kind and caring, a beautiful person both inside and out. She is the light of my life, my whole world. I miss my little girl and I just want to hear her voice again, to know that she is safe and well. Madison, if you are watching, please contact the police and let them know you are okay. You don't have to tell us where you are or why you left, just that you are safe and haven't come to harm. If you have taken Madison, please let her go. Please, I am begging of you, allow my Madison to return to her family. We love her and we miss her.*

Sarah then provided the number for a tips line and answered a handful of questions before Ellen wrapped things up.

The press conference hadn't been as bad as Sarah had feared. They never were once the nerves settled. The only tricky moment was right at the start, when she'd spotted a familiar face in the back row, and he'd smiled and winked, and she'd almost knocked over her glass of water. She'd pointedly ignored him for the remainder of the briefing.

The squad room afterwards was a scene of chaos. Phones ringing, calls being answered, notes taken, people rushing around, printers spitting out paper, computer keyboards clattering. Moreno had his desk phone to his ear and his notepad open in front of him and was saying "uh-huh" a lot but not taking any notes.

Sarah settled into the chair at her desk and checked her emails. No footage from the strip mall yet. She opened Twitter and Facebook and read through the responses to the LAPD's posts about Madison James. There were lots of shares and retweets and comments but nothing particularly helpful. She saw that a meme of Madison was proving popular on social media. It was from *Do Not Disturb* and showed her covering her naked breasts and turning her head and saying, "Did you hear something?" The scene was right before the axe man smashed his way into her motel room.

Moreno was off his call and appeared over the privacy divider. "It's been crazy since the presser got underway. The phones haven't stopped."

"Anything useful?"

"Nah, just the usual cranks so far. Marion from Culver City was first to call, to report seeing Madison buying tacos at a truck in her neighborhood."

"Maybe Madison *was* buying tacos?"

"Marion says Madison was with Elvis. Army Elvis, not Vegas Elvis. Marion calls once a week. The missing women are always buying tacos with Army Elvis."

"Right. Gotcha."

"And the guy I spoke to just now? He's confessed to murdering Madison and cutting her body in half, same as he did with the Black Dahlia. The caller is thirty-two years old and lives with his parents. The Black Dahlia was killed in 1947. I know this because I listened to her episode on Creepy Cantwell's podcast last night."

Moreno's phone started ringing again and he rolled his eyes. "Duty calls. More confessions, no doubt."

Sarah powered on her cell phone. She'd missed a call from a number she didn't recognize during the press conference. A ding indicated a new voicemail. The message was from Annie Kline: *Detective Delaney, please call me back when you can. There's something you should know. You have my cell phone number.*

Sarah returned the call and Annie answered immediately.

"I just watched your press conference. Any new leads?"

"Not yet," Sarah said.

"But there's a lot of interest now. Madison is on every news channel. That's a good thing, isn't it?"

"We'll see. You wanted to tell me something. Is this about Cash?"

A pause.

"No," Annie said slowly. "I already told you; I don't know who Cash is."

Sarah suppressed a sigh. "Okay. So why did you call?"

"Madison had a stalker."

"What?" Sarah was incredulous. "And you're just telling me this now?"

"I don't mean recently," Annie said hastily. "It was years ago. But I thought it might be relevant."

"Tell me about the stalking."

"It was harmless to begin with. He was older than Madison. A fan. He'd hang around the studios a lot, ask for her autograph, get his photo taken with her, try to talk to her. She was flattered at first. She thought this was what it was like to be famous, to have adoring fans. Then, while filming one of her movies, she found him inside her trailer."

"Seriously? What did the studio do?"

"Nothing. Not really. He'd managed to get a job on set as a production assistant. Madison complained about his behavior and he claimed it was all a big misunderstanding. He got a warning and kept his distance until the movie wrapped. Madison thought that was the end of it."

"But it wasn't."

"Flowers and gifts started to arrive at her apartment. Huge bouquets. Expensive stuff. Jewelry, perfume, designer purses. It was relentless. Madison was unnerved that this man knew where she lived, but she had two roommates so wasn't overly concerned about her safety. Not until he showed up in her building's garage and attacked her."

"He attacked her?" Sarah was horrified. "What happened?"

"I don't know all the details. Madison doesn't like to talk about it. All I know is that there was a struggle and it got violent, and he tried to get her into his car."

"Did Madison report the assault and attempted abduction?"

"No. The man was injured during the altercation. He set his lawyer on Madison, threatened to sue her if she reported the 'misunderstanding' to the police. This man was rich. I'm talking serious money. His family are extremely wealthy. Madison didn't stand a chance. She let it go and, to the best of my knowledge, she never heard from him again."

"Do you think he could be involved in Madison's disappearance?"

"I don't know," Annie said. "But he's taking an interest, that's for sure."

"What do you mean?"

"He's been posting about her on social media. Kayla has been keeping me updated on what people are saying. She showed me some of his posts and I recognized his name. He hosts a podcast now and he's planning a whole episode about Madison. His name is—"

Sarah cut her off. She already knew what Annie Kline was going to say.

"His name is Jefferson Cantwell."

# 15
# MADISON
## SPRING, 2004

It was late when Madison got back from her shift at the restaurant.

The underground garage in her building was dark and deserted. She always tried to park close to the stairwell that led up to the apartments, but it was almost ten and those spaces were long gone. A back corner bay was all that was available.

Madison was tired and her feet ached. All she wanted was a hot bubble bath and a cold glass of white wine. The restaurant had been busy, Fridays always were, but the tips had been good at least and, God knows, she needed the money. There had been no acting work since the disastrous *Do Not Disturb* shoot last year.

Annie Kline had been right; Ted Clayton had blackballed her. Word had gotten out that she was bad to have on set. The rumors snowballed: Madison James was always late and unreliable; she partied too hard and was using drugs; when she did show up, she was a diva with a foul temper.

None of it was true. Not that it mattered.

When she'd gotten back from North Carolina, the only jobs Madison had been offered were two advertisements, for constipation meds and a sanitary product. She'd flat out refused to do either. Solly had fired her. He was all about the money and Madison wasn't making him any. She was surprised that Annie had stood by her. Madison suspected it was because Annie had known what was going to happen in that hotel suite the day she'd sent Madison to the Fulton Majestic, and she felt guilty.

A few months later and Madison had been wishing she'd done the ads. Her college fund was long gone and the money she still had from the *Do Not Disturb* fee was draining faster from her checking account than water down an unblocked drain. Soon, she'd be struggling to make the rent. Madison didn't want to go to her folks for a handout. Her dad was a plumber, and her mom was a dentist's receptionist, and they didn't have a lot of cash to spare. In any case, she'd have to admit that she wasn't getting any acting work and they'd want to know why, and she would never, ever be able to tell them the truth.

So, she'd taken a waitressing job at a fancy seafood restaurant on Melrose where she served the kind of people she wanted to be. Every night, she delivered lobster rolls and wild jumbo shrimp and crab nuggets to actors and singers and models. She didn't know what was worse—the diners who didn't give her a second glance, or those who recognized her and whispered behind their menus.

*Is it really her? That girl from that movie?*

Madison got out of her station wagon and made her way toward the stairwell. Dim yellow light splashed the black tarmac with jaundiced pops of color. Her tennis shoes squeaked, and the ceiling pipes rattled.

The soft thunk of a car door closing made her stop. Her heart jackhammered. No one had followed her into the garage, and she hadn't spotted another vehicle's lights on when she'd circled for an empty space. Where had the sound come from? She carried on to the stairs, faster now.

A figure stepped out from behind a concrete pillar.

"Hello, Madison."

Even in the half-light, she knew who it was.

Jefferson Cantwell.

He was dressed in light-wash jeans with a crease down the front of each leg and a cashmere sweater, and he was clutching a bouquet of lilies.

Her eyes flitted to the stairwell door and back to him. He was closer to the stairs than she was. Her only route to safety was blocked off.

"What do you want?" she demanded, trying not to show any fear.

"Did you receive my gifts?" he asked pleasantly.

After shooting had wrapped on *Do Not Disturb*, she'd been sent a bouquet of lilies with a card that read: *Madison, I still believe in you. Your biggest fan, Jeff x*. More flowers had arrived. Then bottles of Chanel and Dior perfume. Even a tennis bracelet with real emeralds. She'd dumped the flowers in the trash and sold the perfume on eBay and pawned the jewelry. She'd hated herself for not just donating everything to Goodwill, but she was broke, and she needed the money.

Madison glared at Cantwell. "I don't want your gifts. I don't want you anywhere near me."

He moved closer and Madison instinctively took a step back.

"Are you still mad about North Carolina? I truly am sorry if I scared you. All I want is for us to be friends."

"I don't want to be your friend."

Cantwell tutted softly. "From what I hear, you could do with all the friends you can get right now. And I could be a very influential friend. My family are very wealthy; they have a lot of power in this town. How do you think I got the job with the studio? I could help you, Madison. Please let me help you. It breaks my heart to see you belittle yourself in that restaurant night after night."

He'd closed the gap between them to almost nothing.

"I want you to leave," she said. "I want you to stay away from my building and I want you to stay away from my place of work and I want you to stay away from me."

Cantwell smiled, revealing small pointy teeth. A shudder rippled through her body.

"You've got me all wrong, Madison," he said. "I'm one of the good guys. Spend some time with me and you'll see. We could go for a drive right now. Head on up to the Mulholland Overlook and watch the stars and drink champagne. What do you say?" He winked. "I have a little something for you in the glovebox. A gift to go with the tennis bracelet. Did you know that green is my favorite color? Always green cars for me and always emerald jewelry for my favorite women. And green looks so good on you with that beautiful red hair. Let's go take that drive."

Madison knocked the lilies from his hands. "Leave me the fuck alone, you freak!"

She made a dash for the stairs. But he was on her quickly. One hand clamped hard over her mouth, the other grabbed her arm in a vise grip. He dragged her backward, away from the light of the stairwell and into the shadows. He was surprisingly strong for a slender man. Madison's screams were muffled. She wriggled and squirmed but she couldn't escape his grasp.

He was shouting, his voice echoing around the garage. "We are going on that drive, and we are going to drink champagne and you are going to wear the necklace I bought for you, you ungrateful little bitch."

He dragged her toward a green SUV. In the midst of the struggle, Madison heard the familiar creak of the stairwell door's hinges and the sound of glass shattering and then fast feet on tarmac. A long hissing noise was followed by a sudden pungent odor. Cantwell's grip loosened and she broke free and saw that he was on the ground. He was screaming and clutching at his eyes. Then she watched in disbelief as Taylor Rose aimed a ferocious kick at his torso. He yelped. She kicked again, even harder. Cantwell curled up into the fetal position. Taylor grabbed Madison's arm and yelled, "Let's go!"

They ran for the stairs and raced up the two flights to Madison's apartment. Got inside and jammed all the locks in place.

"What the hell just happened?" Madison asked breathlessly, her back against the door.

Taylor, white-faced and breathing hard, held up a small aerosol can. "Pepper spray. I never leave home without it."

Both of Madison's roommates were out—Lizzie staying at her parents' for the weekend, Carly on a date with her boyfriend. Madison led Taylor to the couch in the communal living room, and they sat.

"Thanks for saving me from that creep." Madison was still shaking. "I dread to think what would have happened if you hadn't turned up." She shook her head in admiration. "I gotta say, I'm impressed by the way you took him out."

Taylor smiled shakily. "I'm impressed myself. I didn't even stop to think about it. I just reacted. I guess I thought I was one of my kickass characters for a moment." She winced, realizing movies were a sensitive subject for out-of-work Madison. "Sorry."

"That's okay. But what are you even doing here?"

"I wanted to clear the air between us. I hate what happened in North Carolina. So, I came here with a peace offering. A nice bottle of Barolo." Taylor scrunched up her nose. "It's in a million pieces on the garage floor now."

"God knows we could both do with a drink after all that drama," Madison said with a small laugh. "I don't have any red, but I do have a chilled bottle of Chardonnay? I'm warning you now though that it's cheap gas station fare."

"Cheap gas station fare sounds good to me."

Madison went to the kitchen and retrieved the screw-top bottle from the refrigerator, and poured generously into two glasses. She returned to the living room and handed Taylor a wineglass and tucked a leg underneath her as she sat back down. "How'd you even know where I live? Cantwell knows my address because he's a professional stalker but I'm guessing you aren't?"

Taylor laughed, all perfect white teeth, and it was like a light being turned on. Even dressed simply in a blouse and jeans and with minimal makeup, she could still have graced the cover of any glossy magazine.

She drank some wine before answering. "The truth is, I had a reservation at your restaurant this evening. I didn't know you worked there. I walked in the door and saw you and ran straight back out again. I know how much you hate me. Then I thought, this is dumb, we can't avoid each other forever. Enough is enough. So, I called my manager, who called your manager, and I got your address. I know the restaurant serves dinner until nine, so I guessed you'd be home around ten. I bought that nice bottle of wine, drove to your apartment, and then I guess I saved your ass."

Madison laughed, then turned serious. "I don't hate you, Taylor. If I'm being truthful, I was jealous of you. And I was angry about you getting the final girl part in *Do Not Disturb*. Clayton promised it to me."

"Really?" Taylor said. "I didn't steal it from you, Madison. Ted sent the script to my manager, I read it, loved it, tried out for the Maya Swanson character and was offered the part. That's the truth, I swear."

"I believe you. When did Clayton send you the script? When did he offer you the part?"

Taylor told her. It was weeks before Madison had been summoned to his suite at the Fulton Majestic. He really had played her.

Taylor said shyly, "I'd really love it if we could be friends, Madison."

"That's what Cantwell just said."

Taylor snorted wine out of her nose and they both laughed until tears streamed down their faces. Madison had been wrong about Taylor Rose. All that time resenting her, being envious of her, and she'd never actually taken the time to get to know her.

"I'd like us to be friends too."

They hugged. Then Taylor said, "What about Cantwell? You're going to report him to the police, right?"

"I guess so."

"He can't get away with it, Madison. That guy's a danger to all women."

She nodded. "You're right. I'll go to the cop shop first thing tomorrow."

Madison's phone shrilled. She pulled it from her purse and frowned. It was an unknown number. It was late. "Who's calling at this time?"

Taylor waggled her eyebrows. "Booty call?"

Madison rolled her eyes. "I wish."

She answered. Listened. Felt the color drain from her face. She said, "Okay, I understand." Then she closed the phone.

"Are you okay, Madison?" Taylor asked, concerned. "Who was it?"

"A guy called Marvin Sparks. He's Jefferson Cantwell's lawyer. Cantwell is in hospital and threatening to have us arrested for assault and to file a personal injury lawsuit against us."

Taylor's mouth dropped open. "Are you serious? He attacked *you*. He tried to abduct you. You need to tell this Sparks guy where to go."

Madison shook her head. "Cantwell will destroy us both. His family are loaded."

"So he gets away with it? He wins?"

Madison smiled sadly. "Men like Cantwell—like Ted Clayton—always win."

# 16
# MADISON
## SUMMER, 2004

Madison assessed herself in front of the full-length mirror. Cropped blue satin cowl-necked top and matching skirt that sat low on her hips and showed off her toned stomach. Hair down and loose. Smoky eyes and a deep-burgundy lipstick. Taylor had said to dress fancy.

They'd spent a lot of time together since the night Jefferson Cantwell had attacked Madison in the parking garage. She had grown to like Taylor a lot. Her friend's star continued to rise while Madison continued to work shifts at the restaurant, but it didn't matter. They usually kept their get-togethers low-key. Dinner and drinks at local neighborhood haunts or hanging out at each other's apartments.

A triple *honk* drew Madison to the bedroom window. She looked down at the street below. Taylor was behind the wheel of a brand-new Audi TT with the top down. She waved up and Madison gave herself a final once-over in the mirror before making her way downstairs.

"Sweet ride," she said, climbing into the passenger seat. "Is it new?"

Taylor grinned. "I decided to treat myself. I always wanted a car like this. Too much?"

"Definitely not. You deserve it. There's just one thing wrong with it."

"Oh?"

The radio was tuned to a country station that was playing a twangy song about a teen finding out his girlfriend was pregnant and thinking that his life was over. Madison messed around with the dials until she hit upon "This Love" by Maroon 5. She cranked up the volume.

"Much better! Now we're good to go."

Taylor laughed and pulled away from the curb with a delicious growl of the engine.

The evening was warm, and a light breeze tousled their hair. The air smelled of citrus and exhaust fumes. They started to climb into the Hollywood Hills, beautiful homes flanking each side of the street, and Madison turned to Taylor in surprise. "We're not going to dinner?"

"Nope." Taylor smiled mysteriously. "We're going to a party."

Taylor wasn't a party girl. She didn't drink a lot of alcohol and she never touched drugs, and she wasn't looking to hook up with guys because she was in a long-distance relationship with Bradley, her high-school boyfriend, who planned on moving out to LA once he graduated from Brown.

They carried on up winding roads until they reached the Bird Streets, an exclusive neighborhood perched above the Sunset Strip, where the street names had avian themes and the homes were owned by A-listers.

The Audi rolled to a stop in front of a mid-century jewel box at the end of a secluded cul-de-sac bordered by lush foliage. They had to park on the narrow street because the huge driveway was crammed with Porsches and Ferraris and Beamers. R&B beats pulsated from the house and a floor-to-ceiling wall of glass showed people drinking and dancing inside.

"Who's hosting the party?" Madison asked as they got out of the car.

"Jimmy Grand. It's his new place. A housewarming thing."

Excitement fluttered in Madison's belly.

Jimmy Grand.

They had appeared together in the movie *The One Year Hitch*, but other than the handful of scenes they had together, Grand had barely spoken to her. They hadn't socialized during or after filming. He had spent most of his time in his trailer playing video games or surrounded by swooning women, and that was just the crew.

"I didn't know you knew Jimmy Grand."

"I don't," Taylor said. "He seems like kind of a douchebag but my manager told me about the party. He thought it would be a good networking opportunity."

The open-plan kitchen and living area was crowded with actors and singers and models that Madison recognized and a lot of groupies that she didn't. A champagne fridge was stocked with bottles of Veuve Clicquot, ice buckets were filled with beer, and liquor bottles were dotted around the room. Two women were bent over a glass coffee table shoveling white powder up their noses. A DJ was spinning vinyl on the decks in a back corner of the vast room.

The drugs, the booze, the music. It was a million miles away from being Taylor's scene. Madison realized why they were here. It was for her benefit. Taylor didn't need to network with these people—but Madison did. It was an opportunity to try to resurrect her career. To show everyone that she was still in town, still relevant, still one of them.

"You hate this party already, don't you?" she said.

Taylor shrugged. "It'll be fun. Let's grab a drink. Maybe give the drugs a miss though."

They went over to the champagne fridge, popped the cork on a bottle, and filled their flutes to the top. Madison was glad it wasn't Dom Pérignon, or she might've choked on it. They took their drinks out to the pool, where it was quieter, and found a couple of unoccupied loungers and perched on them. Madison noticed the necklace Taylor was wearing. It was a gold rose with a tiny diamond in the center.

"Is that new? It's beautiful."

Taylor's hand went to her throat. "My parents had it specially made. It's one of a kind." She blushed prettily. "A gift for my twenty-first birthday."

"It was your birthday? When?"

"Last weekend."

Madison knew Taylor had gone home to visit her folks in Upstate New York the previous weekend, but she'd been unaware of the special occasion. "I had no idea it was your birthday! I'm such a bad friend. I didn't even get you a card."

Taylor waved a hand. "I didn't want to make a fuss."

"At least let me go get you a bottle of champagne that I didn't pay for."

Taylor giggled and Madison went back into the house. She needed to pee and went in search of a bathroom. She found one at the end of the hallway and pushed open the door. Ally Hagen was inside. She was snorting coke off the cistern.

She glanced up and wiped her nose. "Hey, stranger."

Madison hadn't seen Ally in months. She closed the door behind her and locked it. "Coke, Ally? Seriously?"

Ally had always been slim, but she had lost a few extra pounds and it didn't suit her. Her Versace halter dress only emphasized her sharp shoulders and jutting collarbone. Her skin had a sweaty sheen to it. Her hair was lank with an inch of dark roots showing. Her eyes were glazed and bloodshot. To be blunt, she looked like shit.

"Who are you, my mother?" Ally laughed humorlessly. "Oh, wait, my mother did more drugs than I do, so I guess not."

"Are you okay, Ally? You don't look so good."

"Gee, thanks for the compliment," she snapped. "Like you care anyway. Too busy with your boring little blonde pal doing boring stuff to hang out with the likes of me."

"Of course I care. And I'm worried about you. It seems like you're partying a lot. And now the drugs."

"Yeah, well, whatever gets you through. You should know."

"What does that mean?"

Ally smiled nastily. "I heard you took a ride in the elevator. Didn't work out so good for you, did it? Maybe see you around."

She pushed past and left Madison alone—and stunned—in the bathroom.

When she returned to the pool with the bottle of champagne, the sky had deepened from soft orange to rich purple and the lights of the city glowed like a million fireflies down below. Fairy lights strung on palm trees twinkled. Jimmy Grand was on Madison's lounger chatting to Taylor. A modern-day James Dean, he was gorgeous in dark-wash jeans and a white t-shirt that hugged his rock-hard abs. He spotted her and scooched over and patted the seat next to him. "Grab a pew."

Madison sat and refilled her and Taylor's glasses. Grand's body heat and his closeness made her giddier than the fizz.

"It's Mandy, right?" he said. "We did that movie together a while back."

"Madison."

Taylor rolled her eyes. Mouthed the word "douchebag."

"Madison. Right. Are you having a good time?"

"Yeah, it's a great party. Beautiful home."

Grand grinned. "Yeah, pretty neat, huh?"

A shadow fell across the travertine tiles and the actress Rachel Rayner stood over them with her hands on her hips. "Jimmy, I can't find any ice. You know I can't drink wine without ice." She ignored the two women despite having appeared in a movie with Madison.

"Did you try the freezer?" Grand asked.

Rachel pouted.

He said, "Duty calls. I'll be right back."

Madison watched him go, Rachel following him like a devoted puppy. "He's so hot."

"He's a douchebag," Taylor said. "Mandy? Seriously?"

"He can call me Mike for all I care. As long as he's gazing into my eyes with those big baby blues."

"He's gazed into a lot of women's eyes with those big baby blues. He's such a player."

Grand came back with a whisky in each hand and sat down next to Madison, even closer this time. He put the drinks at his feet and a hand on her thigh and her whole body tingled. "So, Mandy. What were we talking about before Rachel interrupted?"

"It's Madison."

He laughed, squeezed her thigh. "I know it is. I'm messing with you. Hey, are you named after that blonde in that old movie? You know, the one that stars that really famous dude?"

"I think you'll need to narrow it down a bit more," Taylor said.

"He means *Splash*. The movie where Tom Hanks falls in love with a mermaid played by Daryl Hannah."

Madison got asked the question a lot. It pissed off her mom, who'd named her after Madison Avenue in New York because she thought it sounded pretty and unique. Then *Splash* came out a couple of years later and thousands of baby girls all over America were named after the Daryl Hannah character.

Grand downed one of the whiskies and nodded enthusiastically. "That's the one! She turns into a mermaid whenever she gets in water, right?" His face lit up. "Hey, do you turn into a mermaid too? Let's find out!" He swallowed the other whisky and grabbed Madison's hand and started pulling her toward the pool.

"What are you doing!" she shrieked.

"Finding out if you're a mermaid!"

He pushed her into the pool and jumped in after her. Madison surfaced to the sound of whoops and cheers from the other guests. She spat out water and slicked her hair back. She was glad she'd worn waterproof mascara otherwise she'd look like that guy from *The Crow*.

"Are you crazy?" she yelled at Grand.

He swam over to her and grinned. Caressed her legs under the water. "Not a mermaid but still beautiful."

Then he leaned in and kissed her. A long, deep, sensual, whisky-flavored kiss.

The whoops and cheers turned to catcalls. The music and voices melted away until it felt like it was just the two of them in the whole world. They kissed for a long time, until their skin pruned. Then they dripped water through the house as they walked hand in hand to the master suite, where Jimmy peeled off her wet clothes and led her to the huge bed.

Madison thought she might be in love.

She also thought Jimmy Grand might just be her ticket back to Hollywood.

# 17

# SARAH

## SEPTEMBER 2022

"Two visits in two days, Detective Delaney? Wow, I must be popular."

Jefferson Cantwell still worked the preppy image and still looked like he was wearing someone else's clothes. It was like he had no sense of personal style and just bought the most expensive item in the store.

"Can I come in?" Sarah said.

"Did you change your mind about the podcast interview?"

"No."

"That's a shame. You have a wonderful voice, Detective Delaney. Authoritative, yet feminine at the same time." Cantwell stuck his head out of the doorway and glanced around theatrically. "Your note-taking sidekick isn't with you today?"

"He's busy."

"Oh, I can imagine. I bet you've had at least ten confessors to Madison's murder since the press conference. Come on through."

It was smoggier today, the vista less impressive. This time Cantwell invited her to take a seat on a beige L-shaped couch and offered her something to drink. She sat and declined the drink offer.

"You won't judge me if I have a small refreshment myself?" he said. "It is past noon and I've just received a shipment from a distillery in Scotland that I'm desperate to try. I guess you could say that fine Scotch is my greatest weakness."

*And pretty young actresses,* Sarah thought. *Especially dead and missing ones.*

Cantwell went over to the bar area that housed a vast collection of Scotch. A FedEx parcel was sitting on the worktop, and he removed a bottle from the cardboard box and opened it. Sniffed appreciatively and poured a finger measure into a crystal glass and added some water from a porcelain jug.

"How the Scots drink it, I believe." He sipped and smiled and nodded his approval. "Worth the wait and the expense." He took the tumbler and perched on an Eames ottoman that was part of a set with the matching chair. "I was very impressed by your performance at the press conference. Professional yet likeable."

"It wasn't a performance," Sarah said. "I was doing my job."

"Every time we present ourselves to the outside world, it's a performance. Terrific outfit choice by the way. A packed stuffy room, with all those hot lights and the nerves jangling? Anyone would perspire under those circumstances, but a black or white blouse conceals the unsightly damp patches. But of course, you knew that. Just like you knew a ponytail would have been too severe and made you less likeable. The lipstick was a small faux pas though. I much preferred the deep-rose shade you wore yesterday. Far more flattering with your dark hair and those chocolate eyes. Anyway, enough small talk. What can I do for you, Detective Delaney?"

"When we spoke yesterday about Madison James, you forgot to mention a small detail."

"I did? What would that be?"

Creepy smile.

"I asked if you knew Madison and you said you'd met a couple of times."

Cantwell brought the tumbler to his lips and regarded her over the rim. "Yes?"

"The time you attacked her and tried to abduct her must have slipped your mind."

The smile vanished.

"That sounds like an accusation, Detective Delaney. Perhaps I should call my lawyer this time. Marvin Sparks. I'm sure you've heard of him."

Sarah had butted heads with Marvin Sparks in court several times on murder cases. She wondered why Cantwell felt the need to have one of the biggest defense attorneys in the city on speed dial.

"This would be the same Marvin Sparks who put the frighteners on Madison James so that she wouldn't report your assault to the cops?"

"As I recall it, I was the only one who required medical treatment following the misunderstanding at her apartment building. A fan delivering a generous gift, and what did I get in return? Two broken ribs and retinal damage, that's what. Madison is lucky that I didn't report her and her little blonde friend to the police and sue them both."

"Her blonde friend?"

He shook his head. "Oh dear, Detective Delaney. You really should listen to my podcast. You might learn something." Cantwell drained the glass, got up, and went over to the bar for a refill. "Are you sure I can't tempt you? It's an eighteen-year-old sherry oak cask."

"Whenever I go to a restaurant, I order the house wine," Sarah said. "If I'm in a bar, I order whatever is on special. I'm not interested in your fancy whisky or your fancy house with its fancy views or your fancy cars in the driveway. What I am interested in is your 'alleged' history of violence against a woman who has been missing for several days. Right now, that makes you the closest thing I have to a suspect."

Cantwell returned to the Eames ottoman with the refilled tumbler. He didn't look worried and that worried Sarah. He looked like he was about to produce an ace when she'd been expecting him to fold.

"Serious question, Detective Delaney," he said. "What would I have to gain from harming Madison?"

"Revenge? She rejected you. She humiliated you. And, according to you, she left you needing hospital treatment. That's a lot of motive."

"You seriously think I'd wait the best part of twenty years to carry out some petty revenge mission? Watching Madison James' career flatline the way it did provided enough satisfaction, believe me."

"Okay. Your podcast then. The new episode featuring Madison. It could garner a bigger audience than what you already have, which is apparently not a lot."

Creepy smile.

"Look around you, Detective. My podcast is my passion, but it doesn't pay the bills. Whether an episode has ten listeners or ten thousand, it makes no difference to my bank balance. My ego? Yes, but not enough to execute an elaborate kidnapping plot. You want a motive? How about a comeback movie with everything riding on it? How's that for motive?"

"What movie? What are you talking about?"

Cantwell picked up a remote control from a glass-topped coffee table. "May I?"

Sarah shrugged.

He pointed the remote at a seventy-inch flat-screen TV above the marble fireplace. The screen woke up and displayed a rolling news channel. The current item was about climate change.

"What am I looking at?" Sarah asked impatiently.

"Patience, Detective Delaney. It's been playing on a loop all morning if you'll just wait a moment or two."

Sarah waited. Climate change. Corrupt politicians. Then it was back to their top story: the vanishing of Madison James. They played an excerpt from the press conference and Sarah tried not to cringe at seeing herself onscreen. Then the image switched to a video clip tagged "Exclusive" and Sarah tried not to gawp.

There onscreen was Jimmy Grand. Twenty years older and twenty pounds heavier. The floppy black hair now had the unnatural sheen of a drugstore dye kit. The flame-blue eyes were bloodshot and hooded. The sharp square jaw had been softened by wobbly jowls. He was perched on a Porsche in front of a house that made the one she was sitting in look like a beach hut.

Jimmy Grand was rambling on about Madison James being "a beautiful soul" and "a super-talented actress" and "an absolute hoot" and how he hoped she would be found safe and well so that they could maybe work together again one day. Then he shamelessly plugged his new movie—his first in a decade—that would be shown in select theaters around the country later in the month.

Cantwell paused the TV with a triumphant look. "Jimmy Grand has a new movie to promote at the exact same time that Madison James has vanished and is all over the news? Tell me that's a coincidence, Detective Delaney."

"So, the guy has a new movie out? So what? It hardly makes him a suspect."

"There's the other stuff too. The rumors."

Sarah sighed, weary of Cantwell's game-playing. "What rumors?"

"Well, seeing as you've just accused me of being a violent criminal in my own home, maybe I shouldn't be repeating unfounded speculation about someone else."

"Spit it out."

"Jimmy Grand wasn't just a lover; he was a fighter too. If you catch my drift?"

"I don't."

"He beat his girlfriends. Allegedly."

"And?"

"Oh, Detective Delaney. You disappoint me. You really haven't done your homework, have you?"

"Meaning?"

"Meaning Madison James was Jimmy Grand's lover once upon a time. Although, 'fiancée' may technically be more accurate. What's that old saying again? 'What happens in Vegas, stays in Vegas.' And a lot happened there one night if you believe the stories."

# *THE ONE NIGHT HITCH?*

*Co-stars Grand and James rekindle romance and tie the knot in Vegas!*

DID YOU HEAR? MAGAZINE

By Zoe Wilde, Entertainment Reporter

October 13, 2004

What's that we hear?

Is it wedding bells ringing or the sound of a million hearts breaking across America?

That's right—Hollywood's favorite bachelor Jimmy Grand is off the market after getting hitched to actress Madison James in Las Vegas at the weekend, as our exclusive photo shows.

The pair first met on the set of rom-com *The One Year Hitch*, where Madison's character falls head over heels for Grand's boy-next-door only for him to wed her sister and relegate her to the role of maid of honor. Ouch!

They dated briefly recently—long after filming wrapped—before Jimmy moved on to Madison's *Survive the Night* co-star Rachel Rayner, and then moved on again and again with a bevy of beauties . . .

Madison's movie career appears to have stalled with no acting credits since last year's slasher flick *Do Not Disturb,* and nothing else in the pipeline according to our sources.

But it certainly hasn't been a case of "always the bridesmaid" for blushing bride MJ, who now appears to have bagged her biggest and best role to date—as Mrs. Jimmy Grand!

The fiery redhead was starring in a show in Sin City when she hit the love jackpot with a visit to the famous Little White Wedding Chapel with old flame Grand on her arm.

Ding! Ding! Ding!

Flame-haired Madison wore a not-so-traditional white minidress that showed off her shapely legs, while Grand gave off smokin' hot Jimmy Dean vibes in black jeans and shades.

Has Madison James tamed Hollywood's biggest bad boy? It sure looks that way!

**Turn the page for our photo special on other celeb Vegas weddings featuring Britney, Sarah Michelle Gellar, Liz Taylor, and more**

# WIRE NEWS 24

OCTOBER 18, 2004

ENTERTAINMENT

Grand, James rep denies Las Vegas wedding

Los Angeles—Jimmy Grand and Madison James have refuted claims that they married in a Las Vegas ceremony earlier this month.

Reports last week suggested the actors, who met on the set of the 2003 romantic comedy *The One Year Hitch*, exchanged vows after being photographed outside the Little White Wedding Chapel.

The pair, who share a representative, briefly dated earlier this year but have quashed rumors of marriage.

A statement, released on behalf of Mr. Grand and Ms. James by Annie Kline Talent Management, read: "Jimmy Grand and Madison James are not married.

"Jimmy and Madison have remained close friends since filming *The One Year Hitch* together.

"Madison has been starring in a sellout show in Las Vegas and Jimmy was in town to make a personal appearance at a nightclub.

"The two met up socially as friends. The photograph which appeared in the media has been taken completely out of context.

"There was no wedding ceremony. Jimmy and Madison are fully focused on their careers, and both have exciting projects in the works."

# 18
# MADISON
## FALL, 2004

Taylor tossed a copy of a trashy tabloid magazine onto the table.

It was open at a page showing a photo of Madison in a white mini puffball dress and holding a floral bouquet. She was standing at the entrance to the Little White Wedding Chapel in Las Vegas with Jimmy Grand.

"Please tell me you didn't."

"I didn't," Madison said.

"Is this"—Taylor tapped the magazine—"the reason why you're wearing sunglasses inside a bar? You know it's only douchebags and divas who wear shades indoors?"

The waitress saved Madison from having to answer.

"Are you ready to order?" Her eyes strayed from her notepad to the Vegas photo and then to Madison and back to the photo.

Taylor flipped the magazine shut. "A small glass of the Barolo, please."

"Vodka tonic. Double."

Taylor's eyebrows lifted a fraction at the order. When the waitress left, she leaned in close and said in a low voice, "I didn't know you were even still dating Jimmy Grand."

"I wasn't. I'm not."

After the housewarming party, Madison and Jimmy had hooked up a few more times. He'd taken her to dinner at the best restaurant in town and for drinks at The Volcano Club, and back to his house in the Bird Streets for marathon lovemaking sessions. Madison had been smitten. She'd been getting noticed. They'd been papped together out on the town and Annie had started getting calls about her availability. Annie had been hoping two of her clients would soon be crowned Hollywood's new golden couple by the press. Madison had hoped so too.

Then Grand had been snapped "canoodling" (the article's word, not Madison's) with Rachel Rayner in the best restaurant in town, and the studios had dropped their interest in Madison fast. All Annie had been able to line up for her was a Las Vegas dinner show. It was a short run, but the restaurant wouldn't keep her job open for her. Madison didn't have a choice, though. She had to act again, so she'd quit the waitressing gig. Plus, the Vegas show was throwing in free accommodation on the Strip and the chance to escape Hollywood—and Jimmy Grand—for a while. Or so she'd thought.

Taylor said, "Tell me what happened."

"You know I was doing the show in Vegas? On the final night, the cast were in the casino having a few drinks to celebrate the end of a successful run. You know what it's like there, the cocktails just keep on coming. Then I heard someone yelling the name Mandy from across the bar."

Taylor sighed. "Jimmy Grand."

"I told him I didn't want to speak to him. I was still pissed at finding out I'd been dumped by reading about it in the papers.

He said he regretted the whole Rachel thing. He missed me. He thought I was looking hot."

"And you fell for his lines?"

"You know what I'm like around him. I couldn't help myself. He bought a bottle of champagne for me and a bottle of Scotch for him. We took the booze to his room. Got drunk, fooled around, and then I guess Jimmy proposed."

The waitress reappeared just at that moment with their order on a tray. She took her time laying a napkin in front of each of them and then placing their drinks on top. She hovered for a few moments like she thought she might be invited to join in the conversation before finally saying "enjoy" and reluctantly moving on to the next table.

"Did he get down on one knee?" Taylor asked. "Did he give you a ring?"

Madison sucked some vodka through the straw. It was good and strong. "No, he was lying in bed naked. He didn't have a ring. It was spur of the moment. He said 'Let's get hitched, Mandy. The press will love it.'"

Taylor made a face. "Romantic."

"I'd sunk a whole bottle of Veuve Clicquot. It seemed like a good idea at the time. I went shopping at Caesars and bought a dress with a bundle of crumpled bills he gave me, and we met outside the chapel."

"And then you got cold feet?"

"I started to sober up is what I did. Realized this wasn't exactly the wedding I'd always dreamed of."

"I'm so glad you didn't go through with it. What happens now?"

Madison said, "Annie will issue a denial on behalf of both of us. But she wants to wait a few days. Her phone's been ringing off the hook. She's thrilled. She's already booked me two auditions with major studios."

Taylor beamed. "Well, that's fantastic. Maybe this Vegas wedding thing wasn't such a bad idea after all. You get headhunted by the big guys, and you don't even have to be Jimmy Grand's wife. A win-win situation."

"I told Annie I'm sick and can't go to the auditions."

Taylor's smile dropped. "But you're not sick. Are you?"

Madison shook her head. She glanced around the bar to make sure no one was watching. Then she slid her shades down to the end of her nose.

Taylor gasped. "Grand did that to you?"

Madison nodded and pushed the sunglasses back into place. "He was furious after I left the chapel. Wild with rage. He followed me to my hotel room and pushed his way inside. Accused me of humiliating him. Then he clocked me with the kind of right hook those Vegas fight fans pay good money to see."

Taylor was horrified. "That fucking bastard."

Madison blinked. It was shocking to hear her friend curse, because she never cursed unless it was in a script. The worst Taylor ever called anyone was a douchebag.

"So, no auditions until the shiner heals," Madison said. "And no restaurant job either. Maybe I should just quit Hollywood. Go back home to Dutton."

"You're not going to quit," Taylor said firmly. "You're too good an actress to give up. And you want it too much. We're both alike that way. You're not Ally Hagen."

"Ally?" Madison asked, surprised. "What happened with Ally?"

"I heard she left Los Angeles. Went back home to sort herself out. Apparently, she'd been living in some old motel out on the highway. She left a note."

Madison frowned. "Ally wouldn't go back to her hometown. Her mom's a junkie and her dad used to beat her."

"Maybe she went to rehab somewhere. I don't know. The point is, Ally was a mess. You're not. You're going nowhere."

Madison shook her head. "Maybe Ally had the right idea, getting out. This town is toxic. The things we have to do to have any chance of making it. It makes me sick."

"What do you mean?"

"Ted Clayton."

"I don't follow."

Madison said, "You know what happens in his suite at the Fulton Majestic. You've been there too. Ally and I saw you ride the elevator that day at the auditions."

Taylor nodded slowly and drank some wine. "Yes, that was a horrible day. He asked how I felt about nudity, and I told him I wasn't a nudity actress. Then he asked me to go down on him and I refused and left."

"You said no? But he gave you the lead role. And the final girl part in *Do Not Disturb*. The same part he promised me after I . . ."

Madison let the words trail off.

Maybe Clayton saw Taylor as a challenge, a prize to be won over time. Maybe he just liked being around that special kind of beauty. Maybe he actually respected the ones who said no and rewarded them with the better roles.

Taylor said, "You didn't . . . ?"

Madison dropped her head and was glad she still had the Jackie O shades on to hide her shame behind.

"Oh, Madison. That's why you were so angry on set that day. No wonder. How awful for you."

"That day when I . . . When he made me . . . he'd already offered you the lead. I told you, Taylor, men like Ted Clayton always win. Jefferson Cantwell and Jimmy Grand too."

"Not anymore." Taylor's cheeks were pink with anger. "Ted Clayton abused you and then he blackballed you. Now I'm going to blackball him. I'll never work with him on another movie ever again. Or Jimmy Grand. Not after what they both did to you. And that's a promise."

# HOLLYWOOD HOTLINE

CASTING NEWS

Taylor Rose and Jimmy Grand Board Dark Thriller *The Murder Book*; Ted Clayton to Direct

By Zak Springer

December 9, 2004

EXCLUSIVE: Taylor Rose (*Do Not Disturb*) and Jimmy Grand (*I'm Your Guy*) have closed deals to lead *The Murder Book*, a dark police procedural thriller.

Ted Clayton (*The Blood Moon Murders*) is slated to direct in what will be a change of direction for the filmmaker best known for his work in the horror genre.

The Huxley Brothers wrote the script and will also produce.

In the film, a haunted detective battles the demons of his past while trying to save the life of a beautiful young woman who has been targeted by a sadistic killer.

Additional casting is currently underway, with production set to kick off in the spring.

*The Murder Book* sees Rose and Clayton team up for a third time, having previously worked together on slasher movies *Dead Like Her* and *Do Not Disturb.*

Grand's notable recent projects include *Town Full of Secrets, The One Year Hitch,* and *I'm Your Guy*.

Clayton told *Hollywood Hotline*: "I couldn't be more thrilled to have Taylor Rose and Jimmy Grand on board for *The Murder Book*. They are the brightest young stars in Hollywood right now and I know we're going to make a great movie together."

Taylor Rose stated: "Some of my best work has been under the guidance of Ted Clayton and I can't wait to get started on this exciting new project."

Grand added: "*The Murder Book* is going to be awesome. Audiences will get to see a different side to Jimmy Grand in this mean and moody cop thriller."

Taylor Rose is repped by Lister Long Entertainment, and Jimmy Grand by Annie Kline Talent Management.

# *THE BEST OF FRENEMIES!*

*It looks like Taylor Rose and Madison James have gone from being best buddies to feuding friends after a VERY public spat . . .*

DID YOU HEAR? MAGAZINE

By Zoe Wilde, Entertainment Reporter

December 15, 2004

Would you like a side of fury with your burger?

Patrons at a trendy WeHo eatery were treated to more than just the specials this week when they found themselves with front row seats to a sensational showdown between starlets Taylor Rose and Madison James.

Sources say fiery redhead Madison stormed into the restaurant and angrily confronted blonde beauty Taylor, who was dining with an unknown female companion.

One onlooker told us: "Madison James completely lost her s**t. She was yelling 'How could you do this to me? With him! After what I've been through? I'll never forgive you!' Taylor was practically crying into her crab cakes. She was trying to apologize but Madison was like a woman possessed."

Another eyewitness added: "I couldn't believe what I was seeing! You ask me, the fight was about Jimmy Grand. He broke Madison's heart and now Taylor is starring in a movie with him. Awkward!"

Taylor Rose and Jimmy Grand have just been announced as the stars of big-budget thriller *The Murder Book*, which is expected to cement the gorgeous pair's status as Hollywood's hottest property.

Jimmy and Madison had a brief summer fling before teasing fans with hopes of a wedding after being spotted at the famous Little White Wedding Chapel in Las Vegas in the fall.

The nuptials were later denied in what appears to have been nothing more than a crass publicity stunt.

Taylor and Madison both starred in gory slasher flick *Do Not Disturb* and have remained firm friends despite Taylor being a rising star and Madison fast becoming a Hollywood has-been.

A source, who didn't want to be named, told *Did You Hear?*: "Madison had a reputation for bad behavior on the set of *Do Not Disturb* and was a real diva by all accounts. I can't say I'm surprised by this latest tantrum, but I feel bad for Taylor. She stood by Madison and look how Madison has repaid her friendship."

Poor Taylor Rose! Who knew public humiliation was on the menu at the fanciest restaurant in town?

# 19

# SARAH

## SEPTEMBER 2022

The ghosts of Madison's past were reappearing one by one.

First Jefferson Cantwell, now Jimmy Grand.

A podcast.

A movie.

Both trying to capitalize on her misfortune for their own gain.

Cantwell was right. Sarah should have dug deeper where Jimmy Grand was concerned. A past relationship between him and Madison? How had she missed it? Her face burned with anger and embarrassment.

"Sloppy, Delaney. Very sloppy."

Sarah started the car and pulled away from the Mulholland mansion, Cantwell watching her leave from the doorway. She called Moreno on speaker.

He said, "If you're calling to tell me you just spotted Madison James sharing buttermilk hotcakes with Marilyn Monroe in Du-Par's, you're too late. Janice from Echo Park already beat you to it."

"I need you to get me a current address for Jimmy Grand."

"On it."

She killed the call and carried on down the narrow tree-lined two-lane until the street opened up and she found a shoulder wide enough to pull over. Sarah took the phone from the dashboard charger and opened Madison's Wikipedia page and scrolled to the "Personal life" section.

There was a paragraph about her twice winning the annual Dutton beauty pageant and being crowned prom queen at her high-school senior prom. Another paragraph was dedicated to her philanthropic efforts, namely fundraising for the American Stroke Association after her father died after suffering a massive stroke.

But there was no information about romantic relationships and no mention of Jimmy Grand. Then again, Madison's Wikipedia page was hardly accurate. It still gave her age as thirty-one. Anyone could edit it, including Madison herself. Maybe she'd airbrushed Jimmy Grand from her past now that he was a nobody and she still aspired to be a somebody.

Sarah opened Grand's Wiki next. His filmography was more extensive than Madison's, with twelve movies listed. The eleventh had been released in 2012. The twelfth was this year's comeback film, a low-budget indie production called *My Name Is* about an addict's road to recovery and redemption.

Grand had a lot of personal experience to draw on for the part.

His own "Personal life" section detailed his long battle with drug and alcohol addiction, including an overdose while filming *The Murder Book*. That had led to his first spell in rehab. Grand was back at the expensive facility in Arizona a year later—and back off the wagon less than six months after that stay. His movies had bombed and so had his career. His third spell in rehab was just two years ago and he had been sober since, hence the comeback attempt.

There was also a long list of Hollywood starlets whom Grand had romanced during his heyday—including Madison James. According to the passage, they had briefly dated and had sparked speculation of a quickie wedding after being photographed at the Little White Wedding Chapel in Las Vegas, but the nuptials had been denied by both parties. Sarah clicked on the hyperlinks that navigated to the citation resources.

An article headlined "The One Night Hitch?" was illustrated with a paparazzi photo of Madison wearing a white minidress with a bustier top and puffball skirt and carrying a small bouquet. Grand was dressed in a white t-shirt and black jeans.

The second article—"Grand, James rep denies Vegas wedding"—showed them leaving a hotel separately the following morning. Madison was in jeans and a long-sleeved top, her face mostly obscured by huge Jackie O sunglasses. Grand had swapped the black jeans for blue denim and looked like he was nursing the world's worst hangover.

Moreno called with an address for Jimmy Grand in Sylmar.

"Sylmar?" Sarah frowned. "Are you sure?"

Sylmar was a suburban neighborhood in the San Fernando Valley, and as north as you could go while still being within the city of Los Angeles. It wasn't the most desirable zip code in the Valley by a long stretch, and definitely not where Sarah would have expected to find the multimillion-dollar white-box dream home that had been the location for Grand's TV interview.

"I'm sure," Moreno said. "I also checked out his socials. Did you know he has a new movie out this month?"

"I do now. He's been all over the news, using Madison's disappearance to plug it."

"I also got Madison's bank and cell phone records. No major red flags with regards to her checking account or credit card. A few cash withdrawals. Otherwise, it's mostly grocery shopping, gas station payments, utility bills, and so on. The florist's charge for the mother's flowers is there but there are no payments to Lyft or Uber or any other cab companies on the day she vanished. I'm about to start on the cell phone statements."

"Keep me posted."

The northbound 405 took Sarah deep into the Valley, and thirty minutes later she turned onto a street where modest homes nestled in the hills of Sylmar. The views were pretty enough but it wasn't the Hollywood Hills, and no one, including Jimmy Grand, had a Porsche 911 sitting in their driveway.

His house was a low single-story construction with light-blue siding and a one-car garage and had probably been built sometime in the '80s. The patch of grass at the front was faded yellow and overgrown and clearly hadn't seen a hose or a lawnmower in weeks. Two plastic trash receptacles stood haphazardly at the foot of the lawn even though it likely wasn't collection day because none of the neighbors had their trash at the curb. A pickup truck held together by rust occupied the driveway. Sarah parked on the street.

Grand seemed unperturbed to find a detective on his doorstep. He cheerfully invited her inside and led her into a cramped living room that reeked of cigarettes and coffee and likely hadn't been redecorated since the house was built. Dead butts spilled from three ashtrays dotted around the room, along with two mugs, one with steam rising from it.

Twenty-two-year-old Sarah would have been freaking out at the thought of being in Jimmy Grand's living room; forty-two-year-old Sarah just wanted a clean space to sit. She gingerly moved aside a stack of laundry from a couch that sagged in the middle and perched on the edge. Grand sat in an armchair facing her.

She said, "Did someone steal your Porsche? I didn't see it outside."

He gave her an embarrassed smile. "You saw the interview, huh? My buddy's place. His car too. He wasn't at home so I figured where's the harm? It's all about projecting the right image with the new movie releasing soon."

Sarah wondered if the buddy knew his home and his wheels were all over the news. She said, "Tell me about your relationship with Madison James. You guys used to be an item, right?"

Grand snorted. "'Relationship' is kind of overstating it. We dated a few times."

"Didn't you almost get married?"

"Oh yeah! We almost did!" He laughed and it turned into a hacking cough. Once he'd recovered, he said, "How fucked up is that? We barely knew each other. Man, things were so crazy in those days."

"What happened with the almost-wedding?"

"We were partying in Vegas, and it seemed like a good idea. You know, the way things do when you're in Vegas and you're off your face on coke and whisky. Then Madison got cold feet at the last minute, and it didn't happen."

"That must have pissed you off. Kind of humiliating being jilted at the altar like that."

Sarah wasn't sure if Vegas chapels even had altars, but the rejection would have been tough to stomach regardless of the setting and size of the wedding.

"Nah. Thank God she did!" Grand mimicked swiping sweat from his brow. "Lucky escape. I had enough problems back then without adding a wife to the list."

He laughed. Sarah didn't.

"You weren't angry?"

Grand frowned. "It was a lifetime ago. Who cares about that stuff now?"

"Did you hit Madison that night? Did you beat her other times too?"

The blue eyes that a million teenage girls had once swooned over flashed with anger. Just for a second. Then Grand quickly rearranged his face into a mask of contrition and he went into full actor mode.

"I was in a bad place back then," he said mournfully, as though delivering a monologue in a daytime soap opera. "I had a quick temper and when I was high or drunk I'd lash out. I don't know if I hit Madison. I don't remember. I probably did. I hate the guy I used to be. He was a grade-A dick. But I'm a different person now. I've changed."

Sarah nodded. "Uh-huh."

*I'll change.*

*I'm sorry.*

*I didn't know what I was doing.*

*It won't happen again.*

She had heard her father feed her mother those lines a hundred times. He never did change. He never was quite sorry enough. He never stopped hitting her mom until the day he died. Sarah didn't believe Grand had changed either. Men like that never did.

She felt her phone vibrate in her pocket with a message.

"You mind if I smoke?" Grand asked. "It's the one bad habit I haven't been able to kick yet."

"Knock yourself out. It's your home."

Sarah figured she'd be addicted herself soon enough, with all the passive smoking she was doing.

He patted his jeans pockets and came up empty. "I think I left my smokes and lighter in the kitchen. I'll be right back."

Grand got up and left the room. Sarah checked her phone. The message was from Moreno: *Just came across these. Might be useful.*

He'd attached screen-grabs from Madison's Instagram account. Jimmy Grand had left comments on some of her posts. They were all from five years ago.

*Hey Madison! How goes it? Let's hook up. DM me!*

*Looking good, Madison! Drink sometime?*

*We should do another movie together babe. We were so good together. DM me . . .*

*ANSWER ME YOU RUDE FUCKING BITCH!!*

Grand returned with a pack of Marlboro Reds and sparked up.

Sarah said, "When was the last time you saw Madison?"

"Probably Vegas?" Grand scratched his head. "Maybe we ran into each other at a party or a red-carpet event afterwards. I don't know for sure. My memories are kind of hazy. I'm pretty sure we never hooked up again though. You know, in the bedroom."

"You haven't spoken to her recently?"

He blew out a long plume of smoke. "Nah, not for years."

"But you did try to get her to meet with you."

"Did I?"

"And it seems like you got real mad when Madison wasn't interested."

"What the hell are you talking about?"

Sarah showed him her phone with the photos of the Instagram comments.

"That was years ago! I already told you, I was in a bad place. I don't even remember writing that stuff."

"This new movie of yours, it's the first in how long?"

"Ten years."

"Ten years? That's a long time. And now your former co-star and lover has vanished. Just as your movie is about to be released."

Grand smoked furiously. "So?"

"So, it gets you some nice free publicity."

"What the fuck are you trying to say?"

"I'm saying the timing has worked out well for you. That's all."

Grand stabbed out the cigarette in one of the overflowing ashtrays. His fingers were stained yellow from all the smoking; his cheeks were flushed pink from all the anger.

"You think I had something to do with her going missing?" he yelled. "Are you kidding me? I haven't given that bitch a thought in years. Why would I? She's a fucking waitress. So, she took off or got snatched or got herself murdered or banged her head and is wandering around someplace with no fucking clue who she is. Yeah, it's sad. But I tell you what else is sad—my life, that's what. Do you have any idea what it's like to have everything and then wind up with nothing? So yeah, I saw an opportunity to get some promo for the new picture, sell a few tickets, get some folks in the theaters. So what?"

The act was over. Mr. Contrite was long gone, and Mr. Angry was stealing the show.

"Do you know where Madison is?" Sarah asked calmly.

"No! And I don't care either."

"Do you know who Cash is?"

"What?" Grand was taken aback. "Why are you asking? Where'd you get that name?"

"So, you know who he is then?"

Grand stared at her and then he huffed out a short laugh when he realized he had information that she needed. He wasn't about to give it up.

"Nah, no idea." He stood. "Let me show you out. I have three more interviews lined up today and I need to go get ready."

Outside on the doorstep, Sarah turned to face him. "Is Annie Kline still your manager?"

Grand said, "Yeah she is."

Then he shut the door in her face.

◆ ◆ ◆

"How'd it go with Grand?" Moreno asked when she returned to the office. "Did you get that stuff I sent you?"

"I did, thanks. He's bitter. Can't accept that he screwed up his own career, thinks the whole world still owes him something. Still has a mean temper too. I can't believe I used to have a crush on that guy."

Moreno couldn't hide his amusement. "You had a crush on Jimmy Grand?"

"Big-time," Sarah said. "Every teenage girl and young woman in America did. Quite a few men too."

"I'll take your word for it. Did he give you anything useful?"

"I think he knows who Cash is. Or maybe he is Cash. He's still repped by Annie Kline."

Moreno said, "I've been through Madison's cell phone records, and it's mostly calls and texts to and from Kline, Larissa, the restaurant, and her mom's care facility in Indiana. She also called the SoulCycle place and the property rental company for her building and a hair salon. That's it."

"We should check six weeks ago too. See if there are any calls or texts that would explain the Palm Springs trip."

"I already did. Nada."

"So, the cell phone records are a bust?"

"Yes and no. It's what else that's missing that confuses me. The audition wasn't arranged through Annie Kline, right? So, how'd Madison find out about it? There are no calls from any studios or production companies or any individuals that don't check out."

Sarah thought about it. "An email or social media message to arrange the meet?"

"Maybe. But without a phone or a laptop, our tech guys can't do shit." Moreno's desk phone shrilled, and he groaned. "More Confessing Sams, no doubt. I'm up to twenty now."

He disappeared behind the privacy divider and Sarah opened her emails and saw that she had a response from the strip mall security company. She viewed the footage. Rewound it and watched it again. Checked that they'd sent her the correct day's feed. They had.

Just like the Fulton Majestic video, there was no sign of Madison James.

She had set off on foot in the direction of the strip mall, but she hadn't entered its lot or any of its stores and she hadn't walked past it either.

The Joneses and the strip mall were separated by a block that comprised the laundromat, the auto shop, and the liquor store.

And the alleyway.

An alleyway with no CCTV at either end.

◆ ◆ ◆

Sarah spent the weekend at her dining table trawling through feeds from LAPD cameras closest to the streets either side of the alleyway. But she didn't see a redhead in a blue dress or Cantwell's SUV or Jimmy Grand's old pickup truck or any other suspicious vehicles.

She watched Grand's interviews and listened to some of Cantwell's podcast episodes. She ate takeout food and avoided doing any housework. She went over the lists of cast and crew from Madison's movies again and briefly got excited when her gaze snagged on the director Buck Bendich's name.

A buck was a type of money and money was cash. Then she discovered that Buck Bendich had died of a heart attack two years after directing *The One Year Hitch.* He wasn't the Cash she was looking for.

Sarah badly needed a break in the case.

On Monday morning, she got it.

# 20

# SARAH

## SEPTEMBER 2022

Sarah and Moreno were huddled around the desk of an MPU detective by the name of Hendricks.

Hendricks and his partner, Dessers, had just finished working a custody case where a ten-year-old girl had been abducted by her father. The kid had been found safe and well after two weeks on the run and had been returned to the mother. It was the kind of happy ending Sarah craved, one of the reasons she'd transferred over from RHD. Working homicides, the best she'd been able to offer the families of the victims was justice and some form of closure. She couldn't bring their loved ones back from the dead. With missing persons, she was able to offer something else: hope.

Now that Hendricks and Dessers had cleared their own case, it was all hands to the pump in the search for Madison James. They'd both been helping man the tips line, which continued to be busy with a lot of callers but no real leads. Until now.

"The call came in at 8:07 a.m.," said Hendricks. "I knew straightaway this one was different. The level of detail got my 'Spidey senses' tingling. She was also keen to get off the line fast which is unusual. Most of the cranks are talkers. The Confessing Sams and the dead-celebrity worshippers, like Marion in Culver City and Janice in Echo Park, will chew your ear off all day if you let them. This woman was different. I tried to get her to stay on the line and provide her name and she hung up. Here, listen for yourselves."

Hendricks set up his computer to play the recording. Sarah and Moreno and Dessers all leaned in closer to hear better. The caller was female, with a Southern accent. It was difficult to place her age. There was muffled background noise, traffic going by, voices of passersby. The woman spoke with a sense of urgency.

> *I'm calling about Madison James. She was only supposed to be gone until Saturday. Something's gone wrong. Go to the Stargaze Motel. Room fifteen. Look for her there.*

The words chilled Sarah. She asked Hendricks to play the recording again. The caller's voice was familiar somehow, but she didn't know why. Sarah couldn't place it.

Hendricks spun around in his chair to face them. "'She was only supposed to be gone until Saturday'—what the hell does that even mean?"

Sarah said, "She's calling from outside. You can hear the traffic. A Southern accent. Hard to place the age but I'd say young."

Dessers said, "No way that's a Southern accent." He spoke with a rich Matthew McConaughey drawl. "I grew up in the South, spent the first twenty-five years of my life in Texas. Her accent is about as genuine as a trunk full of Rolexes in Venice Beach. It's not a bad fake but it's a fake all the same."

Moreno said, "She doesn't want to be recognized."

"Could still be a crank though," Hendricks said thoughtfully. "Maybe she's discovered her old man is playing away from home at this motel. Figures a bunch of cops bursting into the room when he has his pants around his ankles will scare the shit out of him."

Moreno said, "Her voice seems kind of familiar."

Sarah said, "Uh-huh. Get your jacket. I'm driving."

◆ ◆ ◆

The Stargaze Motel was a traditional L-shaped motor lodge off the I-105. It comprised a long line of fifteen ground-floor drive-up rooms with an office building making up the short side. Gray cinder block contrasted with red-painted doors that might have once been cheerful but now looked tired. It was early, the day bright and warm, so there was no way to tell if the motel lived up to its lofty name. Even if it did, there was no pool or courtyard or even a lawn chair outside each room to enjoy the spectacle if the sky did put on a show after dark.

Just like the Fulton Majestic, the motel's office was a monument to the past, but it had none of the grandeur of the hotel. Here, the '70s still reigned, with plastic plants and glass block walls and an ancient wooden vending machine. There was no computer, just a book for guests to sign. A corkboard with numbered hooks and keys hanging from them was on the wall behind the desk along with a clock that was frozen forever at ten to two.

They asked the man behind the counter if they could speak to whoever was in charge after showing their badges. He eyed them suspiciously. "That would be me. I'm the manager. Rick Bird."

While there were some doubts over the legitimacy of the motel's moniker, its manager couldn't have been more appropriately named. He was in his sixties and skinny and hawkish, with a hook nose and a pointed chin and tiny black eyes that constantly darted around the room.

"Room fifteen," Sarah said. "Who's staying there?"

Bird got twitchy. He thumbed through the guest book with shaking hands. "No one. It's vacant."

Moreno indicated the corkboard. "There's no key for room fifteen on the board."

Bird glanced over his shoulder and scowled.

"Are you sure it's empty?" Moreno asked.

"It damn well should be. The last guest should be gone by now. She only paid until Saturday."

Sarah and Moreno exchanged a look.

*She was only supposed to be gone until Saturday.*

Sarah said, "You need to tell us everything you know about the guest in room fifteen."

The tip of Bird's tongue poked out between cracked lips like a lizard's. He licked the lips. The eyes darted faster. "She arrived Monday, paid cash, signed the book, didn't want to be disturbed, not even for fresh laundry and bedding. That's it. That's all I know. I wasn't on shift at the weekend. I thought she'd left already."

Sarah grabbed the book, flipped to last Monday. Ran her finger down the page until she reached room fifteen. The signature was illegible.

"Describe her."

Bird shrugged. "Blonde hair. Big sunglasses. I don't remember what she was wearing. Maybe dark pants and a dark shirt. I didn't pay a whole lot of attention. She was a guest, same as any other."

"Show us the room."

Bird got antsy. "No way. There could be another guest in there now. I told you, I wasn't here at the weekend. They could've checked in while my assistant manager was on duty and that's why the key's gone. My guests are entitled to their privacy."

Sarah flipped through the book to the weekend's entries.

"No one signed in for that room on Saturday or Sunday. Take us there right now."

"You got a warrant?"

Sarah sighed. Everyone was an expert on the law these days. Bird wilted under her stare but he didn't offer to take them to the room. She turned to Moreno. "Detective Moreno? Could you execute a warrant for the Stargaze Motel, please."

He took out his phone. "On it."

"And make sure it's for the whole motel. Every single room, and the office too. We're going to tear this place apart."

"Okay, okay," Bird said. "I'll show you. Jeez. Fucking cops."

He opened a drawer filled with spare keys and rummaged around but didn't find one with a "15" fob attached. Bird swallowed hard, his Adam's apple bobbing up and down. "The spare is gone."

"Gone where?"

"I don't know. Someone must have taken it."

"Wait here," Sarah ordered.

Room fifteen was the farthest away from the office, right at the end of the long line of the L. There was no vehicle parked in the bay outside.

The curtains were drawn shut. A plastic bag with clean towels and extra toilet paper was untouched outside the door. A "Do Not Disturb" sign hung from the doorknob and swayed in the breeze. The faint burble of TV voices drifted from inside. Sarah knocked hard. No answer. She tried the doorknob. The door was unlocked.

"We need to get in there and see what we're dealing with," Sarah said. "Ready?"

"Ready," Moreno replied grimly.

They took up position on either side of the door and hugged the wall. They both pulled their weapons. Sarah's body thrummed with adrenaline. Moreno's face was taut with tension and he suddenly looked ten years older. He met her eye. She nodded. He placed the hand not holding the gun flat against the door and sucked in a big deep breath.

Then he pushed open the door to room fifteen.

# 21

# SARAH

## SEPTEMBER 2022

Moreno burst inside, leading with his Beretta. "LAPD!" he yelled. "Don't move!"

Sarah followed him into the gloom, her weapon also drawn. Her nerves had nerves.

No one shot at them.

There was no gunfight.

The bedroom was unoccupied.

Moreno crossed the space quickly to an open bathroom door, both hands still wrapped tightly around the gun. He disappeared inside. A few seconds later, he shouted, "Bathroom is clear. Madison isn't here. I'm going to have a look around."

Sarah lowered her Glock, holstered it, and took in the scene. Her heart rate had just about returned to normal.

The room was dimly lit because of the thick curtains that were drawn tightly across the only window, blocking out the daylight. A TV was tuned to a rolling news channel, the screen's glare the only light source. The current news item was Madison James' disappearance. A couple of news anchors were discussing the missing actress in the studio, while her photograph was displayed in the top right corner.

A trash can under the desk was stuffed with empty food cartons and snack bar wrappers and crushed soda cans and empty water bottles. A Cup Noodle container and a plastic fork were next to a small kettle. Also on the desk was a well-thumbed paperback by the same author as the book on the nightstand in Madison's apartment.

There was a closet without a door. A blue floral dress was the only item of clothing hanging on the rail. A pair of gold strappy sandals were lined up neatly below it. Sarah recognized them from the camera footage of Madison James at The Joneses on Monday morning.

A pink and yellow neon duffel bag was on the floor near the closet—just like the one Larissa Jones had said Madison usually kept her gym stuff in for her yoga and SoulCycle classes but was missing from the trunk of her Ford Mustang. A platinum-blonde wig was lying on the floor. It was a short bob style with bangs, like the one Julia Roberts wore in *Pretty Woman* when she was dressed as a hooker and picked up Richard Gere on Hollywood Boulevard.

Kitty Duvall's Julia Roberts wig.

The one Madison had borrowed for a play and hadn't returned.

A set of silver metal handcuffs lay next to the wig, a teeny key still in the lock. Another of Kitty's props.

The realization of what she was looking at hit Sarah hard.

Madison James had been here. And she had come here of her own free will.

She hadn't been taken. She wasn't being kept prisoner. It seemed highly unlikely that she'd banged her head and was wandering around with amnesia and had no idea of her own identity like Jimmy Grand had suggested.

She had checked into the Stargaze Motel on Monday wearing Kitty Duvall's wig and she had hidden out in this room for days, watching the news coverage about her own disappearance.

She had been aware of the TikToks, the other social media posts, the search efforts to try to locate her. She had eaten instant noodles and Snickers bars and drank Diet Coke while her own mother and her best friend and her manager had all feared the worst. She had probably delighted in how the whole country had become obsessed with the vanishing of Madison James.

Moreno called out from the bathroom. "There's hair in the sink. Like it's been chopped off. It's auburn and curly. Some ladies bath stuff in here too. A new toothbrush, an almost full tube of toothpaste. No blood or sign of foul play. No towels either though, which is weird."

Madison had cut off her hair—and what? Had she planned on using the handcuffs to fake an abduction and an imprisonment before claiming she had somehow escaped her captor?

Why?

And where was she now?

Sarah's eyes travelled around the room. A pay-as-you-go burner phone was on the nightstand, suggesting at least one accomplice in the deception. A room key with a "15" fob was next to the phone. A lamp had been knocked to the floor, its shade askew, the bulb shattered. A glass tumbler was also upturned on the threadbare carpet.

Something had happened in this room. A struggle. Violence.

A thick brown blanket was draped over the queen bed. It was the kind of blanket that would be stored on a closet shelf and taken down for extra warmth in the winter. It was late summer and ninety degrees out.

*She was only supposed to be gone until Saturday.*

There had been a plan and it had changed.

*Something's gone wrong.*

Moreno emerged from the bathroom. "What the hell is that smell?"

Sarah was aware of it too.

In among the mustiness and old sweat and stale cigarettes and junk food stink, there was something else. A metallic odor, the smell of old pennies.

Sarah took gloves from her pocket and snapped them on. Hit the light switch on the wall. Blinked in the sudden glare. Her eyes adjusted and she saw red stains on the fabric headboard that weren't part of the pattern. There were more red splotches on the pine nightstand. Red spatter decorated the faded wallpaper like a kindergarten kid's first attempt at artwork.

Sarah walked over to the bed and peeled back the heavy brown blanket.

"Oh fuck," Moreno said from the bathroom doorway.

The once-white sheet beneath the blanket was completely covered in blood that had dried and hardened and caked into a dark carmine stain.

There was a lot of blood.

Too much blood.

No one could have survived what had happened in this room.

# 22
# SARAH
## SEPTEMBER 2022

Blue lights swirled in the motel parking lot.

Two black and white LAPD cruisers and a forensics van were zigzagged haphazardly outside of room fifteen. There were no media trucks yet because Bird hadn't tipped them off, probably because a serious crime wasn't the best advertisement for his business. But it wouldn't take long for word to get out and for the press pack to start circling. Sharks, sniffing out blood, hungry for food.

There was no ambulance or coroner's wagon either, because there was no body. But just because there was no one to tag and bag, that didn't mean they weren't dealing with a homicide.

Sarah thought again of the blood on the bed and felt sick. So much blood. She knew in her gut that there would be no happy ending here. The hope was gone. There would be no repeat of Hendricks and Dessers and the ten-year-old kid in the custody dispute. Her first case with the MPU, and missing had very likely just turned to murder.

Uniformed officers were knocking on the doors of the other occupied rooms and interviewing guests. Forensic techs were inside the room, dusting and swabbing and photographing and bagging evidence.

Sarah didn't like Kitty Duvall's chances of seeing her wig and handcuffs any time soon.

Moreno was outside room fifteen getting an update from one of the white-suited techs. Sarah was interviewing Rick Bird in the glare of the sun, because his office was also being treated as a crime scene, seeing as the missing key from the desk drawer had most likely been stolen to provide access to Madison James' room.

She showed Bird a photo of Madison. "Is this the woman who checked into room fifteen last Monday?"

Bird's eyes darted frantically. He looked as sick as Sarah felt. The eyes landed on the photo. "Nah, she's a redhead. The guest was blonde."

"The guest was wearing a wig. Take a closer look. I need you to confirm if this was the woman staying in room fifteen."

The eyes flicked to Madison's picture. The lizard tongue licked lips that were drier than the desert. "Yeah, maybe. It's hard to say for sure. I told you she had the big sunglasses on, like the ones Kennedy's wife used to wear."

"This woman has been all over the news. People have been looking for her for days. You didn't recognize her? You didn't think to tell anyone she was staying here all this time?"

"I don't watch the news, okay? Or read the papers. All doom and gloom and depressing shit. How was I supposed to know she was missing? Even if I did, it's none of my business. As long as they pay and don't wreck the place, I don't care who stays here."

"Any cameras?"

A place like this, Sarah already knew the answer.

"Nope. My guests are entitled to their privacy."

More like Bird didn't want a record of the drug deals that happened here and the sex workers who were hustled into rooms by johns who paid by the hour.

"You said she paid cash. Is this a cash-only establishment?"

"Nah, I got one of those card reader things. It was her choice to pay cash."

*No paper trail*, Sarah thought.

She said, "There was no car parked outside the room. We're just off the highway here so she didn't walk. Did you see her arrive in a vehicle?"

"I don't remember. It's like I said, she was a guest like any other."

"Cut the crap, Mr. Bird. She checked in on a Monday. Today is Monday. Right now, there are only six other guests. Last week would have been similar. That's not a lot to keep track of. She paid cash for five nights, which I'm guessing is unusual. I doubt the Stargaze Motel ranks highly on TripAdvisor for tourists. You would have remembered her. So, tell me what you know, or we can continue this chat in a hot windowless room downtown."

Bird glared at her with the beady black eyes. She glared right back. "She got dropped off, okay?" he said. "The driver didn't stick around."

"Did you get a look at the driver?"

"No."

"What kind of car was it?"

"A bright yellow sedan."

"Do you remember anything else about the car?"

"Yeah. It had the word 'taxi' on top."

Sarah sighed. She thought of the burner phone on the nightstand. Madison had likely used it to book the ride and had paid in cash. She hadn't been dropped off by an accomplice. That lead was a dead end.

The motel's assistant manager had been dragged from his bed by a couple of uniforms knocking on his door. He had worked Saturday and Sunday. No one had asked him about room fifteen. He hadn't given anyone the key. He said he only left the desk unattended when he had to take a leak and admitted it was possible someone could have swiped the key when he was in the john. The drawer was kept unlocked. A college kid had worked the overnight shifts at the weekend, and they were still trying to reach him.

But Sarah thought whatever had happened in that room had gone down before Saturday. Saturday was when Madison was supposed to reappear according to the anonymous tips-line caller. Sarah guessed the attack had taken place earlier in the week, and most likely when Bird had been on duty. The office had a big picture window with a clear view of the line of rooms. She thought that Bird saw plenty that went on in the motel.

"Did you see the woman again after she checked in?"

"Nope."

"She didn't leave the room?"

"Not that I saw."

"Did she have any visitors?"

Bird was sweating. He pulled at the damp collar of his yellowed shirt. Scratched at his arms. "Not that I saw."

Sarah was sure he was lying. Maybe he was scared. Maybe he was hiding something. Maybe he was covering for someone. "Are you sure about that?"

"Positive. No visitors that I know of."

She saw Moreno duck under the yellow crime-scene tape strung around room fifteen and head her way. She walked to meet him, out of earshot of Bird.

"Anything?" she asked.

"They haven't found a weapon. There's only one room key, the one on the nightstand. Either the one Madison was given when she checked in or the one taken from Bird's office. We don't know yet. The other key is missing."

"What do you think happened here?"

"I think Madison was hiding from someone. And they found her."

"Do you think there's a chance she could still be alive?"

"I don't know. That room, Sarah. It's bad. Really bad."

A blue Chevy Impala roared into the parking lot, spitting gravel, and screeched to a halt in front of them.

"Shit," Sarah said.

A tall, good-looking man with dark curly hair got out. He was late forties and wore a charcoal dress shirt tucked into black jeans, and Ray-Ban aviators. The shirtsleeves were rolled up to the elbow, showing off tanned, toned forearms. Sarah knew for a fact that the rest of the body was just as tanned and toned thanks to daily runs and thrice-weekly weight sessions.

Her stomach did a little flip. Then the familiar anger took over.

He slammed the door and strolled toward them. Took off the sunglasses and tucked them into the shirt's breast pocket. He jutted his chin at Bird.

"Is he the motel manager?"

Sarah folded her arms across her chest. "He is."

"I am," yelled Bird. "And I got a name. The name's Bird."

The man ignored him. "Thanks for babysitting my witness," he said to Sarah. "I'll take it from here."

Moreno said, "Who the hell is this asshole?"

The asshole introduced himself. "Detective Nick Delaney from Robbery-Homicide. This is our case now."

"Delaney?" Moreno repeated, confused.

Sarah said, "This asshole is my husband."

# 23

# SARAH

## SEPTEMBER 2022

"I didn't know you were married."

Moreno's gaze drifted to Sarah's left hand, no doubt to see if a ring he hadn't noticed before had suddenly appeared.

There was no wedding band. Not anymore.

Not since she'd taken it off six months ago.

"Homicide?" Bird looked like he might faint. "You never said anything about the woman being dead. You said she was missing."

"She is missing," said Sarah.

"She's dead," said Nick Delaney.

Sarah grabbed his arm and steered him away from the motel manager. Tried to ignore the jolt of electricity that surged through her when she touched him. Tried to stay angry.

"What do you think you're playing at?" she hissed. "We don't know that she's dead. This remains a missing persons investigation until we do. There's no body. We don't even have a weapon yet. Stop shooting your goddamn mouth off and get back in your Chevy and leave. RHD has no right being here."

Nick said, "The way I hear it, there's no way anyone could have survived that amount of blood loss. This is a homicide investigation for sure. You know it is. It's my case. Don't make this personal. Don't make this about us, Sarah."

They had first met when Sarah was still in uniform and Nick was a newly minted detective. He'd asked her out and they'd gone for a drink, and they had talked and laughed all evening until the bar shut. Nick had given her a ride home and they'd sat in his car outside her apartment, still talking and laughing, until dawn lightened the sky. They had kissed.

Then she'd turned him down for a second date. Not because she wasn't attracted to him. She was. That was the problem. Nick Delaney was smart, funny, gorgeous, and everything she wanted. Over the course of a single night, Sarah had fallen so hard and so fast that it terrified her. She didn't return his calls and eventually he'd stopped calling.

Two years later, they'd found themselves both working the murder table at Hollywood Division. Sarah, a detective herself by now, couldn't deny the feelings she still had for him. It was hard to breathe around him. It hurt to look at him. It was impossible not to want to touch him. When he'd asked again for a belated second date, she'd agreed. Six months later they were married.

Sarah knew the other cops had been surprised when she took Nick's surname. She also knew that some of her female colleagues were disappointed, that they felt like she'd surrendered her identity for a man.

The way Sarah saw it, the name she'd been given at birth had been courtesy of a man too. A man who was a drunk and a bully. Her father. The truth was, she couldn't wait to be rid of it. Nick Delaney showered her with love, whereas her father had showered her mom with drunken blows. Sarah had been proud to take her new husband's name.

Delaney and Delaney.

They weren't officially partners in a work sense, but they were a team in every other way. The best team. She'd thought they were unbreakable. And for almost ten years they had been. Until Nick broke them.

She glared at him now. "I'm not making it personal. This isn't about us. It's about Madison James. This is my case, and finding out what happened to her is my responsibility. Now if you don't mind, I have a missing woman to find."

"No, Sarah, you don't," Nick said softly. "You have a dead woman to find. Scratch that. *I* have a dead woman to find."

She shook her head and looked away. She could feel tears threatening. She forced them back. She wouldn't give him the satisfaction of seeing how much the case was affecting her. But he knew her too well.

"I know this is tough," he said. "It's your first case with MPU. You wanted a different outcome. Of course you did. But you've done your part. You did everything you could. You need to let it go now. Don't do what you always do and get too involved."

"Don't get too involved?" she shouted. "You've got a fucking nerve, Nick Delaney. I'm not the one who screwed around with a murder victim's sister."

"Keep your voice down." His own voice was low and angry. "We've been over this a million times. This isn't the time or place."

Sarah and Nick had never worked a case together, but they had often discussed what they were working on. They had bounced ideas and theories off each other. Helped each other deal with the really bad ones. The cases they couldn't close. The ones that cut the deepest. The ones they couldn't let go of.

Irina Gonzalez had been one of those cases for Sarah.

Irina was a twenty-five-year-old single mom who had been raped and then bludgeoned to death by an unknown intruder while her toddler son slept in the next room. As the weeks passed without a suspect or any real leads, the case began to consume Sarah. The dining table at home was papered with images of Irina and crime scene photos and witness statements and forensic reports.

She spent hours in the kitchen going over and over those same pages and photos, searching for something she had missed, a tiny detail that would crack the case wide open. Something—anything—that might help secure justice for Irina's family, for her little boy.

Nick had warned her it wasn't healthy, said she was getting too involved, that she was becoming obsessed. Sarah knew he was right. Irina was the latest in a long list of dead girls whose murders she had investigated. It was taking a toll.

But Nick was getting in too deep himself.

Alexis McAdam had gone on a date and never returned home. Her body had been found two days later in an alleyway. Alexis's sister Laura was the key witness in building a case against Nick's prime suspect. He dropped whatever he was doing any time she called, jumped in the car to meet her whenever she remembered another detail that might be important.

Sarah was used to Nick receiving calls and texts at all hours. It came with the job. But there had never been any secrecy between them, nothing to hide. Suddenly, Nick was leaving the room to take a call. The texts were becoming more frequent. He had never had a passcode on his cell phone before and then he did.

It hadn't taken long for Sarah to work out the passcode. She was a detective; it was what she did. She found dozens of messages exchanged between her husband and Laura McAdam. Messages that went way beyond the case. Sarah confronted Nick and he admitted getting too close, but claimed he'd never slept with Laura. It was clear from the texts that he'd wanted to. As far as Sarah was concerned, Nick had still betrayed his vows. He had cheated on her emotionally and, in her book, that was a hundred times worse than a drunken one-night stand with a stranger.

Sarah had told him to leave, which he had. She avoided him at work and their split provided plenty of water cooler gossip for the RHD dicks. Then she returned home from a late shift one night and found Nick in the living room, drunk and weeping. He begged her to take him back. She told him she'd think about it. After she poured him into an Uber, Sarah called a locksmith and changed the locks.

Then she put in for a transfer. She was done with homicide investigations, and she was done with Nick Delaney. MPU would be a fresh start all round.

That had been the plan anyway. It wasn't working out too good so far.

But Nick was right. Now wasn't the time or place to rake over the embers of their marriage. She was letting him get under her skin. It was unprofessional. And they had an audience. She glanced over to where Moreno was suddenly very interested in his shoes, while Rick Bird had seemed even twitchier since Nick had showed up claiming a woman had died in his motel. He looked like he was waiting for a grenade to go off.

Then Nick pulled the grenade's pin.

"Look, there's another reason why I think Madison James is dead," he said. "As well as all the blood, I mean. She's not the first."

"What do you mean?"

"Another actress died in this motel. She was murdered. Her name was Taylor Rose."

# SILVER SCREAM MAGAZINE

THE RED ROSE: A TRIBUTE

By Seth Midnight, March 2005

*She was draped in red satin, her flaxen hair fanned out on the pillow. Beneath the scarlet lipstick, her rosebud mouth had taken on a blue hue. Her slender throat was decorated with a necklace of bruises.*

Sadly, this is not a scene from a movie. This is real life.

The actress Taylor Rose is dead at just 21. Brutally murdered in a Los Angeles motel. Another victim of the City of Angels.

Naturally, comparisons have already been made with the infamous unsolved murder of Elizabeth

Short aka The Black Dahlia, whose body was discovered in Leimert Park in 1947.

Like the Dahlia, Rose was drawn to the bright lights of Tinseltown in search of fame and fortune. She was desired, she stood out, she was memorable. And just like Short, her sparkling light has been dimmed far too soon.

Rose was a year younger than the Dahlia when she met her tragic demise.

The Black Dahlia had no known film credits but Taylor Rose did. Fans of this magazine will best remember her for her roles in slasher flicks *Dead Like Her* and *Do Not Disturb*.

*Dead Like Her* saw Rose play a college student who finds herself targeted by a masked killer hunting young women on campus who look just like her.

In *Do Not Disturb*, she earned a legion of fans for her portrayal of plucky Maya Swanson, who takes on a crazed axe murderer—and wins.

Real name Rose Taylor, she was born in Upstate New York in July 1983, the only child of Ned and Jocelyn. Her parents were too distraught to comment on their daughter's death.

Her long-term boyfriend, Bradley Huffman, told us: "Rose and I were high-school sweethearts.

"It took a whole year for me to build up the courage to ask her out. She was beautiful, of course, but she was also smart and funny and kind.

"I couldn't believe it when she agreed to go on a date with me to the movies.

"That night, she told me her dreams of being a Hollywood actress. For anyone else, it would have been a pipe dream. But not Rose. She was special.

"I always knew I'd have to share her with the rest of the world but that was okay—a talent like hers was meant to be shared.

"She made everything in the world brighter and better just by being in it.

"I don't know what I'm supposed to do without her. My heart has been shattered into a million pieces."

Her manager, John Lister, added: "I guess you could say I 'discovered' Rose when she was just 14.

"She was visiting Disneyland with her folks and I was there with my own kids and I saw her and I just knew she was going to be a star.

"Rose wanted to finish her schooling in New York before even considering an acting career. I was happy to wait.

"I signed her when she was 18 and she stayed with my family and I in our spare room for several months before the offers started rolling in.

"Rose was like a daughter to me. I'm utterly devastated."

Onscreen, Taylor Rose was brave, beautiful, fearless, luminous, invincible.

That's how everyone at *Silver Scream* magazine will remember her—as the ultimate "Final Girl."

Rest in Peace, Red Rose.

# 24

# MADISON

## SPRING, 2005

Madison stayed in bed for days.

Her roommates didn't ask what was wrong. They knew. Everybody did. It was all over the news. Lizzie and Carly left sandwiches and soup and tea outside her bedroom door, but she couldn't stomach any of it.

Taylor was dead.

Murdered in a filthy motel room.

Her best friend. The only real friend she had.

Or used to have.

Madison hadn't spoken to her in months, not until the night Taylor died.

She'd been so angry when she'd discovered Taylor had agreed to star in *The Murder Book*. The betrayal had hit like a wrecking ball, landed so much harder than Jimmy Grand's right hook in Vegas. Taylor hadn't even had the guts to tell Madison herself. She'd let her read about it in a magazine, the same way Madison had found out that Grand had moved on from her to Rachel Rayner.

There had been an ugly scene in a restaurant. Madison had confronted Taylor and lost her temper. Jimmy Grand *and* Ted Clayton. Why stick one finger up at her when she could stick up two? Taylor had sat rigid in her seat, napkin folded primly on her lap, her food going cold in front of her. She had taken everything Madison had thrown at her. Didn't try to interrupt or defend herself or offer an explanation.

When Madison was done venting, all Taylor said was, "I'm sorry. But I had to."

Ted Clayton apparently wanted to move on from slasher flicks. *The Murder Book* was going to be a dark thriller in the style of *Se7en* and *The Bone Collector* and *Along Came a Spider*. It was about a haunted detective (Grand) who got sent a murder book, like the ones cops used for homicide investigations, but this book detailed a murder that hadn't happened yet. The detective then faced a race against time to track down the girl in the book (Taylor) before the killer struck in the same way he described in its pages.

There was going to be a huge budget thrown at the movie. It was going to make Taylor Rose a household name. It was supposed to propel her onto the A-list.

Now she was in a murder book for real.

◆ ◆ ◆

*Madison replayed their final conversation repeatedly in her head:*

*A soft knock at the door. Almost hesitant.*

*Madison got up on tiptoes and peered through the spyhole. She hadn't heard from Jefferson Cantwell since the "misunderstanding" in her parking garage, but she always checked first before opening the door now. Just in case he was on the other side, brandishing a bouquet of lilies.*

*It wasn't Cantwell with flowers.*

*It was Taylor Rose with a bottle of wine.*

*Madison almost didn't open the door. It had been months since the showdown in the restaurant. The press had had a field day. They'd gobbled up the argument like it was the crab cakes on Taylor's plate. It was humiliating. The only time the papers and magazines showed any interest in Madison was when there was a whiff of scandal involving a bigger name. A Vegas wedding with Jimmy Grand; a public spat with Taylor Rose.*

*She wanted out. She was done. Madison would do what Ally Hagen had done and leave Hollywood in her rearview mirror. She would go back to Dutton and live a normal life and she might even be happy. She had given it her best shot and it hadn't been good enough.*

*Madison had returned to Indiana but not for the reason she'd planned. Her dad had suffered a huge stroke and never recovered. She went home for the funeral and slept in her old bedroom, where posters of Leonardo DiCaprio and the Backstreet Boys were still thumbtacked to the wall and her battered teddy still sat on a wicker chair by the door. She wrapped herself in her comforter with its familiar fabric softener scent and watched the snow fall outside the window, and she wanted to stay there forever. Her home, with her family, and the familiar streets and stores and people, was where she belonged. It was where she had always felt safe and loved.*

*Then her mom, frail and bowed by grief, had perched on the edge of her bed and told Madison how proud her dad had been of her for chasing dreams that were bigger than Dutton, Indiana.*

*So here she was, back in her shared apartment in Los Angeles, with one of the "50 hottest stars of 2005" on her doorstep.*

*Madison opened the door.*

*Taylor smiled nervously. "Peace offering." She held up the bottle of Barolo. "I didn't smash it this time."*

*"What do you want, Taylor?"*

*"To explain. To make things okay between us."*

*"You don't have to explain. You want to be rich and famous, and Ted Clayton is going to make that happen. I get it. I just don't think we can be friends anymore. I trusted you. I loved you. And you let me down."*

*Taylor's fingers worried at the little gold rose pendant around her neck that she never took off. "I'm not doing it for me. I'm doing it for my mom and dad. They're getting old. They both still have jobs that mean working long hours just so they can pay the bills. They should be taking it easy at their age. I'm doing* The Murder Book *for them. I want to be able to look after my parents the way they've always looked after me."*

*Taylor was an only child like Madison. She'd told her once how her parents had tried for a long time for a baby without any success. The doctors didn't know why they weren't getting pregnant, couldn't find any medical reason. Eventually her mom and dad had given up hope, accepted that it was God's will not to bless them with children. Then, both in their forties, it finally happened. Taylor was their miracle baby. They both absolutely adored her.*

*It was such a Taylor reason for doing the movie that Madison felt her anger lose its sharp edges and soften into sadness.*

*"Why didn't you just tell me?"*

*"I wanted to, and I kept putting it off and then it was too late. I know it was a horrible way to find out. You must have felt awful."*

*"It was. I did."*

*"I'm so sorry, Madison."*

*Madison just nodded.*

*Taylor pulled her gold shawl tighter around her bare shoulders. It was March and it was cold out. Beneath the shawl was a red dress. It was not a color she usually wore, but, as always, she looked stunning.*

*"You look pretty," Madison said. "Is Bradley in town?"*

*"No, he's visiting next weekend." Taylor stared at the floor. "I'm going to a party. In the Hills."*

*Taylor didn't invite her to the party and Madison knew why. Not her kind of people. Madison no longer fitted in. Maybe Jimmy Grand was the host again. Or Ted Clayton. They both had fancy houses up in the neighborhood.*

*"Right. I hope you have fun."*

*Taylor looked at her then, her lake-blue eyes pleading. "Do you think we can still be friends?"*

*Madison answered truthfully. "I don't know, Taylor. We'll see. Maybe I'll see you around."*

*She closed the door. The next day she found Taylor's bottle of wine on the mat.*

*Madison wouldn't see Taylor around. She'd never see her again.*

The detective leaned his notepad on his beachball belly like it was a desk. He'd wedged himself into an armchair. Madison faced him on the couch.

His name was Mulgrew, and he was old with bulging eyes and more salt than pepper in his hair. His shirt was starting to untuck from his pants and there was a ketchup stain on his tie. He licked the tip of his pencil whenever he wrote anything down and said "hmmm" a lot.

Mulgrew had taken his time in speaking to her, seeing as Madison had been one of the last people to see Taylor alive.

"So, Rose Taylor came to your apartment around seven p.m.?"

It was strange to hear the detective call Taylor by her real name. She had flipped it around when she'd moved to Hollywood because Taylor Rose sounded starrier.

"That's right."

"How long did she stay?"

"Not long. Ten, maybe fifteen, minutes."

"What did you talk about?"

"Taylor came to clear the air. We'd had an argument over a movie role and hadn't spoken in a while."

Pencil lick.

"Hmmm. And did you?"

"Did we what?"

"Clear the air."

"Kind of."

"Is that all you spoke about? Clearing-the-air stuff?"

"Taylor told me she was going to a party. In the Hills."

"Hmmm. A party in the Hills."

"The Hollywood Hills," Madison clarified. "Lots of rich people."

"Yeah, I know the Hills. Don't let the Men's Wearhouse clearance suit fool you. Did she mention a street name? Tell you who was hosting this party?"

"No."

Mulgrew turned the frog eyes on her. "So, Rose Taylor was a party girl?"

"Huh?"

"Booze. Drugs. That kind of thing."

"No, definitely not! Taylor didn't drink a lot. One or two glasses of wine or champagne. She never took drugs."

Pencil lick.

"Hmmm. The tox report and bloodwork say otherwise. You ever see her do some Special K?"

"I don't even know what that is."

"Ketamine."

"I still don't know what it is."

"It's a kind of anesthetic used by docs and vets. Some kids take it recreationally to get high. I'm guessing the young Hollywood crowd would have no problem getting their hands on it."

Madison was appalled. "Taylor would never take anything like that. She must have been drugged."

"Hmmm. How about boyfriends?"

"Taylor's boyfriend is at Brown. Bradley Huffman. They've been together for years."

"I mean boyfriends here in Los Angeles. When the Ivy League guy isn't in town."

"No way. She would never cheat on Bradley."

Pencil lick.

"Hmmm. Did Ms. Taylor have any Latino friends?"

"She was friendly with the actress Luna Sanchez."

Mulgrew stared at her. "I meant men. Latino men."

"No."

"Any other dark-skinned men?"

"No! Taylor didn't hang around with other guys. I told you. She was totally into Bradley."

"We have a witness who saw Ms. Taylor entering the room at the Stargaze Motel with a dark-skinned man. The witness says they seemed very . . . friendly."

"Your witness is lying!" Madison said angrily. "You've got Taylor all wrong."

"Have I? You said it yourself—you hadn't spoken in months. Maybe you didn't know your friend as well as you thought you did."

Madison didn't have an answer to that.

Mulgrew pocketed the notepad and pencil and stood, hiking up his pants. Madison showed him to the door.

"One last thing," he said like he was in an episode of *Columbo*. "Her folks asked about a necklace with a gold and diamond rose pendant. Was she wearing it when she visited your apartment?"

"Yes, she was," Madison said. "She never took it off."

"Hmmm. Well, she wasn't wearing it when we found her."

# 25

# SARAH

## SEPTEMBER 2022

"Taylor Rose?" Sarah said. "I know that name. She was in a movie with Madison James. *Do Not Disturb*. I watched it a couple of nights ago. Taylor Rose was the star. A beautiful blonde girl."

Nick nodded. "The press called it 'the Red Rose Murder.' She was wearing a red dress when she was murdered and, with the name, I guess it was a slam dunk for a headline."

"When did it happen?"

"Around seventeen or eighteen years ago."

Sarah did the math. She'd have been mid-twenties and still a rookie boot working out of Topanga Division at the time.

"I don't remember it," she said. "I was probably too busy breaking up bar brawls and attending domestic disputes to pay much attention to a homicide case, even one involving a Hollywood actress."

Nick said, "Taylor Rose made the news for about a month before the press pack moved on to something else and everyone kind of forgot about her."

"What happened to her?"

"Strangled, I think. I was a beat cop, I didn't work the case. I don't know the details." He gestured around him. "But I remember this dump was where she died. The place has always been hinky."

A crime scene tech exited the office building. "I've got everything I need," he said. "It's all yours."

"Finally!" Bird darted inside and slammed the door like he thought it would save him from any more questions. He immediately stuck his head back out again. "There's black powder everywhere. Who's gonna clean this shit up?"

Sarah said, "That would be you."

"Fucking cops."

Bird slammed the door again.

Sarah said to Nick, "Was Bird the motel's manager when Taylor Rose was murdered?"

"I don't know. I need to pull the murder book out of storage. If he was, he'll be in there. Once I've been through the book, I'll decide what to do about him. But first, I want to take a look at the room."

"It's my crime scene," Sarah pointed out. "Still my case."

Moreno cleared his throat, either to unblock some phlegm or remind them he was still there.

Nick ignored him. He said to Sarah, "We both want the same outcome—to find out what happened to Madison James. Why don't we both work the case? You do your thing, I'll do mine, then we can trade notes. What do you say?"

Sarah sighed. She knew it made sense for MPU and RHD to work together. At least until they'd established what exactly had happened to Madison James. Just so long as Nick didn't piss her off.

"Okay."

He winked. "Delaney and Delaney. The best team."

He was pissing her off already.

She said to Moreno, "Let's go."

"Where?"

"To find out who Madison James' accomplice is."

◆ ◆ ◆

Moreno didn't ask any questions about Sarah's detective husband on the way back to the PAB. He was learning. Instead, he called Hendricks for the location of the tips line call.

Hendricks had the information by the time they walked into the office.

"Pay phone on Victory Boulevard in Van Nuys," he said. "Didn't even try to *67 the call."

Sarah said, "We need to pull recordings from every LAPD camera in the vicinity of that pay phone ASAP."

"On it," Moreno said.

Sarah called Ellen Downey, the LAPD's head of media relations.

"I need a favor."

Ellen sounded stressed. "It had better be a quick favor. We've been inundated since the Madison James presser."

"Can you put together a file of press cuttings on Madison James and another actress by the name of Taylor Rose?"

Ellen sighed. "How far back?"

"Twenty years."

"You're kidding, right?"

Sarah said, "We have a crime scene at a motel off the I-105. We might be dealing with a homicide now."

"Might?"

"No body. Not yet."

"Shit."

"Can you help?"

"Leave it with me. You owe me dinner at Musso & Frank. Martinis included."

Ellen hung up.

The mention of dinner reminded Sarah to eat. She decided to go in search of a burrito while they waited for the Van Nuys camera feeds. Moreno declined the offer of delicious Mexican food in favor of a couple of energy bars and a protein drink he had stashed in his desk drawer. His PT would be so proud.

Sarah was in a restaurant around the corner from the PAB and on her last bite of a chicken burrito when Moreno called.

"We have the footage."

"Back in five. Don't start without me."

"Like I'd even dare."

Five minutes later, Moreno had the footage cued up and ready to go on his computer.

They'd lucked out. The pay phone was attached to a wall between a 7-Eleven and a coin laundry. No booth. Nice and exposed. And right next to a busy intersection.

"Hendricks said 8:07 a.m.," Moreno said. "Here we go."

He hit the play button. The feed was from a camera mounted on a traffic light that showed a main thoroughfare busy with rush-hour traffic. The sidewalks were also bustling with foot traffic.

The time stamp on the screen read 8:06.

They watched and waited.

A figure dressed in dark clothing came into shot from behind the camera. They jogged across the parking lot in front of the coin laundry and 7-Eleven. They looked to be of medium height and a slim build.

Sarah's pulse quickened.

The figure went straight to the pay phone.

"Our mystery caller," said Moreno.

The person faced the wall for the duration of the call.

"Turn around!" Sarah said, frustrated.

The dark-clad figure hung up, glanced around, and then jogged in the direction they'd come from, heading straight for the camera. They were wearing black jeans and a hoodie and a ball cap. The brim of the cap was pulled down low.

Then the caller looked up. Just for a second.

Sarah said, "Pause it right there."

Moreno did as he was told.

"Can you zoom in?" she asked.

Moreno zoomed in on the image until it began to pixelate. It wasn't great quality but it was enough. Sarah recognized the face onscreen.

"Wait," Moreno said. "Is that who I think it is?"

Sarah said, "Yes, that's exactly who it is."

# 26

# SARAH

## SEPTEMBER 2022

Chloe Reid watched from behind the Jack in the Box counter as Sarah and Moreno approached.

"I guess you're not here for a cheeseburger?" the young blonde said. Her sassy tone indicated she had no idea just how much trouble she was in.

There was a small line of people waiting to be served. A guy at the front yelled, "Hey, no cutting in!"

Sarah ignored him. "No, Chloe, we're not here for a cheeseburger. We need to talk."

"If this is about the prints, I already went to the station and gave them. I need to serve this guy."

Chloe looked past them to the line as though the conversation was over.

"It's not about the prints. It's about the phone call you made to the tips line."

"I don't know what you're talking about."

Sarah sighed. "Chloe, we have you on camera making the call. The disguise wasn't very good. And the pay phone is a three-minute drive from where you work. You're not exactly a criminal mastermind."

"I'm not a criminal," she snapped.

"That's for us to decide."

The hungry guy was shouting again. "Is no one serving in this place? Do I need to go to Burger King?"

An older woman emerged from the kitchen area. She was wearing a burgundy shirt with a scarf knotted under the collar instead of the red Jack in the Box t-shirt Chloe was wearing. Her breast pocket had a pen caddy poking out and Sarah guessed she was some kind of supervisor.

"Is there a problem, Chloe?" the woman asked. "Why are the customers not being served and threatening to go to Burger King?"

"No problem, Jacey," Chloe called. She said to Sarah, "I can't talk about this just now. I'm working. You're going to get me fired."

"You're going to get yourself arrested. Outside. Now."

Chloe swallowed. "I'm taking my break now, Jacey."

"You already had your break."

"I'm taking another one."

"It's coming out of your wages."

"Whatever," Chloe muttered under her breath.

She left the counter and trudged toward the exit. Sarah and Moreno followed. They stepped outside into heavy heat. The restaurant was flanked by a drive-thru on one side and a small lot with a strict thirty-minute limit on the other. A kid who was Chloe's age and wearing the same red tee was leaning against a hatchback eating a Jumbo Jack cheeseburger.

"Go stuff your face someplace else, Freddy," Chloe said.

"I'm on my break," Freddy complained through a mouthful of meat and bread.

"I mean it, beat it."

She was trying to sound tough but there was a wobble to her voice.

Freddy shook his head and tutted, but pushed himself off the bumper and went back into the restaurant.

They stood in a loose triangle, cars trundling past on Van Nuys Boulevard.

Sarah said, "How did you know Madison James was staying in the Stargaze Motel?"

"I didn't. I had no idea where she was."

"This is serious, Chloe. You need to start telling the truth."

"I am. I swear, I didn't know where she was. Not until this morning when I was told to call the tips line."

"Who told you to make the call?"

Chloe shook her head.

Sarah sighed again.

"It was only supposed to be the purse," Chloe said. "The phone call wasn't supposed to be part of the deal."

"Tell us about the purse," Moreno said.

"I was told where to find it, in a stinking alleyway in Fairfax. I was to take it to Griffith Park and stash it somewhere and pretend I'd found it. Then I was to post a couple of TikToks. Mention who the purse belonged to and say the woman was missing. Make it sound really dramatic. The plan was to get everyone talking about her and for her face to be all over the news. I guess it worked."

Sarah said, "You set this up with Madison James?"

Chloe shook her head. "No, I didn't even know who the purse belonged to until I saw her ID. I was telling you the truth when I said I'd never met her, had never heard of her. Honestly? I was disappointed. I thought it was going to be someone more famous."

"Did someone pay you to do all this?" Sarah asked.

"No. I didn't do it for money."

"So, why do it then? Why risk getting yourself into trouble?"

"Am I in trouble?"

"That depends on you telling us the name of the person who put you up to this."

Chloe pulled off the Jack in the Box visor and rubbed her forehead.

"The name," Sarah urged.

Chloe nodded, resigned. "I'm an actress. That's why I did it. I've already been in a couple of commercials after answering ads in the local paper, but I don't want to be stuck doing air freshener and cat food commercials forever. I want to be in TV shows and movies and that only happens with an agent or a manager."

Sarah had a pretty good idea where this was going.

Chloe went on, "I worked as her assistant for a month. She knew how ambitious I was, that I would do anything to be famous. A couple of months after she fired me, she called me out of the blue and told me what she wanted me to do. She said to think of it as an audition, like playing a witness in a crime drama. She promised she'd represent me once the dust settled. Yeah, it all sounded kind of nuts, but I figured girls like me had to do a lot worse back in the days before #MeToo. It was a harmless publicity stunt. No one would get hurt. Her client would get really famous—and I'd have a manager. Everyone would win."

Annie Kline.

"Madison's manager set it up?"

"Yeah, I guess Annie Kline and Madison James cooked up the scheme together."

"What about Cash?" Sarah asked. "Where does he fit into it?"

"Who? I don't know who that is."

Either Chloe Reid was an exceptionally talented actress or she was telling the truth.

"Where is Madison now?"

"She wasn't at the motel?" Chloe asked, surprised.

"No, she wasn't."

"I don't know where she is. Annie told me what to say in the call. I told her I'd need to buy a burner and she said that I had to make the call ASAP and to use a pay phone." Chloe chewed her bottom lip. "She sounded worried."

*No one would get hurt.*

Somewhere along the way, the plan had changed.

Someone *had* got hurt.

Someone had died.

# 27
# MADISON
## SEPTEMBER 2022
## (ONE WEEK EARLIER)

Today was the day.

Madison got up at dawn. She'd barely slept. Most of the night had been spent staring at the ceiling, contemplating what she was about to do. She knew it was crazy. She also knew she had no choice.

The apartment needed to be cleaned and tidied. She dusted and polished, and smoothed over the bed sheets, and plumped up the cushions on the couch, and washed the dishes, and emptied the trash.

Her home would be searched eventually, after the planted purse was found and the cops started taking an interest in her disappearance. Madison didn't want strangers judging her for a dirty plate or an unmade bed. A silly thing to worry about given everything else that was going on, but still.

More importantly, she wanted to make sure there was no clutter to distract them from finding Taylor Rose's necklace.

Madison opened the closet and pulled out two dresses. A green wrap-over and a navy shirt dress. She laid them on the bed and tried to decide which one to wear to the audition that didn't exist. Neither seemed right. She went back to the closet and saw the blue floral dress hanging there. It had been in the back of the closet, forgotten for years, until six weeks ago when she'd worn it for the visit to Palm Springs.

Palm Springs.

Where everything had changed.

The real reason for the elaborate fake disappearance.

The reason Annie Kline didn't know about.

Madison wriggled into the blue dress and slipped the gold strappy sandals onto her feet. Took down the blue leather purse from the closet shelf.

Over by the dressing table, she lifted the jewelry box lid so that the freezer bag with the necklace would be in plain sight. She'd been careful never to touch it. She picked up the frame that held the photo of her with her mom and dad and she gently traced their faces with her finger.

Madison almost changed her mind for the hundredth time, knowing the distress she would cause her mom. Then she reminded herself that the alternative was so much worse.

Madison wrote the note that she hoped a smart cop would be able to decipher and slipped it into the back pocket of the purse. She'd read an article once about a missing actress, Jean Spangler, whose purse had been found in Griffith Park with a cryptic note inside. That detail had stuck in her mind. She'd liked how the cops had tried to find the "Kirk" mentioned in Jean's note.

She wanted them to try to find the "Cash" in her own.

Madison gave her reflection a final look in the mirror. Hopefully, in a matter of days, this would be the image the whole country would be seeing.

In the kitchen, she took a Sharpie from the drawer and drew a big black circle around today's date on the calendar she'd purchased a few days ago.

Yesterday, Madison had emptied the contents of her gym bag into the Mustang's trunk. She had taken the duffel upstairs to her apartment and filled it with everything she would need.

Kitty's blonde wig, sunglasses, and dark clothing for the disguise.

Food and water, so she wouldn't have to leave the motel room. PJs to sleep in. A paperback to relieve the boredom when she wasn't watching the news and hoping to make the headlines.

A small bundle of cash—all she could afford to withdraw from the ATM over a period of weeks—wrapped tightly in an elastic band to pay for the room. A burner phone with the number of Annie's burner stored in the contacts.

The handcuffs, also courtesy of Kitty, that Madison would wear throughout her motel stay, one wrist at a time and tight enough to chafe and leave ugly welts. Scissors to chop off her hair. All to make the bogus abduction seem more authentic.

She had then taken the duffel bag to her car and made the familiar drive in the direction of The Joneses. She had parked several streets away from the restaurant. Madison wasn't on shift and she didn't want Larissa or Tre spotting her car in the neighborhood and asking awkward questions.

Then she had slipped into the stinking alleyway and hidden the duffel under a pile of cardboard boxes.

Today, Kitty was smoking by the pool as usual. Madison stopped to speak to her. Witnesses were important.

"Morning, Kitty. It's a beautiful day, isn't it?"

The old woman eyed her through a cloud of cigarette smoke. "You look fancy. Those tips are going to be rolling in today, sweetheart. You should make an effort more often."

"Oh, I'm not going to work. I have the morning off. I'm heading to an audition."

"An audition, huh? Another community play?"

Madison forced an excited smile. "No, it's for a big-budget production. Kitty, this is the breakthrough role I've been waiting for—it's going to make me a star."

Kitty waved the cigarette. "Well, good luck with that."

"I have my lucky dress on and a good feeling about this one. I'll tell you all about it later!"

"You do that, sweetheart."

Madison's acting skills were tested at the restaurant too.

She shouted a hello to Tre and Carlos in the kitchen and hopped on a stool at the counter while Larissa served a customer.

"I didn't expect to see you today," Larissa said when she was free.

"I wanted your approval on the outfit. What do you think?"

"You look terrific, but you always do, Madison James. And you're going to smash this audition."

Madison smiled brightly. "God, I hope so. It'll be fantastic to be back on the big screen after so many years. And lead actress too!" They chatted for a few more minutes and then Madison climbed off the stool. "I'd better go, I'm getting a Lyft to the audition. Can't show up in that old banger. What would people think?"

They hugged over the counter and Madison felt a crushing guilt. She knew Larissa would be the first to worry; the one who would go to the police and report her missing.

"I'll see you this evening," Madison said.

Another lie.

Madison left the restaurant and checked the time on her phone. She was on track. She set off in the direction of the strip mall. The laundromat had been closed forever and the auto shop was shuttered, the mechanics still on vacation. She reached the mouth of the alleyway and glanced around. The street was empty. Madison already knew there were no cameras nearby or covering the street on the other side of the alley, because she'd scoped out the neighborhood for CCTV days ago.

It was why she'd chosen this location for the vanishing act.

She stole into the dark. Found the duffel she'd hidden the day before and ducked down behind a stack of tires and quickly changed into black jeans, a sweater, and sneakers. Pulled on the wig and the shades. Stuffed her dress and sandals into the duffel. Then she left the blue purse under the cardboard for the girl to find.

She'd been one of Annie's many receptionists. Annie had said the girl reminded her of Madison when she was that age. Ambitious, willing to do anything to make it in the movies. Annie was confident the girl could be trusted to carry out her role and keep her mouth shut.

A car engine was idling on the other side of the alleyway. It would be the cab Madison had booked with the throwaway burner phone she'd purchased with cash. No paper trail or electronic record.

As she walked through the alleyway, dodging puddles of vomit and urine, Madison removed the SIM card from her own cell phone and snapped it in two. She emerged into the sunshine, bent down, and dropped the SIM into a drain. The phone would be tossed into a dumpster at the motel. She'd trash all her belongings there too in five days' time.

Then—on Saturday—she would be found at dawn, staggering along the side of the highway, her dress torn, her hair hacked off, her wrists bruised and swollen from her restraints. She would be tearful and disoriented and scared and shaking and she would give the performance of her life.

Madison and Annie had come up with the plan together after Madison had suggested a fake disappearance to garner media interest and resuscitate her almost-dead career. She'd been unsure if her manager would go along with a plot that was so risky and audacious and downright crazy. But, after some consideration, Annie had been willing to get on board. Madison figured the woman was every bit as driven by success and fame and money as the actors she represented.

And maybe a small part of Annie felt like she owed Madison for sending her to that hotel suite with Ted Clayton all those years ago.

They'd agreed that Annie would feign ignorance about everything when the cops came calling about Madison's disappearance. She would tell them she knew nothing about an audition, or who Madison was planning on meeting, or where she might be. The less information Annie was able to offer, the less interest the police would have in her.

As far as Annie was concerned, Madison would then tearfully recount how she'd been snatched off the street, bundled into a car and blindfolded, and held hostage in an unknown location, by an unknown abductor, before being dumped by the side of the road days later.

Only that wasn't the story Madison was going to tell the police.

# 28

# SARAH

## SEPTEMBER 2022

Sarah and Moreno were back in Annie Kline's office with the artificial floral smell and the view of the brick wall. Annie was dressed sharply in another skirt suit and her hair was perfectly styled, but she was pale and drawn and the bags beneath her eyes betrayed the lack of sleep.

"Have you found Madison?" she asked.

"No, not yet."

Annie looked even more worried.

"She wasn't at the motel," Sarah added.

Annie's face twitched. "What motel?"

"We spoke to Chloe Reid. She told us everything. At least, everything she knows. You and Madison faked the disappearance."

Annie nodded, resigned. She didn't try to deny it. "She wasn't at the motel? Are you sure? Room fifteen."

Moreno said, "We found evidence that Madison had been staying there. She's not there now."

Annie was distraught. "Where is she? What's going on? This wasn't part of the plan."

"Tell us about the plan," said Sarah.

Annie sighed long and deep and weary. "It was something we'd joked about in the past. How we should stage a disappearance, get the media interested, and make Madison a household name. Then, once she was found, the movie and TV parts would start rolling in. But that's all it was, a joke. Like a plot from a movie."

"What changed? Why did it stop being a joke?"

"Madison came to my office about six weeks ago. She said she wanted to do it for real. She was turning forty this year. It was her last chance. She'd spent two decades trying to make it in Hollywood and time was running out. She felt like something drastic had to happen. She suggested a fake abduction. I asked if she was serious, but I could tell from the look on her face that she was. I told her she was crazy. But a part of me was thinking: could this actually work? Everybody is obsessed with true crime shows and podcasts. Social media has made it easier than ever to garner interest in a story. Madison was adamant that she wanted to do it. We talked about how we would make it happen. I still wasn't convinced. But, by the time we'd come up with a plan, I was on board. I actually thought it might work."

Annie Kline talked them through it.

There would be a quick outfit change in an alleyway. Madison would have a taxi waiting to take her to a motel to hide out for several days before showing up on the side of the road and claiming she'd been grabbed off the street and abducted by an unknown assailant who'd then let her go. Annie knew a girl who would plant the purse in Griffith Park, pretend to find it, and then post about the discovery on social media—that would get the ball rolling on the media interest.

Annie said, "Once the dust settled, I planned to take Chloe on as a client. That would be her payment for carrying out her part of the plan. She'd made it clear that she didn't want money, she wanted representation. There would probably be some photo call with Chloe and Madison—the girl who found the vital clue and the woman who disappeared—and I could say that's how we met and that I'd decided to offer Chloe representation. She worked here for a month. I didn't think anyone would remember the prior connection between us."

"You were prepared to take on Chloe Reid as a client just so you could help Madison James relaunch her career?" Sarah asked. "That seems like a big ask."

Annie shrugged. "The kid does have some talent. She's got a lot to learn but the potential is there. So, no, it didn't seem like a huge ask. In fact, she reminds me a lot of Madison when she was Chloe's age. That same raw talent and ambition and determination. The problem with Chloe, the reason why I didn't take her on before, is how she looks."

Moreno frowned. "You mean slim, blonde, and pretty?"

"Exactly. She looks just like every other girl who walks through my door hoping I'll make them rich and famous. But I believed Chloe's role in Madison's disappearance would boost her profile and I'd be able to secure her some auditions off the back of all the attention. It seemed like a situation where everyone would win."

"You had it all worked out, huh?" Sarah said. "But it didn't go to plan. Something went wrong."

Annie nodded. "Madison was supposed to reappear early on Saturday morning. I was glued to the TV waiting for the breaking news. But they just kept playing the same footage from the press conference and all the interviews Jimmy Grand was doing."

"An added bonus for you, what with him also being your client."

"Well, yes, I suppose," Annie said, as if she hadn't already considered all the ways she would benefit. She went on, "I tried calling Madison on her burner phone, but it rang out. I called all weekend.

She didn't pick up. By this morning, I was frantic. That's when I told Chloe to make the call to the tips line."

"When was the last time you spoke to Madison?" Moreno asked.

"Thursday. I told her about your visit and we discussed how it was all going. We were both pleased. There was a lot of interest. Chloe had done well with the socials. I was already getting calls from the media wanting to line up interviews with Madison if she was found safe and well. Some of the studios were in touch too."

"Why the Stargaze Motel?" asked Sarah.

"I don't know," Annie said. "I guess Madison thought it fit the bill. Somewhere with no cameras; the kind of establishment that doesn't take a lot of interest in the guests and what they get up to; close by a highway for Madison's reappearance."

"So the Stargaze Motel was Madison's idea?"

"It was. I'd never heard of it."

"Do you know the name Taylor Rose?"

Annie was thrown by the change of subject. "Of course. It was tragic what happened to that girl. She and Madison were friends. Madison was devastated. Why are you asking about Taylor Rose?"

"Did you know Taylor Rose was murdered at the Stargaze Motel?"

Now Annie Kline looked shocked. "No, I didn't. I mean, I knew the girl was found in a low-rent motel, but I couldn't have told you which one. It must be nearly twenty years ago. I had no idea that Madison was staying at the same place."

Sarah said, "When we spoke to you, you seemed surprised about the note we found in Madison's purse."

Annie frowned and the little upside-down V appeared. "I was surprised. It wasn't part of the plan. I have no idea why it was in her purse. Maybe it was from before, a previous appointment, and she forgot it was in there."

"Maybe. You said you called Madison after we spoke to you last Thursday."

"That's right."

"But you called someone else first, didn't you?"

"Uh, no. I don't think so."

Sarah's cell phone vibrated in her butt pocket with an incoming call.

"Who is Cash?" she asked.

"I've already told you, I don't know."

"That's who you called, isn't it?"

"No."

"Did you tell anyone that Madison was staying at the Stargaze Motel?"

"No."

Annie Kline was starting to look unwell.

Sarah said, "Room fifteen at the Stargaze Motel is a crime scene—and not just because Madison was hiding out there. We have reason to believe a homicide took place in that room."

Annie gripped the edge of the desk for support and swayed like she might keel over.

"Who is Cash, Annie? What did you tell him?"

Annie Kline's face shut down. "I'm not saying another word without my lawyer."

Sarah said to Moreno, "Arrest her for obstruction of justice. That's just for starters. We'll see what else we can add."

She stepped out of the office while Moreno read Annie Kline her Miranda rights. Saw that her missed call was from Nick Delaney.

Sarah stalked past an open-mouthed Kayla and went outside and returned the call.

"I have Taylor Rose's murder book," Nick said. "I've just started reading, but I've already come across something interesting."

"What's that?"

"Guess what room at the Stargaze Motel Taylor Rose's body was found in?"

"Room fifteen."

"Yep."

Sarah said, "Madison and Taylor were friends. She would have known the details of the murder. And she wouldn't have forgotten about it like everyone else."

Nick said what Sarah was thinking. "So, why hide out in that very same room?"

"That's what we need to find out."

# 29
# SARAH
## SEPTEMBER 2022

Tuesday morning.

Annie Kline, as expected, had lawyered up and wasn't talking. But plenty of other folk were. The media was abuzz with news of her arrest: *Agent of missing actress arrested!* Sarah guessed Kayla had earned herself a few bucks for the tipoff. Thankfully, the press still didn't know about what had gone down at the Stargaze Motel.

Moreno was working on the warrant application to access Annie Kline's phone records. Bribing judges with sexual favors and Dodgers tickets wouldn't be necessary to get it signed off. The woman was neck-deep in this mess and the only confirmed person so far who knew where Madison James had been hiding out.

Sarah was going through the cuttings file on Madison and Taylor Rose that Ellen Downey had compiled and left on her desk, when Nick strolled into the office with a battered blue three-ring binder under his arm. He pulled a chair from another desk over to where Sarah sat and made himself comfortable in her cubbyhole. Having him so close to her again made her feel woozy. The familiar scent of his cologne and soap and shampoo was intoxicating. She gulped down the shitty coffee from the vending machine like she was trying to sober up after too many wine coolers.

He tossed the blue folder onto her desk. "Taylor Rose's murder book. I was up until after midnight reading through it all. How's this for irony? She'd recently been cast in a movie called *The Murder Book* when she died. Her character actually appeared in a murder book just like this one. Spooky. Anyway, the film bombed. Moviegoers thought it was insensitive to push ahead with the project after the real-life murder."

Sarah flashed back to a framed poster in Annie Kline's office. Jimmy Grand with a brunette actress by the name of Rachel Rayner. Now she remembered why it'd been familiar. The brief scandal over the recasting and the movie going ahead. It had looked like cashing in on a tragedy. Then it had all been consigned to a distant, hazy memory, at least for Sarah.

Nick said, "Mulgrew was the lead on the case."

Sarah made a face. "No wonder it went cold."

Nick nodded his agreement.

Mulgrew had been a lazy cop who was more interested in counting down the days to his retirement than he was in closing cases. Sarah was pretty sure he never had victims' photos and case files spread across his dining table when he clocked out for the night. He had died on the eighteenth hole of the golf course less than two years after pulling the pin.

"Rick Bird was manager at the Stargaze Motel when Taylor Rose died," Nick said. "He was on duty that night and, get this, was Mulgrew's star witness. He claimed Taylor was with a 'dark-skinned' guy who paid cash for the room. The guy was young, tall, and muscular. Possibly Latino. According to Bird, the girl had seemed a bit wobbly on her feet as they'd walked to the room, but was definitely into the guy and entered the room voluntarily with him."

There was a photofit of the suspect included in the file, but it looked pretty generic to Sarah. The man had never been found.

Nick went on, "Madison James was another witness. She had spoken with Taylor just hours before the murder. She disputed the suggestion that Taylor would have been fooling around with a guy at a motel. She also claimed Taylor never took drugs. The toxicology report showed alcohol and ketamine in her system. She'd had intercourse shortly before her death. Whether it was rape or rough consensual sex was inconclusive. Cause of death was strangulation."

From his notes, it was clear that Mulgrew had been working the theory that Taylor Rose had been partying, had hooked up with the Latino guy, and they had gone to the Stargaze Motel to party some more and have sex. The fun had turned nasty and Taylor had wound up dead.

Nick said, "The boyfriend and the parents were all interviewed and backed up what Madison James said. Taylor was very straight-laced, didn't get blind drunk, never did drugs, didn't have any problems in her relationship with Bradley Huffman."

"Mulgrew had tunnel vision," Sarah said. "He was fixated on the Latino guy and didn't want to look at any other suspects. He took Bird's statement as gospel and ignored the people who knew Taylor Rose best."

"He also didn't follow up too much on the party in the Hills that Madison said Taylor was planning on attending that night. Mulgrew was the worst kind of cop. Lazy and sloppy."

Sarah had googled Taylor Rose the night before. Her death was condensed into a single paragraph on her Wikipedia page. The photo that appeared in most of the image search results was a professional head shot. That and stills from her movies.

Sarah flipped to the front of the murder book. A different photo of Taylor Rose had been slotted into a clear plastic pocket. It wasn't from a studio shoot and Taylor looked a little older than she had in the head shot. She was wearing a gold rose pendant with a tiny diamond in the center.

Sarah had seen that necklace before.

"That necklace Taylor Rose is wearing in the photo. It's in Madison James' apartment."

"There's a note in the murder book about the jewelry." Nick pulled the binder toward him and found the relevant section. "Here it is. The parents asked about the necklace. They said she never took it off. It wasn't on the body. Madison confirmed Taylor had been wearing it when she saw her that night."

Sarah stood and leaned over the privacy divider and brought Moreno up to speed. "We need that necklace recovered from the apartment and bagged ASAP."

"On it," he said.

She sank back into the chair. "So what now?"

Nick said, "I want to have a go at Rick Bird. Something is off about that guy. I'm not buying the Latino hookup story for a minute. Bottom line is, Bird was present when one—possibly two—women died at his motel. And he had access to the room on both occasions." He stood and picked up the murder book. "I'll keep you posted."

Sarah returned to the cuttings file. She'd already read the articles about the Vegas wedding that never happened. She worked her way through the rest. A horror magazine had declared Madison James the next great scream queen following her performance in *Survive the Night.* Photos from the premiere showed Madison posing on the red carpet with a bottle blonde called Ally Hagen who Sarah recognized as having also been in the film.

There were a lot of negative reviews of *The One Year Hitch*, albeit with some complimentary statements about Madison's performance. Jimmy Grand didn't fare so well. "All smolder but no spark," one reviewer observed. There was some standard press stuff for *Do Not Disturb* that included both Madison and Taylor Rose. A few gossipy entries about their friendship and some papped shots of them "out on the town" that looked more like dinner in a quiet restaurant. Taylor featured in a lot more cuttings than Madison because her career had clearly been more successful.

Sarah read the announcement about Taylor Rose starring in *The Murder Book* and a follow-up in a trashy magazine gleefully detailing a spat between her and Madison over Taylor's involvement in the movie.

Press coverage of Madison James dried up completely after that story. The "Red Rose Murder" articles dried up quickly too when the case turned cold with no exciting new developments.

Then *The Murder Book* had been released and bombed, like Nick had said. One final headline caught Sarah's eye:

> Money talks? "Cash" is keeping schtum on box office bomb!

Sarah read the story quickly, her excitement growing. She zeroed in on one particular paragraph:

> Dubbed "Cash" within the industry for his legendary generosity while entertaining guests at his favorite nightspots, Ted Clayton might not be feeling so generous now that his big budget picture just bombed big-time at the box office in its first weekend. Cash declined to comment on the flop.

Cash was Ted Clayton.

# 30

# SARAH

## SEPTEMBER 2022

Sarah rolled to a stop in front of a gigantic soulless white box in the Hollywood Hills that probably didn't offer much change from ten million.

She figured she would be happy to live in a home with no soul if it meant a prestigious zip code and calling the likes of Lady Gaga and Quentin Tarantino her neighbors.

Even though these super-luxe pads all looked the same to her, she thought the great palms and jacarandas flanking the double-wide black-ash front door were familiar. A black Porsche 911 was in the drive, all sexy curves and a mirror-like sheen.

Sarah was fairly sure the house and the car were the same ones used by Jimmy Grand as the backdrop for his TV interview. She assumed Ted Clayton was the "buddy" who hadn't been at home to object to Grand's cheeky opportunity grab.

A Honda Accord was parked next to the Porsche. Even with Sarah's Chevy adding to the mini fleet, there was room for another three cars.

A man who wasn't Ted Clayton answered the door.

He was late twenties and of slim build with fair hair sprayed stiffly in place. He wore a cornflower-blue shirt and very tight jeans and Nike Dunk sneakers that Sarah knew cost a fortune because Nick owned a pair and she had freaked out when she'd found the receipt.

"I'm looking for Ted Clayton," she said.

"Aren't we all?" the man retorted.

"And you are?"

"Jeremiah. I'm Ted's assistant."

Sarah introduced herself and showed her badge. "Can I come in?"

"Nope. Not unless I legally *have* to let you in, and I'm guessing I don't."

"Seriously? It's just a chat."

"It's not my place to invite you in. Like, literally. Seeing as I don't live here."

"Mr. Clayton isn't at home?"

"Nope."

"Then how'd you get in?"

Jeremiah rolled his eyes. "Duh, I have a key. So I can drop off Ted's dry cleaning and pick up his mail and make sure there's food in the refrigerator and do anything else that Ted decides he wants doing."

"But you don't know where he is?"

"No," he said slowly. "That's why I'm here, looking for him."

"It's kind of awkward, doing this on the doorstep."

Jeremiah shrugged. "Sorry. Not my home."

"Don't you have access to Ted Clayton's schedule?"

"Of course I have access. I *run* the schedule. But Ted doesn't always stick to the schedule. If he decides he wants to take off and spend all day on the golf course, that's exactly what he'll do. Despite the ten meetings he has planned for that day. When he's on set, it's a different story—Ted is Mr. Reliable. When he's between movies . . . total nightmare. Like looking after a child."

"Could he be on the golf course just now? It's important that I speak to him."

The young man shook his head and the hair didn't move. "Ted isn't on the course. I already checked with the clubhouse. Honestly? He could be anywhere. Meantime, who's left to explain why he didn't show up for a lunch date or a meeting with the scriptwriters or take a call from the studio? Oh yes, that would be me."

"When was the last time you saw him?"

"Thursday afternoon."

"Thursday?" Sarah couldn't hide her surprise. "That was days ago."

The same day Annie Kline made a call right after she found out about the note mentioning "Cash" in Madison James' purse.

"Tell me about it," Jeremiah huffed.

"Did he get a call that day?"

"He would've gotten lots of calls."

"Was one of them from Annie Kline?" Sarah asked.

"Maybe. Maybe not. I couldn't say for sure."

"Have you spoken to Ted Clayton since last Thursday?"

"He's not picking up."

"Isn't that unusual? Aren't you worried?"

Jeremiah shrugged. "It's not unheard of for him to go AWOL like this. One time, he chartered a private jet to Paris with a new girlfriend and didn't tell me. I thought he was in Bel-Air and he was in France."

Sarah said, "Have you ever heard anyone call him Cash?"

"Sure. All the time. I don't, though. I think it's kind of vulgar, but he doesn't seem to mind."

"Is the Porsche his?"

"Well, it's not mine. Not on my salary. The sneakers are as good as it gets."

Sarah frowned. "So, he took off without his car?"

Jeremiah's smile was condescending. "Ted has more than one car. People who live in neighborhoods like this usually do."

Sarah had pulled Ted Clayton's property and DMV records herself. "Only the Porsche is registered in his name," she said.

"The Range Rover is registered to one of his companies. Don't ask me why. Probably something to do with the IRS. Same with his other house."

"Other house? What other house?"

Jeremiah waved a hand dismissively. "Oh, he won't be there. In this heat? Are you kidding? He only stays out there in the winter months."

"Where exactly is this other house?"

"Palm Springs."

The little hairs on Sarah's arms stood on end.

"I'm going to need the address."

# 31
# MADISON
## AUGUST 2022

The dress still fitted.

Madison hadn't worn it in years. It had languished at the back of the closet in a box, following the move from her old apartment to her current home in Studio City seven years ago. It hadn't been unpacked because it was a reminder of one of the worst days of her life, which had ultimately been the catalyst for her acting career ending up as a dumpster fire. Madison didn't know why she'd even kept it.

Now she was glad that she had.

She smoothed the material over her slim hips and turned to assess her reflection. The regular yoga and SoulCycle classes had paid off. Madison was the same size at almost forty that she'd been when she was twenty.

It was the perfect choice. He had liked it once before. She needed him to still like it. To still want her.

When #MeToo had happened and a spotlight was shone on the industry, and actresses were brave enough to come forward and talk about what really went on in those beautiful hotel suites at the hands of men who held all the power in Hollywood, Madison had waited for Ted Clayton to be exposed as an abuser.

She was too insignificant, too cowardly, to strike first. But when others named him—and she was sure there would be many others—Madison would add her voice. She would be vindicated. People would know what Ted Clayton had done in that hotel suite and how he'd destroyed her as a woman and then as an actress. Madison would have a sense of justice and, once his lies fell away and the truth was revealed, she might just be able to salvage her career.

It didn't happen. None of it. No allegations. No truth. No vindication.

Clayton kept on directing movies and casting beautiful young actresses and demanding respect in Hollywood. He was nominated for awards. He posed at his house in the Hills for "at home" features in quality publications. He married for a third time to a woman half his age. The new wife didn't stick around for long, but Ted Clayton was like Teflon.

He was going nowhere.

Cash Clayton was still throwing his money around in VIP bars and clubs all over the Strip.

And Madison was broke.

Her rent had gone up, the Mustang wasn't going to pass its next inspection, and her credit card was maxed out. The "past due" notices were piling up.

The Joneses was busy, it was doing well, but the pandemic had taken a toll and the restaurant had taken a long time to start turning a profit again. Madison didn't want to ask Larissa and Tre for a raise.

She was desperate. She was almost forty and had nothing to show for her life other than a few movies a lifetime ago and a bunch of broken dreams.

Madison had called Ted Clayton.

She had gone to Annie's office when she knew she would be out at a meeting, and sent her latest receptionist off on an errand. Then she had accessed Annie's contacts and made the call from her manager's desk before she could lose her nerve.

Clayton had crushed her career, and he had the power to resurrect it.

One movie role. That's all it would take.

Madison would get down on her knees and beg. She would do more than beg. She would do whatever Ted Clayton asked her to.

He had sounded surprised to hear from her. Then amused. He had agreed to meet her. Madison wasn't sure that he would. The address was in Palm Springs. She knew he had a second home in the desert, because Annie had been there for meetings a handful of times, but she was surprised because he usually went there in the winter months. It was August now and hotter than hell.

Palm Springs was a two-hour drive. Just as she was entering the city, the fuel gauge on the dash blinked red. The Mustang's tank was almost empty. Madison stopped at a small Valero pump station off State Route 111. Filled up and bought a bottle of water.

She was nervous. Her stomach churned. But at least she knew what she was walking into this time. She knew what Ted Clayton was. She wasn't that young girl riding an elevator with no idea what awaited her in a $600-a-night penthouse suite.

His street was quietly rich and comprised candy-colored mid-century modern homes with sharp edges and retro features that were straight out of a *Stepford Wives* fever dream. His house was a pink and cream stucco and stone oasis in the desert, with a rock frontage and succulent lawn, set in an acre of landscaped grounds. Madison knocked and Clayton took his time answering. He was making her wait. Making her sweat.

When the door finally opened, she got her first up-close look at him in years.

Clayton was over sixty now. Expensive platinum highlights blended with gray hair that was thinning. The tan couldn't hide the spider veins on his face, the result of drinking Scotch every day for decades. He was still out of shape. The curve of a belly was visible under his Armani shirt.

He smiled. He'd had his teeth done. Perfectly straight white veneers. The smile chilled her in the warm night breeze.

"Madison James." His eyes travelled the length of her body. "Pretty dress. Come on in."

He showed her into a living room with a rock fireplace and low beams and floor-to-ceiling sliding doors leading to a generous outdoor space with a pool, firepit, and majestic views of the mountains.

He went over to a crystal decanter filled with whisky, like the one in the Fulton Majestic, and asked if she wanted a drink. This time Madison accepted. He poured two doubles and handed her one.

The amber liquid burned her throat and heat spread through her bones.

Clayton sat on an armchair and casually rested a foot on the other knee. She took the couch, back rigid with tension.

"What do you want, Madison?"

He was straight to the point. So was she.

"A role in your next movie."

He smiled, amused. "Why would I do that? I have a million girls who want to star in my movies. Why you?"

Madison wanted to say "because you owe me."

What she said was, "You told me once you could make me a star. I want you to make me a star."

"I have a million girls who want me to make them a star. Pretty young girls who are prepared to do whatever it takes to make it happen."

Madison gulped the rest of the whisky. "I'm prepared to do whatever it takes."

Clayton smiled again. "You're still a very beautiful woman, Madison."

"Thank you."

He got up from the chair and she thought he was going to join her on the couch. Instead, he went over to a vintage teak sideboard and opened a drawer. He removed a small wooden case from the drawer.

Clayton turned to her. "What are you, forty now?"

Madison considered lying. She'd edited her age on her Wikipedia page to thirty-one, but Clayton had known her for too long to be fooled. The math simply didn't add up.

"Not yet," she said.

He nodded once and opened the lid of the wooden case and selected a fat Cuban. He examined the cigar. Replaced it. Picked out another. Returned the case to the drawer. He looked at her. "Still beautiful. But too old."

"What?"

"For the movie. For me."

Madison was stunned. Clayton was turning her down? She flushed hard.

He took the cigar and a box of matches over to the patio doors and slid them open. "The dress was a nice touch. But we're done here. You can see yourself out?"

Embarrassment turned to anger. Now she knew why Ted Clayton had suggested meeting in Palm Springs. He had made her drive all the way out here to make the rejection sting even more. Humiliate her.

"Can I at least use the restroom before I go? It's a long drive back to LA."

"Of course. Second door on the left in the hallway."

He stepped outside into the backyard and lit the cigar. Puffed big fat plumes into the twilight night. Slid the doors shut. She was dismissed.

Madison left the living room. She didn't go to the bathroom. She went looking for the primary suite.

She wasn't leaving empty-handed.

Clayton had been wearing a weighty Rolex. He was a watch fanatic. He had shown off his impressive collection in that "at home" feature about his Hollywood Hills house. Madison bet he had a few here in Palm Springs too.

She headed for the huge walk-in closet. Chinos and jeans and shirts all with designer tags hung on one side. Italian suits cut to perfection and cashmere coats on the other. Shelving was filled with pricy sneakers and buffed leather dress shoes.

In the center of the closet was a dresser island. She pulled open the top drawer. It displayed fifty silk ties. She tried the next one. Jackpot. Six watches still in their chunky cases. She grabbed a Breitling and a TAG Heuer and dropped them into her purse.

Madison was about to leave. But there were two more drawers. She opened the third one. More jewelry boxes. These were smaller and each was decorated with embossed letters. Madison guessed they were items that had once belonged to his wives or old girlfriends. She picked up a red velvet square box with "TR" on the front. Opened it.

Stared at what was inside.

It made no sense.

A tiny gold rose pendant with a diamond in the center.

Madison hadn't seen it in years but she recognized it instantly. A twenty-first birthday gift that Taylor Rose never took off.

Why was it in Ted Clayton's closet?

The delicate chain had been snapped.

Madison tipped the necklace into her purse and returned the empty box to the drawer along with the others.

She opened the final drawer. It was a sock drawer. All navy or black and balled into pairs. Hidden among the socks were other items. Madison realized what she was looking at.

Now Taylor's broken necklace made sense.

# 32

# MADISON

## SEPTEMBER 2022

## (LAST THURSDAY)

After four days at the Stargaze Motel, cabin fever was setting in.

The curtains had been drawn the whole time and the absence of daylight was suffocating. Madison paced the small room for exercise and to loosen her muscles. She had finished the paperback by Tuesday. Mostly she watched the news. They'd showed a clip of Chloe Reid's TikTok when she "found" the purse. The girl was good. Madison had been impressed.

Today's footage of the search party gathering at The Joneses had broken her heart. Larissa had been interviewed and looked dreadful. Madison's disappearance was clearly taking a toll. The guilt was almost unbearable. Her actions were hurting people. Madison tried not to think about how her mom would be feeling right now.

Annie had called earlier and told her two detectives had visited the office. They had asked a lot of questions but she didn't think they suspected what was really going on. Annie had sounded kind of weird. Then she'd asked about the note and Madison had feigned ignorance.

"It's an old purse," she'd said. "Must be a note from years ago."

"That's what I thought," Annie had said, but she didn't sound convinced.

Madison's plan—the one Annie Kline didn't know about—was to frame Ted Clayton for her abduction. She would tell the police that he'd starved and tortured her and kept her captive in room fifteen of the Stargaze Motel, but that she had managed to escape before he'd killed her.

She would frame him because he had murdered her best friend and she wanted him to pay for what he'd done.

The "TR" box that Taylor's pendant had been stored in at his Palm Springs home.

The dozens of small glass vials labeled "Ketamine" hidden in his sock drawer.

Clayton was drugging women and raping them. But something had gone wrong with Taylor. Something had happened that meant she'd wound up being strangled to death.

Madison had planned on reporting Clayton to the police, but by the time she'd returned from Palm Springs, cold hard reality had set in. She had no proof that the necklace had ever been in his closet. Even if she told them about the "TR" jewelry box and the drugs, it wouldn't be enough to justify searching his home. Clayton was rich, just like Jefferson Cantwell. And just like Cantwell, the big-shot movie director would have the best lawyers in the city at his disposal.

He would win.

If she wanted to prove his guilt, Madison would have to become a victim herself.

The star witness in her own abduction.

The plan would have to be plausible, believable. Clayton would deny it all, so her story had to be as convincing as possible.

Her DNA would be all over room fifteen at the Stargaze Motel from her "captivity"—having trashed her own belongings first before making her "escape."

Madison had also left the note in the purse and Taylor's necklace in her apartment for the police to find. The note would hopefully put the cops on "Cash" Clayton's trail, so that when she accused him of being her abductor his name wouldn't be completely out of the blue. The note would be a little early clue.

The necklace would be Clayton's "motive" for the kidnap and planned murder that she would fabricate. She would tell the police that Clayton had figured out she'd found the jewelry and suspected his role in killing Taylor Rose, so Madison had to be eliminated.

She'd say he'd kept her handcuffed to a bed with hardly any food or water and he had tortured her to find out if she'd told anyone else about Taylor's pendant. Her weight loss and injuries—all self-inflicted—would compellingly back up her claims.

Madison knew the police would still ask difficult questions and she'd need an answer for all of them.

First up, they'd want to know why Ted Clayton would invite her to an audition—one that she could tell other people about—and then abduct her.

The simple answer was that he wouldn't—so there had to be some confusion over who she was auditioning for.

Madison would tell the cops she'd been approached at The Joneses by a production assistant who claimed to be working on behalf of a famous director. The director wanted Madison to try out for the lead in his new movie. The project was so top-secret that the production assistant couldn't even divulge the identity of the director yet for fear of it being leaked to the media. It had all sounded hinky to Madison until the woman told her where and when the audition would be held—Monday at noon at the Fulton Majestic. Madison knew Ted Clayton had once favored the venue, and she'd visited him recently to ask for a role in his next movie, so she thought the mystery director might be Ted "Cash" Clayton but didn't know for sure. Hence the note with the question marks.

Madison knew the cops would also ask why she'd agreed to audition for Ted Clayton after finding Taylor's necklace at his home. She'd thought long and hard about that one. Decided she'd tell them she'd found the necklace and taken it and then realized there was probably a perfectly innocent explanation.

All these years later, Madison would tell them, she wasn't even sure that Taylor *had* been wearing the rose pendant the night she died. Madison had been so used to seeing Taylor wearing it that maybe she'd assumed and got it wrong. Maybe her friend had lost it at Ted Clayton's Palm Springs home days or weeks earlier. Maybe he'd found it and didn't even know it was hers. He probably had a lot of women in that house. Maybe he'd put it in a box to get fixed and had forgotten all about it.

Madison would tell the police that she'd seen no reason not to meet the director. The idea that he could have been involved in the murder was ridiculous, surely? Taylor Rose had been murdered by a tall, muscular, Latino man. Not Ted Clayton.

It was all bullshit.

Madison hadn't been mistaken. Taylor had been wearing the necklace the last time she saw her. Clayton had had the necklace and he'd had the exact drug they'd found in Taylor's system. He had killed her. Madison just needed to prove it.

Everything appeared to be going to plan. Madison was restricting her food intake to a single Cup Noodle meal and a Snickers each day. The waistband on her PJs was starting to feel looser. The cuffs had raised the skin on her wrists into angry welts. The cheekbone under her left eye was bruised and swollen where she'd punched herself. Not as hard as Jimmy Grand had once punched her, but hard enough to leave a mark.

There would be one other crucial question the cops would throw at her: Why had her abductor faked an audition instead of just snatching her outside her apartment or the restaurant?

Annie had already asked the question when they'd discussed their plan. Madison had told her the mention of an audition would remind everyone that she was an actress. If she was snatched from outside The Joneses, the media would call her "the waitress." If she vanished on her way to an audition, she would be known as "the actress." Annie had seen her point.

Of course, Madison would need to come up with a different answer for the cops.

She stood in the bathroom now, under a bare yellow lightbulb, and faced the mirror. Practiced a little shoulder shrug and a sad expression. "I guess Ted Clayton wanted to get my hopes up one last time that I was going to be a star. He'd kill the dream one more time. And then he'd kill me."

Madison picked up a pair of scissors from the washbasin. Her hair had always been her thing, but it had to go. This had to look real. She grabbed a fistful and, before she could change her mind, chopped it off. Hair floated into the basin like confetti in the wind. She cut off another chunk, even longer this time. It couldn't be neat. It wasn't a haircut at a salon.

Snip, snip, snip.

She heard a creak from the other room.

Madison froze.

Listened.

Had she imagined it?

She went into the bedroom, the carpet sticky under her bare feet. Stood there in the middle of the room. All she could hear was the TV burbling with the volume down low. She tossed the scissors onto the nightstand next to the room key and picked up the burner phone. There had been no calls or texts from Annie while she was in the bathroom. Madison started toward the window to peek out the curtain. She'd made it halfway across the room when she heard something else.

The scrape of metal against metal.

Then the creaking sound again as the doorknob turned.

The door opened.

Ted Clayton stepped into the room. He was holding a key with a "15" fob just like her own. He used it to lock the door behind him.

"Surprise."

"What . . . what are you doing here?" Madison stuttered.

She backed away from him until she hit the queen bed.

"I'm here to fix a problem. One that you've created."

Fear ripped through her. "I don't know what you mean."

"Oh, I think you do," Clayton said. "When I discovered the necklace was gone it was weeks after your visit. I couldn't be sure it was you who took it. Then I got a call from Annie Kline today. The cops had been to see her about your so-called disappearance. They'd shown her a note that mentioned Cash and the Fulton Majestic. Annie knew what it meant but she didn't tell them. She wanted to warn me that the cops might want to speak to me. She told me not to worry. Assured me you were fine. Wouldn't say anything else."

"How did you know where to find me?"

"If you were fine, you were hiding out someplace. I gave it some thought. I considered the note and the missing necklace and I called my friend Mr. Bird on the front desk, who confirmed a woman had checked in Monday and had specifically asked for room fifteen. Now what conclusion do you think I came to?"

Tears rolled down Madison's cheeks. "You killed Taylor," she whispered. "Why?"

Clayton looked sad, just for a moment, then he shrugged. "I didn't plan it. She wasn't meant to die. I didn't even plan on slipping some Kit Kat into her drink. She was coming to my house in the Hills to talk about the movie. That's all."

"She told me she was going to a party."

Clayton smirked. "I guess she didn't want to hurt your feelings by telling you the truth. Sweet Taylor Rose. Too sweet for her own good. When she showed up that night wearing that red dress, I knew I had to have her. I'd always wanted her, ever since the first day I set eyes on her. Do you know, she's the only actress who's ever rejected me during a visit to my hotel suite? It made me want her even more. She was special. She was different. She was *better* than the rest of you. But I'd resisted for years. Then . . . that night . . . that red dress. So, I mixed a little Kit Kat into her champagne. Figured it would loosen her up. That's what it does, produces dissociative sensations and hallucinations. Often leaves users with no memory of events while under its influence. Which is handy for me."

"But something went wrong."

He nodded. "I guess I fucked up the dosage. She wasn't as out of it as I'd thought when I took her into the master suite and started making love to her. She fought back like a little wild animal. Wouldn't stop screaming."

"So, you strangled her. You murdered her. Then you brought her here to this filthy motel to dump her body."

"I had no choice. I told you, it wasn't planned. I was sorry she had to die. That girl was going to be a star. Not like you."

Madison tried to swallow but her throat had gone dry. She could barely breathe. "What are you going to do?"

Clayton reached into his pocket and pulled out a knife. The blade was long and sharp. He said, "You know, you never were final girl material."

Then he lunged so fast that Madison didn't know what was happening until she was on the bed and Ted Clayton was on top of her.

He squeezed her throat with one hand and raised the knife with the other.

# 33

# SARAH

## SEPTEMBER 2022

Sarah called Moreno from the Ventura Freeway.

"Ted Clayton isn't at his Hollywood Hills home. His assistant hasn't seen or heard from him since last Thursday."

Moreno said, "The same day Madison James stopped answering her burner phone."

"Also the same day we think Annie Kline tipped off Clayton about the note."

"I'm still working on Kline's call records."

"Clayton has a second home in Palm Springs," Sarah said. "I'm heading there now."

"Do you think Madison visited him in Palm Springs the night of Kitty Duvall's book club?"

"That's exactly what I think. He has a second car too. A black Range Rover. The assistant thinks it's registered to one of his companies rather than Clayton himself."

Moreno said, "I'll see what I can find out. Try to track the Range Rover."

"Keep me posted."

Sarah pulled up Nick's number next. "Any update?" she asked.

"Bird is sticking to his story. Still claims Taylor Rose entered the room with a Latino guy the night of the murder. Still says he hasn't seen Madison James since she checked in on Monday. He's hiding something—he's shifty as hell with those crazy eyes—but I'm not sure he's our doer."

"Anything else?"

"We have one guest at the Stargaze Motel unaccounted for. He stayed in room fourteen, right next door to Madison. Checked in Friday lunchtime, left on Saturday. None of the other guests saw or heard anything. You ask me, most of them are probably in the system and wouldn't tell us even if they did. It's that kind of quality establishment. Where are you? Sounds like you're on the road."

Sarah brought him up to speed. She said, "I've got a bad feeling about this."

"What's the address? I'm coming out there too."

"No, Nick. You're not. If I need backup, I'll contact the local cops."

"Just give me the address, Sarah."

She sighed. Gave him the address.

The smoggy suburban sprawl gradually gave way to dry, flat desert and a clear tanzanite sky. Dozens of wind turbines sliced through the hot, dry air. Moreno was back on the speaker system.

"What do you have?" Sarah asked.

"Annie Kline's phone records—and confirmation that she did call Ted Clayton last Thursday. And that's not all."

"What else?"

"I found the company that owns the Palm Springs property and got the details of the Range Rover. There's a BOLO on the car now. I also had a look at the traffic cameras nearest to the Stargaze Motel. There was a black Range Rover close by the motel late on Thursday and then again on Friday."

"Nice work, Moreno."

"Don't get too excited. The plates don't match the one registered to Clayton's company."

"He could have switched them. Trying to cover his tracks. Clayton is our man, Moreno. I can feel it."

She disconnected.

A while later, Sarah passed the pump station where Madison had filled up seven weeks ago—right before something had happened that had left her scared and shaken.

The GPS led her down a quiet Palm Springs street and then announced she had reached her destination. She was in front of a pink and cream single-story construction with a rock frontage. It was very 1950s and reminded her of the houses in the trailer for the new Harry Styles movie *Don't Worry Darling*, where bad shit happened in a seemingly idyllic town. All the blinds were pulled down despite it being the middle of the day. A black Range Rover was in the driveway.

Sarah called Moreno. "I'm at the house. The car is here."

"What's the license plate?"

She read it out.

"That's not the plate for the car registered to the company. It's a match for the Rover that was in the vicinity of the Stargaze Motel."

Sarah got out of the Chevy, the phone still at her ear, and approached the house. As she got closer, she noticed the trunk of the car hanging lower than it should be. A few more steps and the smell confirmed her worst fears.

She said into the phone, "We have a body in the trunk." A shadow passed across the front window. "Someone's in the house."

"Okay, Sarah. I'm hanging up now and contacting Palm Springs PD. Don't do anything. Wait for backup."

She retreated to her car.

Nick arrived before the local black-and-whites. He slid into the passenger seat.

"How'd you get here so fast?"

He grinned. "Blue lights all the way on the freeway."

Sarah said, "Madison James is dead. She's in the trunk."

The grin vanished. "Oh, fuck."

Nick's cell phone rang. He answered.

Sarah's own phone shrilled. It was Moreno.

The wail of sirens shattered the calm of the quiet neighborhood as two cruisers rounded the corner and careered to a stop next to them.

Sarah and Nick ended their calls.

He said, "We finally tracked down the missing guest. He says he saw the woman in room fifteen. He helped her load a very heavy suitcase into the trunk of a black Range Rover around noon last Friday."

Sarah nodded. "We just got the forensics back. The blood in the motel room doesn't belong to Madison James."

# 34

# MADISON

## SEPTEMBER 2022

## (LAST THURSDAY)

Madison couldn't breathe. Couldn't force air into her lungs.

The room was suddenly dimmer. A thicker darkness crept into the edges of her vision. White sparks exploded in front of her eyes.

Somewhere, far away, TV voices spoke her name and sounded like they were underwater.

Her hands clawed frantically at Clayton, scratching his skin, trying to free the hand from her throat. Through the cloudiness and tiny explosions, she saw the knife raised above her, its blade glinting wickedly in the glare from the television screen.

Madison reached desperately for the nightstand and knocked over a glass tumbler. She fought to stay conscious, battled against the blackness. Her fingers closed around the scissors. She gripped them. Swung them at Clayton.

A warm wetness enveloped her. Sharp pain shot through her shoulder. There was a gasp. A hiss. The pressure on her throat slackened and Madison sucked in a raw, painful breath. Then another.

The air tasted metallic. The cloying scent was thick in her nostrils. Her chest heaved. She drank in the rancid air like it was cold water in the desert. Her vision cleared. She became aware of the heavy weight still on top of her. Madison heaved Clayton to the other side of the bed.

The scissors were blade-deep in his neck. A small fountain of red spurted from the wound. She had hit an artery. His eyes were glazed. His face had a waxy, gray sheen in the gloom. He was making a terrible gargling sound.

He was still alive.

Madison pulled the scissors from his neck and held them two-handed above his shuddering body, and then she brought them down hard into his heart. She did it again. And again. The shuddering stopped. The gargling silenced. His eyes stilled and became empty.

Ted Clayton was dead.

Madison dropped the scissors. Sweat and blood soaked her pajamas. Her shoulder felt like it was on fire. Clayton's knife was on the pillow, blood on its sharp point. It had nicked the skin. Her blow had knocked his off target. Otherwise Madison would be dead instead of him. The lamp was on the floor, its bulb shattered, but she could see that the once-white sheets were now crimson red.

Her brain inexplicably flashed to the scene in *A Nightmare on Elm Street* when Freddy Krueger sliced up Johnny Depp's character and he was sucked into his own bed, leaving behind only a horrific bloody mess. That's how the motel room looked now. Except Clayton's body was still here.

Madison climbed off the bed and crawled across the filthy carpet and leaned against the far wall. She sat there for a long time until the shock wore off and the reality of what she'd done hit her like an eighteen-wheeler.

She had killed a man. She had taken a life.

No.

She had saved herself. Clayton had tried to kill her.

He had murdered Taylor.

Madison thought of the other jewelry boxes in his closet drawer, all bearing different initials.

She was sure he had killed others too.

The burner phone was still on the dresser. Madison should call 911. It'd been self-defense. She'd done nothing wrong.

But what if the police didn't believe her?

She had stabbed him four times.

Then there was the motel manager. Rick Bird had lied once before to protect Clayton. What if he lied again? What if he claimed Madison had set the whole thing up to murder in cold blood the famous film director who had destroyed her career?

She sat there against the wall for a long time, until milky light began to bleed through the gap in the heavy curtains as a long terrible night gave way to a new day.

Madison knew what she had to do.

She peeled off the pajamas that had hardened with Clayton's blood and removed her underwear. Got under the hot shower and washed her hair and scrubbed her skin until it hurt and the water ran clear. Toweled herself dry and then wiped down the stall.

Back in the bedroom, Madison tried to ignore the body on the bed. She dressed in the black jeans, sweater, and sneakers she had changed into on Monday. She tied her hair in a band and tugged on the blonde wig. Then she took a big breath and went over to Clayton. Didn't look at his face as she searched his pockets. Came up with a keyring that included a fob for a Range Rover.

Madison could leave Clayton here while she gathered evidence of his crimes. It would be a whole lot easier. But what if Bird checked the room? It would be even worse for her. It would look like she was on the run. Madison needed to buy herself time. She needed to move the body.

She slid on the sunglasses and cracked open the door. There was no Range Rover in the parking bay.

*Shit.*

She stuck her head out. No one was around. She glanced down the line of motel rooms to the office. No one behind the desk either. She pocketed the key Clayton had used to access her room and stepped outside. Her sneakers crunched on the gravel as she rounded the building. The Range Rover was in front of the row of dumpsters at the gable end.

Madison got in behind the wheel and went in search of the biggest roller suitcase she could find.

◆ ◆ ◆

When she returned to the motel, she expected to find flashing blue lights and yellow crime scene tape. Cops waiting to arrest her.

There was no hive of police activity.

A young guy was behind the desk in the office watching an iPad. Bird hadn't started his shift yet. Madison backed the Range Rover up to the door and removed the suitcase from the trunk.

Inside the room, she placed the suitcase flat on the floor, at the foot of the bed. Unzipped it. Rolled Clayton's body off the bed and into the open case with some considerable effort. Perspiration dampened her brow and top lip. Her scalp was sweaty and itchy under the wig. She pulled it off and cast it aside. It took some time to fold the limbs so they would fit. The metallic stink of his blood mixed with her own sweat made her gag. Madison tried not to vomit. She threw the bloodied pajamas and towels and scissors and knife into the case. Took a thick brown blanket from the closet shelf and covered the bloodied bed sheets. Unlocked the door and tossed the key Clayton had used to access the room into the case too. She zipped it up. Clayton was not a slender man and she groaned and heaved and finally managed to get the suitcase upright. Her muscles burned and she was breathing hard.

Madison put on the sunglasses and opened the door of the room, then popped the trunk of the Range Rover with the key fob. She half pushed, half dragged the heavy case outside, wondering how the hell she was going to lift it into the car.

Then she stopped dead.

Room fourteen's parking bay was occupied. The room door was wide open. A middle-aged man in a cheap shiny suit appeared in the doorway. He spotted her and said, "Hey, let me help you with that."

Before Madison could object, he took hold of the suitcase and tried to lift it.

"Jeez." He laughed. "You got a dead body in there or something?"

Madison smiled weakly. "I guess I overpacked."

"My wife is always the same. A weekend break and she takes enough clothes and toiletries for a month."

They took an end each and managed to heave the case into the trunk.

She climbed behind the wheel and slammed the door and hit the gas and realized she hadn't even thanked the man.

Madison drove to Palm Springs, to the pink and cream house with the rock frontage and cactus-filled lawn. She left the Range Rover and Ted Clayton in the driveway. She tried all the keys on the ring she'd taken from his pocket and none of them fitted the front door.

*Shit.*

She returned to the car. Rummaged in the glovebox. Found another set of keys with a Palm Springs fob. Once inside, Madison made her way directly to the primary suite. She entered the closet. Pulled open the third drawer down of the island dresser.

It was empty.

# 35

# SARAH

## SEPTEMBER 2022

More cruisers arrived.

A coroner's wagon was parked at the end of the street. A forensics unit was also on standby. But first there was a live situation to deal with.

Madison James hadn't died in room fifteen of the Stargaze Motel. She was not in the trunk of the Range Rover. Sarah thought Madison was inside the house. She was also pretty sure that Madison had killed Ted Clayton.

Relief battled with despair.

The property was surrounded now. There was no escape. No way to steal through the backyard and through the palm trees and out into the vast desert. There was nowhere to run.

But Sarah didn't think that was the plan anyway.

Madison James could have been long gone by now. She could have been in the wind for days, but she wasn't. She could have had a head start, but didn't. Sarah had no idea if Madison was armed. Had no idea what her endgame was.

She said to a uniform, "Can we find out if there's a phone inside the house? We need to speak to her."

"Roger that."

"I'm guessing Clayton is the stiff in the trunk," Nick said. "What a fucking mess."

"We don't have an ID on the blood yet but it looks that way. What the hell happened in that motel room, Nick?"

He didn't answer. His eyes strayed to the street behind her and he sucked in a breath. "Fuck. SWAT are here. Shit just got serious."

Sarah heard the roar of an engine and turned to see a big black Lenco BearCat screech to a halt. A team of eight piled out of the tactical vehicle decked out in helmets and bulletproof vests and wielding riot shields and assault rifles.

"Who the hell called in SWAT?" she said.

"That would be me."

The voice belonged to a man in his fifties who was wearing an ill-fitting pinstriped suit and an ill-advised mustache. At least the facial furniture was more Tom Selleck than Errol Flynn.

"And you are?" Sarah snapped, even though she knew immediately that the guy in the suit was a local dick looking for a territorial pissing contest.

He pulled his ID. "Detective Lou Kelly from Palm Springs PD. I gather you two are Detectives Delaney and Delaney from LAPD? Matching names, huh? Cute."

Sarah nodded at the SWAT team, who looked hyped and ready for action as they awaited instructions. "Do you really think the theatrics are necessary? The situation is under control."

"Really?" Kelly scoffed. "You have a stiff in the trunk and a suspect holed up in the house, possibly armed and dangerous. The team will initiate negotiations immediately and, if that doesn't work, they're going in. My turf, my call."

Sarah tried not to show her alarm. "I'm trying to establish contact with the house. Deal with the situation calmly. If she sees a SWAT team outside she could panic. Do something stupid."

"She?" Kelly asked sharply. "This property belongs to Ted Clayton. He's not the one inside?"

"We think he's the stiff in the trunk," Nick said.

"Jesus!" Kelly shook his head. He looked sick.

"You knew him?" Nick asked.

"Everyone in Palm Springs knew him. He was involved with the film festival. He donated money to the city. We golfed together whenever he was in town. He was a great guy." Kelly's gaze wandered to the Range Rover and he shook his head again and tutted softly. "Jeez, Ted." He turned back to Sarah. "Who's in the house?" he asked angrily.

"We believe it's the missing actress, Madison James."

"She killed him?"

"We don't know all the facts yet," she answered carefully.

The uniform returned. "There's a landline registered to the property." He gave Sarah the number.

"Let me speak to her," Sarah said to Kelly. "SWAT isn't the answer here."

The older detective stared at her hard. Then nodded once, curtly. "Speak to her. If she doesn't come out, we're going in. This ends now one way or another."

Sarah plugged the digits into her cell phone. Didn't really expect an answer. It rang and rang loudly in her ear. The ringing echoed more faintly from inside the house. Kelly strolled over to the tactical vehicle. Going by the look on his face when he'd found out his buddy Ted Clayton was dead, Sarah figured he'd be itching to pull the trigger himself if let loose inside the house.

"Come on, Madison," she muttered. "Pick up the damn phone!"

"Hello?"

The voice was small and scared, but Sarah recognized it from *Survive the Night* and *The One Year Hitch* and *Do Not Disturb*.

"Madison?" The word came out in a breath of relief. "You're speaking to Detective Sarah Delaney."

"You're the one who was trying to find me."

"That's right. First up, are you okay, Madison? Are you in need of medical assistance?"

"I'm fine. A knife wound on my shoulder. It's stopped bleeding."

"Can you talk me through what happened, Madison?"

"I killed him."

"Ted Clayton?"

"I killed him," she repeated. Her voice sounded weird, trance-like. "You can't help me now. Maybe I should just die too. You have guns outside, right?" She laughed softly, bitterly. "If I die, I'll finally be famous. If I don't, I'll rot in jail for the rest of my life because of him."

There was a click.

Madison had hung up.

Sarah stared at the cell phone in her hand.

"Fuck."

"What happened?" Nick asked.

Kelly strode toward her. He stood with his hands on his hips, beer belly overhanging his belt. "Is she coming out? Is she armed?"

"I . . . I don't know. We, uh, lost connection."

"Okay, we tried negotiation. It didn't work. Now we go in."

"No! Let me try again."

Sarah redialed the number with shaking fingers.

Again, the phone rang and rang.

*Answer, Madison! Your life depends on it!*

The call connected.

Madison didn't speak. Sarah could hear her breathing on the other end of the line.

"I can help you," she said quickly. "It's not too late to fix this, Madison."

Finally, Madison spoke.

"He tried to kill me." The trance-like voice was gone. She sounded lucid and resolute now. "He killed my friend, Taylor Rose. Ted Clayton killed lots of other women too."

*Shit.*

"Are you armed, Madison?"

"What?"

"Do you have a weapon?"

"No."

"I need you to walk out of the front door with your arms raised. Do you think you can do that, Madison?"

Nick and Kelly watched her intently.

"I can prove it. I have proof that he killed all those women."

"What proof?"

"It's right here. Inside the house."

Sarah hesitated a beat. "Will you show me?"

A long pause.

"You promise you can help me?"

"Yes."

"Okay, I'll show you. Then I'll give myself up."

Madison ended the call.

"What did she say?" Nick asked. "Is she coming out?"

"No. I'm going in."

"Like hell you are. Have you lost your mind?"

Kelly said, "The only people going into that house are the SWAT guys. Don't try to be a hero, missy."

Sarah ignored him.

"I have my weapon," she said to Nick.

"She could pull a gun on you first," he reasoned.

"She said she isn't armed."

"And you're just going to take her word for it? What the fuck, Sarah?"

"She's scared. She's admitted to killing Ted Clayton. We need to end this without anyone else getting hurt. Including Madison."

Nick shook his head. "I still don't like it."

Kelly put his hands up. "If this goes sideways, it's on the LAPD. You made the call."

Sarah walked up the driveway. The stench of Clayton's ripe corpse hit her as she passed by the car, and her stomach roiled. The front door was unlocked. Inside, the house was cloaked in a sepia gloom, just as room fifteen at the Stargaze Motel had been, all the daylight blocked out by the blinds.

She walked down a hallway and saw a living space that looked like it had been ransacked. Drawers hanging open. Cushions pulled from a couch. Shelves emptied of books and ornaments. Artwork that had been ripped from the walls.

She found Madison on the kitchen floor, sitting with her back against the wall, her legs splayed out. The receiver of a wall phone dangled from a curly cable next to her and emitted a beeping tone. Pots and pans and kitchen utensils were strewn across the tiles. On the counter was bread and sandwich meat and an open carton of milk.

Madison had been here for days.

The woman looked like shit. Her auburn hair hung in matted uneven clumps around a drawn face. She had a bruise under one eye and was skinnier now than she'd appeared on The Joneses camera footage a little over a week ago.

She smelled bad too, albeit not as bad as Ted Clayton.

Sarah crouched down next to her. "Madison? I'm Sarah. I'm the one who spoke to you on the phone just now. Can you tell me what happened?"

Fat tears rolled down the woman's cheeks and she nodded.

"Seven weeks ago I found my best friend Taylor Rose's necklace hidden in Ted Clayton's closet," she said. "She was wearing it the night she was murdered twenty years ago. I found ketamine too. He was drugging and raping women. Taylor fought back and he killed her. I knew if I went to the cops and told them what I'd found, that the famous director Ted Clayton was a murderer, they'd laugh at me. I had no real proof. So, I came up with a plan. I was going to frame Clayton for my abduction, say he'd starved and beat me and held me for days, handcuffed to a bed in a motel room—the same room Taylor had been found in. I'd say I'd managed to wear down the metal chain on the cuffs against the bedframe just enough to snap them in two. That I'd smashed the window and climbed out and that's how I'd escaped the room he'd locked me in."

Madison looked at Sarah with a haunted expression. "It all went to shit when he showed up at the Stargaze Motel for real," she went on. "He told me my manager Annie Kline had tipped him off but that she hadn't meant to. Annie didn't know that I was going to frame Clayton. Then he really did try to kill me. What I did to him . . . it was self-defense. You have to believe me."

"Why bring the body here, Madison?" Sarah asked gently. "Why not phone 911 from the motel room after the attack?"

"I knew he wouldn't be able to bring himself to destroy them," Madison said. "They meant too much to him. They had to be here. I had to come here and find them and prove to you what he did."

"What are you talking about? What did you need to find?"

"His trophies. He got rid of the drugs but not the trophies. They were too important."

"Stuff he took from the women he killed?"

Madison nodded. "I had to tear the place apart. It took forever to find the wall safe behind the framed print from *Do Not Disturb*.

It always was his favorite. It took me even longer to figure out the code." She smiled wryly. "It was the movie's release date."

"What was inside the safe?"

Madison said, "On the dining table. The jewelry boxes. And the DVDs."

Sarah stood and went into the adjoining dining room. On the table were nine boxes, all identical except for the initials embossed on them. There were also dozens of slim plastic DVD cases labeled only with initials too. She returned to the kitchen, where Madison was still on the floor. Her face was wet with fresh tears.

"Do the boxes contain items belonging to the women?"

Madison nodded. "I think his second wife is one of them. She died of an accidental overdose, only it wasn't an accident. Another belongs to my friend, Ally Hagen. The 'TR' one is empty because I took the necklace from it."

"And the DVDs?" Sarah asked. "Did you watch them? Do you know what's on them?"

Madison swallowed hard. "Just a couple. Enough to know what he filmed. Young girls completely out of it. Clayton taking advantage of them." She shook her head in disgust. "Always the filmmaker, huh?"

Sarah said, "We have Taylor's necklace. And we're going to get our forensics people in here and we're going to find out what exactly happened to these women. You have my word, Madison. But I need you to come with me now."

She offered a hand and Madison took it and Sarah pulled her to her feet. Madison held out her wrists to be cuffed. They were red and blistered and swollen.

"Okay, no cuffs," Sarah said. "Let's go."

As she led her down the hallway, Madison said, "I called my mom at the care home and told her I loved her. I know I won't see her for a long time."

As they got closer to the front door, Sarah became aware of a commotion outside. Voices booming, vehicle doors slamming, excited chatter.

"I made some other calls too," Madison said. "The whole world should know what he did. What he was."

Sarah opened the door and was blinded by a hundred flash-lights. She blinked the white spots away and saw a half-dozen TV trucks with satellite dishes and rows of cameras and reporters with microphones and photographers clicking cameras. They were huddled behind a hastily assembled police cordon and they were all shouting the same name.

Madison James.

# WIRE NEWS 24

OCTOBER 11, 2022

CRIME; ENTERTAINMENT

LAPD confirm investigations into alleged crimes committed by director Ted Clayton before his death

Los Angeles—The Los Angeles Police Department are investigating claims that Hollywood director Ted Clayton was involved in the deaths and disappearances of a number of women.

Clayton, 64, died last month following an altercation with actress Madison James, 39, at the Stargaze Motel off Interstate 105.

Ms. James had been missing for several days prior to the incident and has since admitted she orchestrated the disappearance because she feared for her safety. She has claimed she was attacked at the motel by the director, whom she worked with on the 2004 film *Do Not Disturb*.

Police sources have told Wire News 24 that Ms. James is unlikely to face charges relating to Mr. Clayton's death under California's self-defense laws.

The LAPD have confirmed a number of investigations into the alleged criminal activities of Mr. Clayton are now underway.

A statement reads: "Following allegations made against Ted Clayton, and as a result of new evidence, the Los Angeles Police Department have launched a number of investigations.

"These include the death of Alessia Bruno, who died of a drugs overdose in 2010 while married to Mr. Clayton; the disappearance of actor Ally Hagen, who was last seen alive in 2004; and the unsolved murder of actor Taylor Rose in 2005.

"These investigations are being carried out jointly by the LAPD's Missing Persons Unit and Robbery-Homicide Division, led by Detective Sarah Delaney and Detective Nick Delaney respectively."

# HOLLYWOOD HOTLINE

CASTING NEWS

Madison James and Dan Cassidy reunite for TV comedy *Our Crowded House*

By Jenny Cruz

November 27, 2022

EXCLUSIVE: Madison James (*The One Year Hitch*) and Dan Cassidy (*Sweet on Her*) have reunited to topline a new TV comedy series.

*Our Crowded House* has been snapped up by a major US streamer, as well as several international territories, and filming is already underway.

Written and directed by Olivia Constantine, the six-parter tells the story of newlyweds Marsha (James) and Matt (Cassidy) who find themselves forced to share a house with their former spouses and their respective offspring.

According to Constantine: "Much hilarity ensues as everyone tries to deal with an extreme blended family situation."

Sources on set say TikTok star Chloe Reid has been cast to play James' daughter on the show.

James and Cassidy first worked together on the 2002 slasher movie *Survive the Night*.

Both have endured high-profile personal issues in recent times.

James hit the headlines following her mysterious disappearance before her involvement in the self-defense death of director Ted Clayton.

Clayton is posthumously being investigated by the Los Angeles Police Department with regards to the deaths and disappearances of a number of women.

Cassidy last year finalized his divorce from former actor Rachel Rayner, whom he shares three children with.

He said: "I was super-impressed by Madison as a debut actor on *Survive the Night*. It was her first film role and I remember thinking: this girl can act! It turns out, she's a terrific comedy actor too. We're having so much fun on the set of *Our Crowded House*."

James added: "It's been a tough two decades but I'm having the time of my life making this TV show. Olivia's script is razor-sharp and Dan is just the best co-star. I'm loving trying my hand at comedy. It's fair to say I'm done with horror, both on screen and off it."

Cassidy is repped by Lister Long Entertainment, and James by Annie Kline Talent Management.

## *THE COMEBACK KID!*

*It looks like Madison James is the hottest property in town with a new man AND a new movie . . .*

DID YOU HEAR? MAGAZINE

By Yasmin Knight, Entertainment Reporter

July 5, 2023

Hollywood sure does love a comeback story!

And Madison James is giving Drew Barrymore, Brendan Fraser, and Winona Ryder a run for their money with a tale every bit as dramatic as one of her movies.

After faking her own disappearance, Madison survived a gruesome knife attack at the hands of serial killer director Ted Clayton that left him dead and the rest of the world reeling.

Talk about taking method acting a shade too far!

MJ is now back with a bang after her show *Our Crowded House* proved to be a smash hit with critics and viewers alike and has just been renewed for a second season.

Fans have loved the sizzling onscreen chemistry between Madison and co-star Dan Cassidy, and it seems like sparks have been flying between the pair behind the scenes too.

After months of rumors, the loved-up couple appear to have finally confirmed their romance by getting cozy in public together all over town.

One source told us: "Madison and Dan only have eyes for each other. They're not even trying to hide it. They're clearly madly in love!"

Dan has three kids with ex-wife and nepo baby Rachel Rayner, while Madison's last high-profile romance was with one-time heartthrob Jimmy Grand, back in the early noughties.

The flame-haired beauty is being hotly tipped for an Emmys nom later this month for her comedy turn in *Our Crowded House.*

And the busy gal has just been confirmed as the

star of the big-budget dystopian movie *Through the Door.*

Based on the bestselling book by novelist Timothy Chase, the story centers on a woman who finds herself twenty years in the future, where all smart technology has been banned and she must use off-grid methods to figure out how to get back home to her family.

Well done, Madison. It looks like it's true what they say—life really does begin at 40!

The only thing Hollywood loves more than a comeback story?

A happy ending.

# ACKNOWLEDGEMENTS

As a youngster, I loved nothing more than spending time at local libraries, picking out books that would keep me enthralled for hours. I never dreamt that one day I'd be writing novels of my own for other people to enjoy. *The Final Act* is dedicated to my readers for a very simple reason—I wouldn't be able to do this dream job without you.

I also wouldn't be able to do it without the support of my family. Mum, Scott, Alison, Ben, Sam, and Cody—you mean everything to me. Thank you for believing in me. And to my dad, I miss you every single day. Thank you for taking me to those libraries and fueling my love of reading.

I'm lucky to work with some truly fantastic people. A huge thank you to my brilliant agent, Phil Patterson, and all the team at Marjacq. Thanks also to everyone at Thomas & Mercer, especially my fabulous editor, Victoria Haslam. A special mention for developmental editor Ian Pindar. You always make the books so much better (especially this one, where your input was needed more than ever!).

Thanks also to my friends, who are also my biggest cheerleaders: Danny Stewart, Lorraine and Darren Reis, Susi Holliday, and Steph Broadribb.